Rarely stirring from his luxurious Manhattan
brownstone and weighing in at an awe-inspiring
one-seventh of a ton, here is Rex Stout's burly,
brainy master of deduction—

NERO WOLFE

assisted by his wiry, tough-talking sidekick,
Archie Goodwin. The caustic clue-hunter, in-
satiable gourmet, dedicated horticulturist, fas-
tidious gentleman and often-reluctant detective
has matched wits with some of the most out-
rageous characters and inventive criminals in
the annals of great detective fiction . . .

NERO WOLFE

SOME BURIED CAESAR

BY REX STOUT

j

A JOVE BOOK

First Jove edition published August 1979

10 9 8 7 6 5 4 3 2 1

Printed in the United States of America

Jove books are published by Jove Publications, Inc.,
200 Madison Avenue, New York, NY 10016

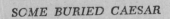

SOME BURIED CAESAR

THAT SUNNY September day was full of surprises. The first one came when, after my swift realization that the sedan was still right side up and the windshield and windows intact, I switched off the ignition and turned to look at the back seat. I didn't suppose the shock of the collision would have hurled him to the floor, knowing as I did that when the car was in motion he always had his feet braced and kept a firm grip on the strap; what I expected was the ordeal of facing a glare of fury that would top all records; what I saw was him sitting there calmly on the seat with his massive round face wearing a look of relief—if I knew his face, and I certainly knew Nero Wolfe's face. I stared at him in astonishment.

He murmured, "Thank God," as if it came from his heart.

I demanded, "What?"

"I said thank God." He let go of the strap and wiggled a finger at me. "It has happened, and here we are. I presume you know, since I've told you, that my distrust and hatred of vehicles in motion is partly based on my plerophory that their apparent submission to control is illusory and that they may at their pleasure, and sooner or later will, act on whim. Very well, this one has, and we are intact. Thank God the whim was not a deadlier one."

"Whim hell. Do you know what happened?"

"Certainly. I said, whim. Go ahead."

"What do you mean, go ahead?"

"I mean go on. Start the confounded thing going again."

I opened the door and got out and walked around to the front to take a look. It was a mess. After a careful examination I went back to the other side of the car and opened the rear door and looked in at him and made my report.

"It was quite a whim. I'd like to get it on record what happened, since I've been driving your cars nine years and this is the first time I've ever stopped before I was ready to. That was a good tire, so they must have run it over glass at the garage where I left it last night, or maybe I did myself, though I don't think so. Anyway, I was going 55 when the tire blew out. She left the road, but I didn't lose the wheel, and I was braking and had her headed up and would have made it if it hadn't been for that damn tree. Now the fender is smashed into the rubber and a knuckle is busted and the radiator's ripped open."

"How long will it take you to fix it?"

"I can't fix it. If I had a nail I wouldn't even bother to bite it, I'd swallow it whole."

"Who can fix it?"

"Men with tools in a garage."

"It isn't in a garage."

"Right."

He closed his eyes and sat. Pretty soon he opened them again and sighed. "Where are we?"

"Two hundred and thirty-seven miles northeast of Times Square. Eighteen miles southwest of Crowfield, where the North Atlantic Exposition is held every year, beginning on the second Monday in September and lasting—"

"Archie." His eyes were narrowed at me. "Please save the jocularity. What are we going to do?"

I admit I was touched. Nero Wolfe asking me what to do! "I don't know about you," I said, "but I'm going to kill myself. I was reading in the paper the other day how a Jap always commits suicide when he fails his emperor, and no Jap has anything on me. They call it seppuku. Maybe you think they call it hara-kiri, but they don't or at least rarely. They call it seppuku."

He merely repeated, "What are we going to do?"

"We're going to flag a car and get a lift. Preferably to Crowfield, where we have reservations at a hotel."

"Would you drive it?"

"Drive what?"

"The car we flag."

"I don't imagine he would let me after he sees what I've done to this one."

Wolfe compressed his lips. "I won't ride with a strange driver."

"I'll go to Crowfield alone and rent a car and come back for you."

"That would take two hours. No."

I shrugged. "We passed a house about a mile back. I'll bum a ride there or walk, and phone to Crowfield for a car."

"While I sit here, waiting, helplessly, in this disabled demon."

"Right."

He shook his head. "No."

"You won't do that?"

"No."

I stepped back around the rear of the car to survey the surroundings, near and far. It was a nice September day, and the hills and dales of upstate New York looked sleepy and satisfied in the sun. The road we were on was a secondary highway, not a main drag, and nothing had passed by since I had bumped the tree. A hundred yards ahead it curved to the right, dipping down behind some trees. I couldn't see the house we had passed a mile or so back, on account of another curve. Across the road was a gentle slope of meadow which got steeper further up where the meadow turned into woods. I turned. In that direction was a board fence painted white, a smooth green pasture, and a lot of trees; and beyond the trees were some bigger ones, and the top of a house. There was no drive leading that way, so I figured that there would be one further along the road, around the curve.

Wolfe yelled to ask what the devil I was doing, and I stepped back to the car door.

"Well," I said, "I don't see a garage anywhere. There's a house across there among those big trees. Going around by the road it would probably be a mile or more, but cutting across that pasture would be only maybe 400 yards. If you don't want to sit here helpless, I will, I'm armed, and you go hunt a phone. That house over there is closest."

Away off somewhere, a dog barked. Wolfe looked at me. "That was a dog barking."

"Yes, sir."

"Probably attached to that house. I'm in no humor to contend with a loose dog. We'll go together. But I won't climb that fence."

"You won't need to. There's a gate back a little way."

He sighed, and bent over to take a look at the crates, one on the floor and one on the seat beside him, which held the potted orchid plants. In view of the whim we had had, it was a good thing they had been secured so they couldn't slide around. Then he started to clamber out, and I stepped back to make room for him outdoors, room being a thing he required more than his share of. He took a good stretch, his applewood walking stick pointing like a sword at the sky as he did so, and turned all the way around, scowling at the hills and dales, while I got the doors of the car locked, and then followed me along the edge of the ditch to the place where we could cross to the gate.

It was after we had passed through, just as I got the gate closed behind us, that I heard the guy yelling. I looked across the pasture in the direction of the house, and there he was, sitting on top of the fence on the other side. He must have just climbed up. He was yelling at us to go back where we came from. At that distance I couldn't tell for sure whether it was a rifle or a shotgun he had with the butt against his shoulder. He wasn't exactly aiming it at us, but intentions seemed to be along that line. Wolfe had gone on ahead while I was shutting the gate, and I trotted up to him and grabbed his arm.

"Hold on a minute. If that's a bughouse and that's one of the inmates, he may take us for woodchucks or wild turkeys—"

Wolfe snorted. "The man's a fool. It's only a cow pasture." Being a good detective, he produced his evidence by pointing to a brown circular heap near our feet. Then he glared toward the menace on the fence, bellowed "Shut up!" and went on. I followed. The guy kept yelling and waving the gun, and we kept to our course, but I admit I wasn't liking it, because I could see now it was a shotgun and he might easily be the kind of a nut that would pepper us.

There was an enormous boulder, sloping up to maybe 3 feet above the ground, about exactly in the middle of the pasture, and we were a little to the right of that when the second surprise arrived in the series I spoke of. My attention was pretty thoroughly concentrated on the nut with the shotgun, still perched on the fence and yelling louder than ever, when I felt Wolfe's fingers gripping my elbow and heard his sudden sharp command:

"Stop! Don't move!"

I stopped dead, with him beside me. I thought he had discovered something psychological about the bird on the fence, but he said without looking at me, "Stand perfectly still. Move your head slowly, very slowly, to the right."

For an instant I thought the nut with the gun had something contagious and Wolfe had caught it, but I did as I was told, and there was the second surprise. Off maybe 200 feet to the right, walking slowly toward us with his head up, was a bull bigger than I had supposed bulls came. He was dark red with white patches, with a big white triangle on his face, and he was walking easy and slow, wiggling his head a little as if he was nervous, or as if he was trying to shake a fly off of his horns. Of a sudden he stopped and stood, looking at us with his neck curved.

I heard Wolfe's voice, not loud, at the back of my head, "It would be better if that fool would quit yelling. Do you know the technique of bulls? Did you ever see a bull fight?"

I moved my lips enough to get it out: "No, sir."

Wolfe grunted. "Stand still. You moved your finger then, and his neck muscles tightened. How fast can you run?"

"I can beat that bull to that fence. Don't think I can't. But you can't."

"I know very well I can't. Twenty years ago I was an athlete. This almost convinces me . . . but that can wait. Ah, he's pawing. His head's down. If he should start . . . it's that confounded yelling. Now . . . back off slowly, away from me. Keep facing him. When you are 10 feet from me, swerve toward the fence. He will begin to move when you do. As long as he follows slowly, keep backing and facing him. When he starts his rush, turn and run—"

I never got a chance to follow directions. I didn't move, and I'm sure Wolfe didn't, so it must have been our friend on the fence—maybe he jumped off into the pasture. Anyhow, the bull curved his neck and started on the jump; and if it was the other guy he was headed for, that didn't help any, because we were in line with him and we came first. He started the way an avalanche ends. Possibly if we had stood still he would have passed by, about 3 feet to my right, but either it was asking too much of human nature to expect me to stand there, or I'm not human. I have since maintained that it flashed through my mind that if I moved it would attract him to me and away from Nero Wolfe, but there's no use continuing that argument here. There's no question but what I moved, without any preliminary backing. And there's no question, whoever he started for originally, about his being attracted by my movement. I could hear him behind me. I could damn near feel him. Also I was dimly aware of shouts and a blotch of something red above the fence near the spot I was aimed at. There it was—the fence. I didn't do any braking for it, but took it at full speed, doing a vault with my hands reaching for its top, and one of my hands missed and I tumbled, landing flat on the other side, sprawling and rolling. I sat up and panted and heard a voice above me:

"Beautiful! I wouldn't have missed that for anything."

I looked up and saw two girls, one in a white dress and

red jacket, the other in a yellow shirt and slacks. I snarled at them, "Shall I do it again?" The nut with the shotgun came loping up making loud demands, and I told him to shut up, and scrambled to my feet. The fence was 10 yards away. Limping to it, I took a look. The bull was slowly walking along, a hundred feet off, wiggling his head. In the middle of the pasture was an ornamental statue. It was Nero Wolfe, with his arms folded, his stick hanging from a wrist, standing motionless on the rounded peak of the boulder. It was the first time I had ever seen him in any such position as that, and I stood and stared because I had never fully realized what a remarkable looking object he really was. He didn't actually look undignified, but there was something pathetic about it, he stood so still, not moving at all.

I called to him, "Okay, boss?"

He called back, "Tell that man with the gun I want to speak to him when I get out of here! Tell him to get someone to pen that bull!"

I turned. The guy didn't look like a bull penner. He looked more scared than mad, and he looked small and skinny in his overalls and denim shirt. His face was weathered and his nose was cockeyed. He had followed me to the fence, and now demanded:

"Who air you fellows? Why didn't you go back when I hollered at you? Where the hell—"

"Hold it, mister. Introductions can wait. Can you put that bull in a pen?"

"No, I can't. And I want to tell you—"

"Is there someone here who can?"

"No, they ain't. They've gone off to the fair. They'll be back in an hour maybe. And I want to tell you—"

"Tell me later. Do you expect him to stand on that rock with his arms folded for an hour?"

"I don't expect nothin'. He can sit down, can't he? But anyhow, I want him out of there right now. I'm guarding that bull."

"Good for you. From what? From me?"

"From anybody. Looky, if you think you're kidding . . ."

I gave him up and turned to the pasture and called: "He's guarding the bull! He wants you out of there right now! He can't pen the bull and no one else can! Somebody will be here in an hour!"

"Archie!" Wolfe bellowed like thunder. "When once I get—"

"No, honest to God, I'm telling you straight! I don't like the bull any better than you do!"

Silence. Then: "It will be an hour before anyone comes?"

"That's what he says."

"Then you'll have to do it! Can you hear me?"

"Yes."

"Good. Climb back into the pasture and get the bull's attention. When he moves, walk back in the other direction, keeping within a few feet of the fence. Was that a woman wearing that red thing?"

"Yes. Woman or girl." I looked around. "She seems to be gone."

"Find her and borrow the red thing, and have it with you. When the bull starts a rush go back over the fence. Proceed along it until you're away from him, then get back in the pasture and repeat. Take him to the other end of the pasture and keep him there until I am out. He won't leave you for me at such a distance if you keep him busy. Let him get the idea he really has a chance of getting you."

"Sure."

"What?"

"I said sure!"

"All right, go ahead. Be careful. Don't slip on the grass."

When I had asked the girl if I should do it again, I had thought it was pure sarcasm, but now . . . I looked around for her. The one in yellow slacks was there, sitting up on the fence, but not the other one. I opened my mouth to request information, but the answer came before I got it out, from another quarter. There was the sound of a car's engine humming in second, and I saw the car bouncing along a lane beyond some trees, headed toward the fence down a ways. It stopped with its nose almost touching the fence, and the girl in the red jacket leaned out and yelled at me:

"Come and open the gate!"

I trotted toward her, limping a little from my right knee which I had banged on the fence, but the other guy, using a sort of hop, skip and jump, beat me to it. When I got there he was standing beside the car, waving the gun around and reciting rules and statutes about gates and bulls.

The girl told him impatiently, "Don't be silly, Dave. There's no sense leaving him perched on that rock." She switched to me. "Open the gate, and if you want to come along, get in. Dave'll shut it."

I moved. Dave moved too and squeaked, "Leave that

gate alone! By gammer, I'll shoot! My orders from Mr. Pratt
was if anybody opens a gate or climbs in that pasture, shoot!"

"Baloney," said the girl. "You've already disobeyed orders.
Why didn't you shoot when they opened the other gate?
You'll be court-martialed. Why don't you shoot now? Go
ahead and blow him off that rock. Let's see you." She got
impatient again, to me, and scornful: "Do you want your
friend rescued or not?"

I unhooked the gate and swung it open. The bull, quite
a distance away, turned to face us with his head cocked
sidewise. Dave was sputtering and flourishing the gun, but it
was obvious he could be ignored. As the car passed through
—it was a big shiny yellow Wethersill convertible with the
top down—I hopped in, and the girl called to Dave to get
the gate shut in a hurry. The bull, still at a distance, tossed
his head and then lowered it and began pawing. Chunks
of sod flew back under his belly.

I said, "Stop a minute," and pulled the hand brake. "What
makes you think this will work?"

"I don't know. We can try it, can't we? Are you scared?"

"Yes. Take off that red thing."

"Oh, that's just superstition."

"I'm superstitious. Take it off." I grabbed the collar of
it and she wriggled out and I stuck it behind us. Then I
reached under my coat to my holster and pulled out my
automatic.

She looked at it. "What are you, a spy or something?
Don't be silly. Do you think you could stop that bull with that
thing?"

"I could try."

"You'd better not, unless you're prepared to cough up
$45,000."

"Cough what?"

"$45,000. That's not just a bull, it's Hickory Caesar Grin-
don. Put that thing away and release the brake."

I looked at her a second and said, "Turn around and get
out of here. I'll follow instructions and tease him down to
the other end along the fence."

"No." She shifted to first and fed gas. "Why should you
have all the fun?" The car moved, and she went into second.
We jolted and swayed. "I wonder how fast I ought to go?
I've never saved a man's life before. It looks from here as if
I've picked a funny one to start on. Should I blow the horn?
What do you think? Look at him!"

The bull was playing rocking horse. His hind end would

go down and then bob up in the air while he lowered his front, with his tail sticking up and his head tossing. He was facing our way. As we passed him about 30 yards to the left the girl said, "Look at him! He's a high school bull!" The car came up from a hole and nearly bounced me out. I growled, "Watch where you're going," and kept my head turned toward the bull. He looked as if he could have picked the car up and carried it on his horns the way an Indian woman carries a jug. We were approaching the boulder. She pulled up alongside, missing it by half an inch, came to a stop, and sang out, "Taxi?"

As Wolfe stepped carefully down from the peak of the boulder I got out and held the door open. I didn't offer to take his elbow to steady him because I saw by the look on his face that it would only be lighting a fuse. He got to the edge of the boulder and stood there with his feet at the level of the running board.

The girl asked, "Dr. Livingstone, I presume?"

Wolfe's lips twitched a little. "Miss Stanley? How do you do. My name is Nero Wolfe."

Her eyes widened. "Good lord! Not *the* Nero Wolfe?"

"Well . . . the one in the Manhattan telephone book."

"Then I did pick a funny one! Get in."

As he grunted his way into the convertible he observed, "You did a lot of bouncing. I dislike bouncing."

She laughed. "I'll take it easy. Anyway, it's better than being bounced by a bull, don't you think?" I had climbed to the back of the seat, since Wolfe's presence left no room below, and she started off, swinging to the left. I had noticed that she had good strong wrists and fingers, and with the jacket off her arms were bare and I could see the rippling of her forearm muscles as she steered expertly to avoid hummocks and holes. I glanced at the bull and saw he had got tired of playing rocking horse and was standing with his head up and his tail down, registering disdain. He looked bigger than ever. The girl was telling Wolfe, "Stanley would be a nice name, but mine is Caroline Pratt. Excuse me, I didn't see that hole. I'm nothing like as famous as you are, but I've been Metropolitan golf champion for two years. This place seems to be collecting champions. You're a champion detective, and Hickory Caesar Grindon is a National champion bull, and I'm a golf champion . . ."

I thought, so that accounts for the wrists and arms, she's one of those. When we got to the gate Dave opened it, and closed it against our tail as we went through. She eased it along under the trees, with overhanging branches trying to scrape me off, and finally emerged onto a wide graveled space in front of a big new concrete building with four garage doors at one end, where she stopped. Dave had come hopping along behind us, still lugging the gun, and the girl in yellow slacks was sauntering our way. I vaulted over the side of the car to the gravel. The golf champion was inquiring of Wolfe if she could drop him somewhere, but he already had his door open and was lifting his bulk to descend, so she got out. Dave bustled up to Wolfe and began to make demands in a loud voice, but Wolfe gave him an awful look and told him, "Sir, you are open to prosecution for attempted murder! I don't mean the gun, I mean jumping off that fence!" Then Wolfe walked around the rear of the car and confronted his rescuer and bowed to her:

"Thank you, Miss Pratt, for having intelligence and for using it."

"Don't mention it. It was a pleasure."

He grimaced. "Is that bull your property?"

"No, he belongs to my uncle. Thomas Pratt." She waved a hand. "This is his place. He'll be here shortly. Meanwhile ... if I can do anything ... do you want some beer?"

"No thanks. I do want beer, but God knows when I'll drink beer again. We had an accident. Mr. Goodwin was unable to restrain our car—I beg your pardon. Miss Pratt, this is Mr. Goodwin."

She politely put her hand out and I took it. Wolfe was repeating, "Mr. Goodwin was unable to restrain our car from crashing into a tree. After inspecting the damage he claimed he had run it over glass. He then persuaded me to trespass in that pasture. It was I, not he, who first saw the bull after it had emerged from behind the thicket. He boasted complete ignorance of the way a bull will act—"

I had known when I saw his face as we approached the boulder that he was going to be childish, but he might at least have saved it for privacy. I put in brusquely:

"Could I use a telephone?"

"You interrupted Mr. Wolfe." She was reproving me. "If he wants to explain—"

"I'll show you the phone." It was a voice behind me, and I turned. The girl in yellow slacks was there close. I realized with surprise that her head came clear to my chin or above, and she was blonde but not at all faded, and her dark blue eyes were not quite open, and one corner of her lips was up with her smile.

"Come on, Escamillo," she said, "I'll show you the phone."

I told her, "Much obliged," and started off with her.

She brushed against me as we walked and said, "I'm Lily Rowan."

"Nice name." I grinned down at her. "I'm Escamillo Goodwin."

2

Wolfe's voice came through the open door, "What time is it?"

After glancing at my wrist watch where it lay on the glass shelf I walked out of the bathroom, holding my forearm steady and level so the iodine would dry where I had dabbed it on. Stopping in front of the big upholstered chair he was occupying, I told him:

"3:26. I supposed the beer would buck you up. It's one of your lowest points when you haven't even got enough joy of life to pull your watch out of your pocket."

"Joy of life?" He groaned. "With our car demolished, and those plants in it being suffocated . . ."

"They're not being suffocated. I left the window open a crack on both sides." I tilted the arm, watching the iodine, and then let it hang. "Certainly joy of life! Did we get hurt when we had a front blowout? No. Did the bull get us? No. We ran into nice people who gave us a swell room with bath to wash up and served you with cold beer and me with iodine. And I repeat, if you still think I should have persuaded one of those Crowfield garages to come and get us and the car, go down and try it yourself. They thought I was crazy to expect it, with the exposition on. This Mr. Pratt will be back any minute, with a big sedan, and his niece says she'll take us and the luggage and the plants to Crowfield. I phoned the hotel, and they promised to hold our room until ten tonight. Naturally there's a mob yelling for beds."

I had got my sleeves rolled down and buttoned, and reached for my coat. "How's the beer?"

"The beer is good." Wolfe shuddered, and muttered, "A mob yelling for beds." He looked around. "This is a remarkably pleasant room . . . large and airy, good windows . . . I think perhaps I should have modern casements installed in my room at home. Two excellent beds—did you try one of the beds?"

I looked at him suspiciously. "No."

"They are first class. When did you say the garage will send for the car?"

I said patiently, "Tomorrow by noon."

"Good." He sighed. "I thought I didn't like new houses, but this one is very pleasant. Of course that was the architect. Do you know where the money came from to build it? Miss Pratt told me. Her uncle operates a chain of popular restaurants in New York—hundreds of them. He calls them pratterias. Did you ever see one?"

"Sure." I had my pants down, inspecting the knee. "I've had lunch in them often."

"Indeed. How is the food?"

"So-so. Depends on your standard." I looked up. "If what you have in mind is flushing a dinner here to avoid a restaurant meal, pratteria grub is irrelevant and immaterial. The cook downstairs is *ipso facto*. Incidentally, I'm glad to learn they're called pratterias because Pratt owns them. I always supposed it was because they're places where you can sit on your prat and eat."

Wolfe grunted. "I presume one ignorance cancels another. I never heard 'prat' before, and you don't know the meaning of *ipso facto*. Unless 'prat' is your invention—"

"No. Shakespeare used it. I've looked it up. I never invent unless—"

There was a knock on the door, and I said come in. A specimen entered wearing dirty flannel pants and a shiny starched white coat, with grease on the side of his face. He stood in the doorway and mumbled something about Mr. Pratt having arrived and we could go downstairs when we felt like it. Wolfe told him we would be down at once and he went off.

I observed, "Mr. Pratt must be a widower."

"No," said Wolfe, making ready to elevate himself. "He has never married. Miss Pratt told me. Are you going to comb your hair?"

We had to hunt for them. A woman in the lower hall with an apron on shook her head when we asked her, and we went into the dining room and out again, and through a big living room and another one with a piano in it before we finally found them out on a flagged terrace shaded with awnings. The two girls were off to one side with a young man, having highballs. Nearer to us, at a table, were two guys working their chins and fluttering papers from a brief case at each other. One, young and neat, looked like a slick bond salesman; the other, middle-aged or a little past, had brown hair that was turning gray, narrow temples and a wide jaw. Wolfe stopped, then in a minute approached nearer and stopped again. They looked up at him and the other one frowned and said:

"Oh, you're the fellows."

"Mr. Pratt?" Wolfe bowed faintly. "My name is Wolfe."

The younger man stood up. The other just kept on frowning. "So my niece told me. Of course I've heard of you, but I don't care if you're President Roosevelt, you had no business in that pasture when my man ordered you out. What did you want in there?"

"Nothing."

"What did you go in there for?"

Wolfe compressed his lips, then loosened them to ask, "Did your niece tell you what I told her?"

"Yes."

"Do you think she lied?"

"Why . . . no."

"Do you think I lied?"

"Er . . . no."

Wolfe shrugged. "Then it remains only to thank you for your hospitality—your telephone, your accommodations, your refreshment. The beer especially is appreciated. Your niece has kindly offered to take us to Crowfield in your car . . . if you will permit that?"

"I suppose so." The lummox was still frowning. He leaned back with his thumbs in his armpits. "No, Mr. Wolfe, I don't think you lied, but I'd still like to ask a question or two. You see, you're a detective, and you might have been hired . . . God knows what lengths they'll go to. I'm being pested half to death. I went over to Crowfield with my nephew today to take a look at the exposition, and they hounded me out of the place. I had to come home to get away from them. I'll ask a straight question: did you enter that particular pasture because you knew that bull was in it?"

Wolfe stared. "No, sir."

"Did you come to this part of the country in an effort to do something about that bull?"

"No, sir. I came to exhibit orchids at the North Atlantic Exposition."

"Your choosing that pasture was pure accident?"

"We didn't choose it. It was a question of geometry. It was the shortest way to this house." After a pause Wolfe added bitterly, "So we thought."

Pratt nodded. Then he glanced at his watch, jerked himself up and turned to the man with the brief case, who was stowing papers away. "All right, Pavey, you might as well make the 6 o'clock from Albany. Tell Jameson there's no reason in God's world why the unit should drop below twenty-eight four. Why shouldn't people be as hungry this September as any other September? Remember what I said, no more Fairbanks pies . . ." He went on a while about dish breakage percentages and new leases in Brooklyn and so forth, and shouted a last minute thought about the lettuce market after Pavey had disappeared around the corner of the house. Then our host asked abruptly if Wolfe would like a highball, and Wolfe said no thanks he preferred beer but doubtless Mr. Goodwin would enjoy a highball. Pratt yelled "Bert!" at the top of his voice, and Greasy-face showed up from inside the house and got orders. As we sat down the trio from the other end came over, carrying their drinks.

"May we?" Miss Pratt asked her uncle. "Jimmy wants to meet the guests. Mr. Wolfe, Mr. Goodwin, this is my brother."

I stood to acknowledge, and became aware that Wolfe was playing a deep and desperate game when I saw that instead of apologizing for not raising his poundage, as was customary, he stood too. Then we sat again, with Lily the blonde doing a languid drape on a canvas swing and a beautiful calf protruding from one leg of her yellow slacks.

Pratt was talking. "Of course I've heard of you," he was telling Wolfe. "Privately too, once or twice. My friend Pete Hutchinson told me that you turned him down a couple of years ago on a little inquiry he undertook regarding his wife."

Wolfe nodded. "I like to interfere with natural processes as little as possible."

"Suit yourself." Pratt took a gulp of highball. "That's my motto. It's your business, and you're the one to run it. For instance, I understand you're a fancy eater. Now I'm in the food business, and what I believe in is mass feeding. Last week we served a daily average of 42,392 lunches in Greater New York at an average cost to the consumer of twenty-three and seventeen-hundredths cents. What I claim—how many times have you eaten in a pratteria?"

"I . . ." Wolfe held it while he poured beer. "I never have."

"*Never?*"

"I always eat at home."

"Oh." Pratt eyed him. "Of course some home cooking is all right. But most of the fancy stuff . . . one of my publicity stunts was when I got a group of fifty people from the Social Register into a pratteria and served them from the list. They gobbled it up and they raved. What I've built my success on is, first, quality, second, publicity." He had two fingers up.

"An unbeatable combination," Wolfe murmured. I could have kicked him. He was positively licking the guy's boots. He even went on, "Your niece was telling me something of your phenomenal career."

"Yes?" He glanced at her. "Your drink's gone, Caroline." He turned his head and bawled, "Bert!" Back to Wolfe: "Well, she knows as much about it as anyone. She worked in my office three years. Somehow she got started playing golf, and she got good at it, and I figured it would be good publicity to have a golf champion for a niece, and she made it. That's better than anything she could do in the office. And better than anything her brother could do. My only nephew, and no good for anything at all. Are you, Jimmy?"

The young man grinned at him. "Not worth a damn."

"Yes, but you don't mean it, and I do. Just because your father and mother died when you were young . . . why I keep spending money on you is beyond me. It's about my only weakness. And when I think that my will leaves everything to you and your sister only because there's no one else in sight . . . it makes me hope I will never die. What do you call it? Immortality. When I think what you would do with a million dollars . . . let me ask you, Mr. Wolfe, what is your opinion of architecture?"

"Well . . . I like this house."

Jimmy cackled. "Ha! Wowie!"

His uncle disregarded him and cocked an eye at Wolfe. "You do actually? My nephew there designed it. It was only finished last year. I came originally from this part of the country . . . was born on this spot in an old shack. There is absolutely no money in architecture and never will be . . . I've looked into it. Where a nephew of mine ever got the idea . . ."

He went on and on, and Wolfe placidly opened another bottle of beer. I myself wasn't doing so bad, because it was by no means pratteria Scotch in my highball, and I had nearly finished my second one, and was so seated that I could take in the blonde on the canvas swing, with all her convolutions and what not. I quit listening to Pratt entirely, and got to wondering idly which was the more desirable quality in a girl, the ability to look as inviting as that stretched out on canvas, or the ability to save a man from a bull, and went on from that to something else, no matter what, when all of a sudden the pleasant sociable gathering was rudely interrupted. Four men came swinging around the corner of the house and tramped across the terrace. With a dim memory of our host's remark about being hounded around the fair grounds, and a dim idea that the look on their faces meant trouble, my hand was inside my coat touching my holster before I knew it, then I came to and pretended I needed to scratch my shoulder.

Pratt had jumped up and was using all his narrow forehead for a ferocious scowl, facing the intruders. The foremost, a wiry little item with a thin nose and sharp dark eyes, stopped right in front of him and told his face, "Well, Mr. Pratt, I think I've got it worked out to satisfy you."

"I'm already satisfied. I told you."

"But we're not." The keen eyes darted around. "If you'd let me explain the arrangement I've been able—"

"It's a waste of time, Mr. Bennett. I've told you—"

"Permit me." The tone was brusque, and came from a solid-looking bird in a gray sport suit that was a dream, with the fitting accessories, including driving gloves on a warm day. "You're Pratt? Lew Bennett here has talked me into this, and I have to get back to Crowfield and out again for New York. I'm Cullen."

Bennett said nervously, "Daniel Cullen."

"Oh." Pratt looked interested and a little awed. "This is an honor, Mr. Cullen. My little place here. Sit down. Have a highball? Jimmy, push up some more chairs. No, you folks stay. Here, Mr. Cullen, meet my niece . . ." He did introductions all around, including titles and occupations. It appeared that Lew Bennett was the secretary of the National Guernsey League. The name of the big-boned guy with scraggly hair and a big tired face was Monte McMillan. Daniel Cullen, of course, was Daniel Cullen, just as J. P. Morgan is J. P. Morgan. The fourth one, who looked even tireder than Monte McMillan, was Sidney Darth, chairman of the North Atlantic Exposition Board. Bert was called and sent for drinks. Lily Rowan sat up to make room on the swing, and I noticed that Jimmy Pratt copped the place next to her. She looked around at the newcomers as if she was bored.

Lew Bennett was saying, "Mr. Cullen's in a hurry to get back, and I'm confident, Mr. Pratt, you'll appreciate what he's doing as well as we do. You won't lose a cent. It will be a happy outcome—"

"I want to say it's a damned outrage!" It was Cullen, glowering at Pratt. "It ought to be actionable! Where the devil!"

"Excuse me," Bennett put in hastily. "I've been all over that aspect of it, Mr. Cullen, and if Mr. Pratt doesn't see it our way . . . he just doesn't. It's quite useless . . . what I mean to say is, thank God you've come to the rescue." He turned to Pratt. "The arrangement is simply this, that Mr. Cullen has generously agreed to take Hickory Caesar Grindon."

Pratt grunted, then was silent. After a moment he asked sullenly, "What does he want with him?"

Bennett looked shocked. "He has one of the finest pure-bred Guernsey herds in the country."

Cullen growled, "You understand, Pratt, I don't need him. My senior herd sire is Mahwah Gallant Masterson who has 43 A R daughters. I have three junior sires who are lined out. I'm doing this as a favor to the breed and to the National Guernsey League."

Bennett said, "About the arrangement. Mr. Cullen is quite correct when he says he doesn't really need Caesar. He is acting very generously, but he isn't willing to pay you the sum you paid McMillan. I know, you've told me you offered it and you paid it and you're satisfied, but the fact remains that $45,000 is a terrific price for any bull. Why, Coldwater Grandee himself sold for $33,000 in 1932, and great as Caesar is, he isn't Grandee. In 1932 Grandee had 127 A R daughters and 15 A R sons. So the arrangement is this: Mr. Cullen will pay you $33,000, and Monte—Mr. McMillan will return $12,000 of the sum you paid him. You'll get all your money back. It can be paid now with Mr. Cullen's check, which I guess you know is good, and there'll be a truck here before dark to get Caesar. Mr. Cullen wants to show him at Crowfield Thursday, if he can be got in shape. I hope he's not upset. I understand you've got him in a pasture."

Pratt turned on McMillan. "You told me this noon that you regarded the deal as closed for good and you wouldn't be a party to any effort to cancel it."

"I know I did." McMillan couldn't keep his hand from trembling a little as he put down his drink. "They've been riding me . . . they've been . . . I'm an old Guernsey man, Mr. Pratt."

"You should be ashamed to admit it!" Cullen exploded.

"They should expel you from the league and freeze you out! Pratt doesn't know any better, he has that excuse at least. But you haven't! You knew what was going to happen to that bull before you sold him!"

"Sure." McMillan nodded wearily. "It's easy for you to talk, Mr. Cullen. What have you got, a couple of billion? What I had, after what the depression did to me, was my herd and nothing else. Just my herd. Then the anthrax came, only a month ago, and in one week what did I have? What did I have left out of my Hickory herd? Four calves, six cows, one junior sire, and Caesar. What could I do with Caesar under those conditions? Live on his fees? Where would that get me? I couldn't even buy grades to breed him to, let alone purebreds. I knew no stockman could pay high enough for him, so I sent telegrams offering him to a dozen of you gentlemen breeders, and what did I get? You all knew I was out on a limb, and the best offer was $9000! For Hickory Caesar Grindon. Then Mr. Pratt shows up and he tells me straight what he wants to do with Caesar, and of course I knew it was impossible, even in the fix I was in, but it was a temptation, so to get rid of him I set a figure so high it was ridiculous. $45,000!" McMillan picked up his glass, looked into it, and put it down again. He said quietly, "Mr. Pratt took out his checkbook and wrote out a check and I took it. It wasn't you, Mr. Cullen, who offered me $9000. As I remember it, your offer was $7500."

Cullen shrugged. "I didn't need him. Anyway, as it stands now, you'll be getting $33,000, or rather keeping that out of what Pratt paid you. Under the circumstances, McMillan, you may consider yourself damned lucky. What I'm doing is in effect philanthropy. I've had my superintendent on the phone, and I'm not even sure I want Caesar's line in my herd. There have been better bulls than Caesar before now, and there will be—"

"No bull of yours, damn you!" McMillan's voice shook with rage. "You damn lousy amateur!" Abruptly he stopped himself, looked around at the faces, and slowly drew the back of his hand across his mouth. Then he leaned toward Cullen and said quietly but pointedly, "How do you like that? Who are you to make side remarks about any bull or any cow either? Let alone Hickory Caesar Grindon! Caesar was the finest bull, bar none, that ever got on the register!"

He passed his hand across his mouth again. "Yes, I say 'was', because he's not mine any more . . . and he's not yours yet, Mr. Cullen. He was a double grandson of Burleigh's

Audacious. He had 51 A R daughters and 9 A R sons. I was up all night the day he was dropped—he sucked these fingers when he was six hours old." The fingers trembled as he held them out. "He took nine grands, the last one being at Indianapolis, the National, last year. At five shows he has taken get of sire. Twelve of his daughters have topped 13,000 pounds of milk and 700 pounds of butterfat. And you say you're not even sure you want his line in your herd! Well, damn you, I hope you won't get it! At least I won't help you pay for it!"

He turned to the secretary of the National Guernsey League, Bennett, and said with his chin stiff, "I'll keep my $12,000, Lew. Count me out of your little deal."

What he got for that was an uproar. Bennett and Darth and Cullen all went for him. It was hard to get details out of all the confusion, but the gist of it seemed to be that McMillan was going back on his word and he couldn't do that, and the honor of the National Guernsey League and of all American stockmen was at stake, and it would put a crimp in the prestige of the North Atlantic Exposition if such a thing happened right next door to it, and McMillan would be keeping $33,000 which was enough anyhow, and so forth and so on. McMillan sat, looking sad and sore but stubborn, without trying to reply to them.

They were shocked into silence by an unexpected bomb tossed into the fray by Pratt.

"Let him alone!" Pratt yelled. "He's out of it anyhow. I don't want my money back from him or Mr. Cullen or anyone else. What I want is the bull, and I've got him, and a bill of sale. That's final."

They glared at him. Bennett sputtered, "You don't mean that. You can't mean it! Look here, I've told you—"

"I do mean it." Pratt's wide jaw was set. "I've paid a good price and I'm satisfied. I've made my arrangements and I'm going to stick to them. I've invited a hundred people—"

"But good God, after what I've . . ." Bennett jumped up, waving his arms, and it began to look as if I might have to reach into the holster after all. He raved. "I tell you, you can't do it! By God, you *won't* do it! You're crazy if you think you can get away with it, and I'll see that you don't! There's a dozen members of the league at Crowfield waiting for me to get back, and when they hear what I have to say, there'll be some action taken, don't think there won't!"

The others were on their feet too. Daniel Cullen rumbled, "You're a goddam maniac, Pratt."

Cullen grunted, and wheeled. "Come on, Bennett. Come

on, Darth. I've got to catch a train." He strode off. The other two followed at his heels. They disappeared around the corner of the house.

After a silence Pratt's jaw relaxed a little and he looked across at the one who was left.

"You know, McMillan," he said, "I don't like the look of that fellow Bennett. Nor what he said either. He might even sneak around to that pasture right now, and I'm afraid the man I've got guarding it isn't much good. I know I wasn't supposed to get anything for my $45,000 except the bull, but I wonder if you'd mind . . ."

"Sure." McMillan was up, big-boned and lanky. "I'll go take a look. I . . . I wanted to look at him anyway."

"Could you stick around a while?"

"Sure."

The stockman lumbered off.

We sat, the nephew and niece looking worried, Lily Rowan yawning, Pratt frowning. Wolfe heaved a sigh and emptied his glass.

Pratt muttered, "All the commotion."

Wolfe nodded. "Astonishing. About a bull. It might be thought you were going to cook him and eat him."

Pratt nodded back at him. "I am. That's what's causing all the trouble."

3

WELL, AS the Emperor of India would say, that
tore it. The children didn't appear to be shocked
any, but I goggled at our host, and I could see by the sudden
tilt to Wolfe's head that he was enjoying one of his real
and rare surprises. He also betrayed it by repeating what
he had already been told, which was equally rare.

"Eat that bull, Mr. Pratt?" he demanded.

Pratt nodded again. "I am. Perhaps you noticed a pit
we have started to dig down by the lane. That's for a barbecue which will occur Thursday afternoon. Three days from
now. I have invited a hundred guests, mostly from New York.
My niece and nephew and their friend Miss Rowan have
come for it. The bull will be butchered tomorrow. No local
man will undertake it, and I'm getting one from Albany."

"Remarkable." Wolfe's head was still tilted. "I suppose
an animal of that size would furnish 7 or 800 pounds of edible
tissue. At $45,000 on the hoof, that would make it around
$60 a pound. Of course you'll use only the more desirable
cuts and a great deal will be wasted. Another way to calculate:
if you serve a hundred guests the portions will be $450 each."

"It sounds terrible that way." Pratt reached for his glass,
saw it was empty, and yelled for Bert. "But consider how
little you can get for $45,000 in newspaper display or any
other form of advertising. The radio would eat it up at a
gulp, and what do you get for it? Nobody knows. But I
know what I'll get out of this. Do you go in for psychology?"

"I . . ." Wolfe choked and said firmly, "No."

"You ought to. Look here. Do you realize what a stir
it will make that the senior grand champion Guernsey bull
of the United States is being barbecued and served in chunks
and slices to a gathering of epicures? And by whom? By
Tom Pratt of the famous pratterias! Let alone the publicity,
do you know what the result will be? For weeks and months
every customer that eats a roast beef sandwich in a pratteria
will have a sneaking unconscious feeling that he's chewing a

piece of Hickory Caesar Grindon! That's what I mean when I say psychology."

"You spoke of epicures."

"There'll be some. Mostly the barbecue guests will be friends and acquaintances and of course the press, but I'm going to run in a few epicures." Pratt jerked up. "By the way, I've heard you're one. Will you still be in Crowfield? Maybe you'd like to run out and join us. Thursday at one o'clock."

"Thank you, sir. I don't suppose Caesar's championship qualities include succulence, but it would be an experience."

"Certainly it would. I'll be phoning my agency in New York this evening. Can I say you'll be here? For the press."

"You may say so, of course. The judging of orchids will be Wednesday afternoon, and I shall probably have left for home. But you may say so. By the way, about this bull. I am only curious: you feel no compunction at slaughtering a beast of established nobility?"

"Why should I?" Pratt waved a hand. "They say this Caesar bull has so many A R daughters, that's the point they harp on. Do you know what A R means? Advanced Register. What a cow has to do to get on the Advanced Register is to produce a daily average of so much milk and so much butterfat over a period of one year. Well, there are over 40,000 A R Guernsey cows in this country, and only 51 of them are Caesar's daughters. Does that sound as if I was getting ready to barbecue the breed out of existence? To hear that bunch over at Crowfield talk you might think I was. I've had over forty telegrams today howling threats and bloody murder. That's that fellow Bennett; he's sicked his members on me."

"Their viewpoint, of course, is valid to them."

"Sure, and mine is to me. —Hey, you want a drink there, Mr. Goodwin. How about you, Miss Rowan? Oh, Bert! Bert!"

When Greasy-face appeared I let him proceed with his function, which I must admit he performed promptly and well. Three highballs were a notch above my ordinary indulgence, but after the blowout and smashup, and the pasture exercise, I felt a little extra would be not amiss. A little fed up with the champion bull, I moved to a chair closer to the champion niece and began to murmur at her. She graciously took it, and after a little I observed the blonde slanting one at me from the corner of her eye, so I tossed her a grin between murmurs. I could have expanded easily, but my prospect was not in fact at all rosy, since what I had to do before

twilight was get Wolfe and the luggage and plants to Crowfield, outride him into a hotel and a room thereof, unpack,
find forage he would swallow without gagging, discuss the
matter of my inability to restrain the car from crashing into
a tree and get it settled once and for all, and probably sit
for a couple of hours and listen to him sigh. I was preparing
to remark to the niece that it was after five o'clock and if
she was going to drive us to Crowfield we had better get
started, when I heard a climax being reached by my employer. Pratt was inviting him to stay for dinner and he was
accepting. I scowled at him, hoping vindictively that the food
would be terrible, for it would only complicate matters and
make him almost too much for one man to handle if we got
to our destination long after dark. He saw me scowling and
let his lids cover half his eyes, and I pretended he wasn't
there and concentrated on the niece again. I had decided
she was all right, wholesome and quite intelligent, but she
looked too darned strong. I mean a girl is a girl and an
athlete is an athlete, though of course there are borderline
cases.

In reply to an invitation from Caroline I was explaining
that I would love to take her on at tennis if I hadn't twisted
my wrist negotiating the fence, which was a lie, when the
second attacking party arrived. Its personnel, as it suddenly
made an appearance at the end of the terrace, left it uncertain at first whether it was another attack or not. In front
was an extremely presentable number, I would say 22 or 3,
wearing a belted linen thing and no hat, with yellowish
brown eyes and warm trembly lips and such a chin. Behind
her was a tall slender guy, not much younger than me,
in brown slacks and pull-over, and backing him up was an
individual who should not have been there, since the proper
environment for that type is bounded by 42nd and 96th
Streets on the south and north, and Lexington Avenue and
Broadway on the east and west. In their habitat they don't
look bad, in fact they help a lot in maintaining the tone, but
out in the country like that, still wearing a Crawnley town
suit including vest and a custom-made shirt and a Monteith
tie, they jar.

The atmosphere they created was immediate and full of
sparks. Our host's mouth fell open. Jimmy stood up with
his face red. Caroline exclaimed something. Lily Rowan
twisted her neck to see and showed a crease in her brow.
The girl got as far as the table which was littered with empty
glasses, let her yellowish brown eyes go around, and said:

"We should have telephoned. Shouldn't we?"

That met denial. Greetings crossed one another through the atmosphere. It appeared that the bird in the Crawnley suit was a stranger to the Pratts, since he had to be introduced as Mr. Bronson. Wolfe and I had our names called, and learned that the girl was Nancy Osgood and the tall slender guy was her brother Clyde. Once more the clarion was sounded for poor Bert, whereupon there seemed to be an increase in the general embarrassment. Miss Osgood protested that they didn't want to intrude, they really couldn't stay, they had been to the fair and had only stopped in on their way home, on an impulse. Clyde Osgood, who had a pair of binoculars dangling on a strap around his neck, gazed down at Pratt in a fairly provocative manner and addressed him:

"We just got chased away from your pasture by Monte McMillan. We were only taking a look at your bull."

Pratt nodded sort of unconcerned, but I could see his temples were tight. "That darned bull's causing a lot of trouble." He glanced at the sister, and back at the brother again. "It's nice of you children to drop in like this. Unexpected pleasure. I saw your father over at Crowfield today."

"Yeah. He saw you too." All at once Clyde stopped talking, and began to turn, slow but sure, as if something had gripped him and was wheeling him on a pivot. He took four steps and was confronting the canvas swing, looking down straight at Lily Rowan.

"How are you?" he demanded.

"I'm fine." She held her head tilted back to see him. "Just fine. You all right?"

"Yeah, I'm great."

"Good." Lily yawned.

That simple exchange seemed to have an effect on Jimmy Pratt, for he took on added color, though as near as I could tell his eyes were aimed at Nancy Osgood, who was passing a remark to Caroline. Caroline was insisting that they stay for a drink. Mr. Bronson, looking a little weary, as if the day at the fair had been too much for him, had sat down. Clyde abruptly turned away from the swing, crossed back over, and got onto the edge of the chair next to Pratt's.

"Look here," he said.

"Well, my boy?"

"We stopped in to see you, my sister and I."

"I think that was a good idea. Now that I've built this place here . . . we're neighbors again, aren't we."

Clyde frowned. He looked to me like a spoiled kid, with a mouth that didn't quite go shut, and moving as if he expected things to get out of his way. He said, "Neighbors? I suppose so. Technically, anyhow. I wanted to speak to you about that bull. I know why you're doing it . . . I guess everyone around here does. You're doing it just to be offensive to my father—you keep out of this, Nancy, I'm handling this—"

His sister had a hand on his shoulder. "But Clyde, that's no way—"

"Let me alone." He shook her off and went after Pratt again. "You think you can get his goat by sneering at him, by butchering a bull that could top any of his in show competition. I'll hand it to you for one thing, you picked a good one. Hickory Caesar Grindon is a hard bull to put down. I say that not only on account of his record, but because I know cattle . . . or I used to. I wanted my father to buy Caesar in 1931, when he was only a promising junior. And you think you're going to butcher him?"

"That's my intention. But where you got the idea that I'm doing it deliberately to offend your father—nonsense. I'm doing it as an advertisement for my business."

"You are like hell. I know all about it . . . from the beginning. It's just another of your cheap efforts to make my father look cheap—you keep out of this, Sis!"

"You're wrong, my boy." Pratt sounded tolerant. "I don't do anything cheap . . . I can afford not to. Let me tell you something. I understand the best bull your father's got is getting pretty old. Well, if your father came to me and asked for that bull I bought, I'd be strongly inclined to let him have him as a gift. I certainly would."

"No doubt! A gift!" Clyde was nearly overcome with scorn. "Now I'll tell you. There was a lot of talk over at Crowfield today. Of course, as a member of the Guernsey League, my father was in on it. He was sure that the plan Bennett arranged with Cullen and McMillan wouldn't work . . . he said he knew you since you were a boy and you wouldn't turn loose. My sister Nancy got the idea of coming here to try to persuade you, and I agreed to come along. On the way we met Bennett and Darth and Cullen going back, and they told us what had happened. I came on anyhow, though it didn't look like there was much chance of talking you out of it. Now I'd like to make a bet with you. Do you ever do any betting?"

"I'm not a gambler." Pratt chuckled. "I'm not exactly

a confirmed gambler, but I don't mind an occasional friendly wager. I won a nice chunk on the 1936 election."

"Would you care to try a little bet with me? Say $10,000?"

"On what?"

They got interrupted. A voice sounded, "Oh, there you are," and Monte McMillan was coming across the terrace. He sounded a little relieved. He approached Pratt: "They were fooling around the fence on the other side, and I told them they might as well go on, and I wasn't sure where they got to. Not that I would suspect the Osgood youngsters of stealing a bull . . ."

Pratt grunted. "Sit down and have a drink. Bert! *Bert!*" He turned to Clyde: "What is it you want to bet about, my boy?"

Clyde leaned forward at him. "I'll bet you $10,000 you don't barbecue Hickory Caesar Grindon."

His sister Nancy exclaimed, "Clyde!" Wolfe's eyes went half shut. The others made sounds, and even Lily Rowan showed some interest. McMillan, who had started to sit down, stopped himself at an angle and held it a second, and then slowly sank.

Pratt asked quietly, "What's going to stop me?"

Clyde turned the palms of his hands up. "It's either a bet or it isn't. That's all."

"$10,000 even that we don't barbecue Hickory Caesar Grindon."

"Right."

"Within what time?"

"Say this week."

"I ought to warn you I've consulted a lawyer. There's no legal way of stopping it, if I own him, no matter how much of a champion he is."

Clyde merely shrugged. The look on his face was one I've often seen in a poker game.

"Well." Pratt leaned back and got his thumbs in his armpits. "This is mighty interesting. What about it, McMillan? Can they get that bull out of that pasture in spite of us?"

The stockman muttered, "I don't know who would be doing it. If there's any funny business . . . if we had him in a barn . . ."

"I haven't got a barn." Pratt eyed Clyde. "One thing. What do we do, put up now? Checks?"

Clyde flushed. "My check would be rubber. You know that, damn it. If I lose I'll pay."

"You're proposing a gentleman's bet? With me?"

"All right, call it that. A gentleman's bet."

"By God. My boy, I'm flattered. I really am. But I can't afford to do much flattering when $10,000 is involved. I'm afraid I couldn't bet unless I had some sort of inkling of where you would get hold of that amount."

Clyde got halfway out of his chair, and my feet came back automatically for a spring, but his sister pulled him back. She tried to pull him away, too, with urgent remarks about leaving, but he shook himself loose and even gave her a shove. He glared at Pratt with his jaw clamped:

"You damn trash, you say that to an Osgood! All right, I'll take some of your money, since that's all there is to you! If my father phones you to guarantee my side, does that make it a gentleman's bet?"

"Then you really do want to bet."

"I do."

"$10,000 even on the proposition as these people here have heard it."

"I do."

"All right. If your father guarantees it, it's a bet."

Clyde turned and started off without even a glance around for good-bye. His friend Bronson put down his drink and followed him. They had to wait at the edge of the terrace for Nancy, who, flustered as she was, managed a darn good exit under the circumstances. As she got away Monte McMillan stood up and remarked to Pratt:

"I've known that Osgood boy since he was a baby. I guess I'd better go and tell him not to do anything foolish."

He tramped off after them.

Lily Rowan said hopefully, "It sounds to me as if there's going to be dirty work at the crossroads." She patted the space beside her which Jimmy Pratt had vacated. "Come and sit here, Escamillo, and tell me what's going to happen."

I lifted the form, strolled gracefully over, deposited it, acquired her left hand, and studied the palm. "It's like this," I told her. "You will be very happy for a while, then you will take a long journey under water and will meet a bald-headed man sitting on some seaweed who you will think is William Beebe but who will begin talking to you in Russian. Not understanding Russian, you will take it for granted that you get the idea, but will discover to your horror that he was talking about something else. Give me the other hand to compare."

Jimmy Pratt, meanwhile, was haranguing his uncle. ". . .

and you sit there and let him call you trash! I'd have liked to smack him! I *would* have smacked him—"

"Now, Jimmy." Pratt waved a hand. He chuckled. "You wouldn't smack an Osgood, would you? Take it easy, son. By the way, since you seem to be feeling belligerent, maybe you'd like to help out a little with that bull. I'm afraid we'll have to keep an eye on him all night. How about a little sentry duty?"

"Well, sir . . ." Jimmy looked uncomfortable. "The fact is . . . I've already told you . . . I don't approve of that. It seems to me a bull like that . . . a champion and so on . . ."

"You wouldn't like to help us guard him?"

"I'd appreciate it if you'd leave me out of that, Uncle Tom."

"All right. I guess we can manage somehow. —What's your feeling about it, Mr. Wolfe? Haven't I got a right to eat my own bull?"

Wolfe obliged with a philosophical lecture on written and unwritten law, degrees of moral turpitude, and the extravagant enthusiasms of bovine genetics. It sounded quite instructive and elevated the tone of the gathering to a plane high above such petty things as smacking an Osgood or eating beefsteak or winning a $10,000 bet. When he had finished, he turned to me with a suggestion: since he had accepted Mr. Pratt's kind invitation to dine there, a change of linen would be desirable, and the luggage was still in our car out by the roadside. Jimmy offered his services, but Caroline insisted it was her job, since it was she who had contracted to drive us to Crowfield, so I followed her from the terrace, across a wide lawn, around some shrubbery and flower beds, and down a path which took us to the graveled space in front of the garage, where a big sedan was parked near the yellow convertible. I stooped to peer under the trees to where I had caught a glimpse of a high long mound of freshly dug soil, with picks and shovels leaning against it. I had noticed it previously, as we drove by in the convertible after escaping from the pasture, but had not then realized its significance.

"Pit for the barbecue?" I inquired.

Caroline nodded. "I think it's pretty awful, but I couldn't very well refuse uncle's invitation to come up for it. Get in."

When she had swung the sedan around and had headed down the drive I said, "I ask this because it's none of my business. I'm interested in human nature. Which is it, advertising, or a Bronx cheer for Father Osgood?"

"I don't know. I'm thinking about something."

So I held myself aloof. The sedan emerged onto the highway and turned left, and in half a minute was swinging around the curve which I had seen from the other direction during my survey of the surroundings after the accident. In the other half of the minute she had arrived at the scene, spun the wheel with her strong wrists, done a U, and pulled up directly behind the relic. I got out. The angle of the low evening sun made long soft shadows with trees and telephone poles on the green of the pasture. Across its expanse, on the other side, I could see the top third of Monte McMillan above the fence, his face turned our way, and moving along this side of the boulder, with slow imperial tread, looking bigger than ever, was the bull. I had to admit he was a beaut, now that I could take an impersonal view.

There were two suitcases, two bags, the sprayer, and the crates of plants. After I got them all transferred I locked the car up again, took another glance at the bull who was soon to be served at 450 bucks a portion, and climbed in beside Miss Pratt. Still aloof, I didn't say anything, but sat quietly and waited for the spirit to move her. After a minute she moved, but only to turn her head to look at me.

"I want to tell you what I was thinking about."

I nodded politely.

"Lily Rowan."

I nodded again. "She calls mè Escamillo. She told me that you and she are going to the fair tomorrow, and suggested that she and I might have lunch together."

"What did you tell her?"

"I told her I couldn't on account of my table manners. I don't like hitch-lunchers."

Caroline snorted. "She wasn't trying to hitch. She would pay the check. She's rich. Very. Maybe millions, I don't know, anyway plenty. She's a vampire. She's dangerous."

"You mean she bites you in the neck?"

"I mean what I say. I used to think the talk about some woman being dangerous, you know, really dangerous, was romantic hooey, but it isn't. Lily Rowan is one. If she wasn't too lazy to make much of an effort there's no telling how many men she might ruin, but I know of at least three she has played the devil with. You saw Clyde Osgood today. Not that Clyde was ever one of nature's noblemen, but he was doing all right. He's just my age, 26. The Osgoods have owned this county for generations, they still have a couple of thousand acres, and after Clyde finished at college he buckled in and handled things for his father, who was away most of the time doing politics and things. People around here say he was really showing some sense. Then during a trip to New York two years ago he met Lily Rowan, and she took a fancy to him and got a spell of energy at the same time. She did worse than bite him in the neck. She swallowed him. Then last spring she spit him out again. That may not be very elegant, but can you describe the activities of a toad with elegance? Clyde hasn't returned to the country; he hangs around New York and tries to see her or tries not to see her. I don't know what he's doing up here now. Maybe he knew she was coming."

She stopped. I remarked, "And that's what you were thinking about."

"No, that only leads up to it." She frowned at me. "You're a detective. That's your business, isn't it?"

"Yep. 24 hour service."

"And you . . . you keep things confidential?"

"Sure, when they are confidential."

"Well, this is. Lily Rowan is after my brother Jimmy."

I raised the brows. "And?"

"She mustn't get him. She hasn't got him . . . yet. I would have supposed Jimmy had too much sense, but apparently that has nothing to do with it. Also I thought he was in love with Nan Osgood; I thought that last winter. A month or so ago Lily Rowan started after him. And even Jimmy . . . even Jimmy will fall for it! How the devil does she do it? Damn her!"

"I couldn't say. I could ask her."

"This isn't a joke. She'll ruin him."

"I don't regard it as a job. You asked a silly question. And her being up here . . . you invited her just to help things along a little and have it over with?"

"I invited her because I thought that seeing her like this . . . out here in the country . . . might bring him to. But it hasn't."

"He still laps it up."

"Yes."

I hunched my shoulders. "Well, granted that I'm a good detective, there doesn't seem to be anything to detect. It seems to be what my employer calls a natural process, and there's no way of stopping it except to send your brother to Australia for a pair of shoestrings or cut her throat."

"I could do that, cut her throat. I could murder her. But maybe there is a way. That's what I was thinking about. She said something about you today while you were upstairs. Something that gave me an idea."

"What did she say?"

"I can't tell you. I couldn't say it."

"Was it . . . well, personal?"

"Very personal."

"What was it?"

"I tell you I won't repeat it. But that, and other things, and her asking you to have lunch with her . . . I believe you could take her away from Jimmy. Provided you don't try. She likes to do the trying, when she gets energy enough. Something about you has attracted her; I knew that when she called you Escamillo."

"Go on."

"That's all. Except . . . of course . . . I don't mean to ask a favor of you. There's no reason why you should do me a favor, even as great a one as this. It's a matter of business. When you send me a bill I'll pay it, only if it's very big I might have to pay in installments."

"I see. First I act coy, then I let her ruin me, then I send you a bill—"

"I tell you this isn't a joke. It's anything but a joke. Will you do it?"

I screwed up my lips, regarding her. Then I got out a cigarette, offered her one which was refused, and lit up.

"Look," I said, "*I* think it's a joke. Let's say she goes ahead and ruins him. In my opinion, if he's worth the powder to blow him to hell, he'll soon get unruined. No man was ever taken to hell by a woman unless he already had a ticket in his pocket, or at least had been fooling around with time-tables. God bless you, you say you want to hire me to pull her off. I couldn't take an outside job even if I wanted to, because I work for Nero Wolfe on salary. But since you want to make it strictly a matter of business, I'll do this for you: I'll eat lunch with her tomorrow, provided you'll pay the check. That will be $2, for which, inclusive, I'll make you a detailed report of progress."

She said briefly, "It isn't a joke. I'll give you the $2 when we get back to the house," and stepped on the starter.

It surely wouldn't have been too much to expect that I might have had a little peace and quiet during the hour that remained before dinnertime, but no such luck. I had unloaded the crates of plants and taken them upstairs to the bathroom, and had carted up the two suitcases, and my final journey was with the two bags. Entering the room with them and hearing a noise in the bathroom, I put the bags down and crossed to the open door and saw Wolfe there, with the lids of the crates lifted so he could inspect the orchids to see if they would require spraying. I said the plants looked to me to be in good shape, and he acknowledged the fact. Then I said that since our shirts and ties were in the suitcases, likewise toilet articles, I presumed it would be unnecessary to open the bags, though I had brought them up. Not looking at me, he murmured casually but distinctly:

"It would be well, I think, to unpack."

I started. "The whole works?"

"Yes."

"You mean take everything out?"

"Yes."

"And put it back in again after dinner?"

"No. We shall sleep here tonight."

I started to improvise a cutting remark, because I am methodical by temperament and like to see plans carried out when they have been made, but then I reflected that after all this place unquestionably had it all over any hotel room they were likely to be saving for us in Crowfield, with the town overflowing with exposition visitors. On the other hand it was always bad policy to feed his conceit by displaying approval, so without comment I returned to the bedroom and began operations on the big suitcase. Pretty soon he waddled in, removed his coat and vest and dropped them on one of the beds, and started to unbutton his shirt.

I inquired pleasantly, "How did you coerce Pratt into having us as house guests? Just turn on the old charm?"

"There was no coercion. Technically we are not guests. Mr. Pratt was eager to adopt my suggestion."

"Oh." I whirled on him with my hands full of socks and handkerchiefs. "You made a suggestion?"

"I did. I'm being perfectly frank about it, Archie; I could let it appear that the suggestion originated with Mr. Pratt, but it didn't; I offered it. Knowing of his difficulty, it seemed a decent thing to do, after his generous hospitality. He approved at once, and proposed a commission to me, and I accepted."

"I see." I was still holding the haberdashery. "What kind of a commission, if you don't mind my asking?"

"Not a very lucrative one. Nor very difficult. Surveillance."

"I thought so." I crossed and opened a drawer of the bureau and arranged the socks and handkerchiefs inside. Then I stood and watched him struggle out of his shirt and heard the seams protesting. "I suspected it the minute you told me to unpack. Okay. That's a new one. Pasture patrol. Bodyguard for a bull. I sincerely trust you'll enjoy a good night's sleep, sir, having this lovely room all to yourself."

"Don't take a tone with me, Archie. It will be dull, that's all, for a man as fidgety—"

"Dull?" I waved a hand. "Don't you believe it. Dull, out there alone in the night, sharing my secrets with the stars? You don't know me. And glowing with satisfaction because just by being there I'll be making it possible for you to snooze in that excellent bed in this big airy room. And then the dawn! Mr. Wolfe, how I love the dawn!"

"You won't see the dawn."

"The hell I won't. Who'll bump me off, Clyde? Or will the bull get me?"

"Neither. I have made arrangements with Mr. Pratt and Mr. McMillan. The man called Dave will be on guard while we are dining. At 8:30 you will relieve him, and at 1 o'clock you will be relieved by Mr. McMillan. You often go to bed that late at home. You had better waken me by knocking when you come in. I am not accustomed to my room being entered at night."

"Okay." I resumed with the suitcase, and laid out a fresh shirt for him. "But darned if I'll lug that shotgun around. I'll take that up with McMillan. Incidentally, I've accepted a commission too. For the firm. Not a very lucrative one. The fee has already been paid, two bucks, but it'll be eaten up by expenses. The client is Miss Caroline Pratt."

Wolfe muttered, "Jabber."

"Not at all. She paid me two bucks to save her brother from a fate worse than death. Boy, is it fun being a detective! Up half the night chaperoning a bull, only to be laid waste by a blonde the next day at lunch. Look, we'll have to send a telegram to Fritz; here's a button off."

4

I DIDN'T get to share any secrets with any stars. Clouds had started to gather at sundown, and by half past eight it was pitch-dark. Armed with a flashlight, and my belt surrounding a good dinner—not of course up to Fritz Brenner's standard, but far and away above anything I had ever speared at a pratteria—I left the others while they were still monkeying with coffee and went out to take over my shift. Cutting across through the orchard, I found Dave sitting on an upended keg over by the fence, clutching the shotgun.

"All right," I told him, cutting off the light to save juice. "You must be about ready for some chow."

"Naw," he said, "I couldn't eat late at night like this. I had some meat and potatoes and stuff at six o'clock. My main meal's breakfast. It's my stommick that wakes me up, I git so derned hungry I can't sleep."

"That's interesting. Where's the bull?"

"I ain't seen him for a half hour. Last I saw he was down yonder, yon side of the big walnut. Why the name of common sense they don't tie him up's beyond me."

"Pratt says he was tied the first night and bellowed all night and nobody could sleep."

Dave snorted. "Let him beller. Anybody that can't sleep for a bull's bellerin' had better keep woonies instead."

"What's woonies?"

He had started off in the dark, and I heard him stop. "Woonies is bulls with their tails at the front end." He cackled. "Got you that time, mister! Good night!"

I decided to take a look, and anyhow moving was better than standing still, so I went along the fence in the direction of the gate we had driven through in our rescue of Wolfe. It sure was a black night. After making some thirty yards I played the flashlight around the pasture again, but couldn't find him. I kept on to the other side of the gate, and that time I picked him up. He wasn't lying down as I supposed he would be, but standing there looking at the light. He loomed up like an elephant. I told him out loud, "All right, honey darling, it's only Archie, I don't want you to get upset," and turned back the way I had come.

It looked to me as if there was about as much chance of anyone kidnapping that bull as there was of the bull giving milk, but in any event I was elected to stay outdoors until one o'clock, and I might as well stay in the best place in case someone was fool enough to try. If he was taken out at all it would certainly have to be through a gate, and the one on the other side was a good deal more likely than this one. So I kept going, hugging the fence. It occurred to me that it would be a lot simpler to go through the middle of the pasture, and as dark as it was there was no danger of Caesar starting another game of tag, or very little danger at least . . . probably not any, really . . .

I went on around the fence. Through the orchard I could see the lighted windows of the house, a couple of hundred yards away. Soon I reached the corner of the fence and turned left and, before I knew it, was in a patch of briars. Ten minutes later I had rounded the bend in the road and was passing our sedan still nestled up against the tree. There was the gate. I climbed up and sat on the fence and played the light around, but it wasn't powerful enough to pick up the bull at that distance. I switched it off.

I suppose if you live in the country long enough you get familiar with all the little noises at night, but naturally you feel curious about them when you don't know what they are. The crickets and katydids are all right, but something scuttling through the grass makes you wonder what it could be. Then there was something in a tree across the road. I could hear it move around among the leaves, then for a long while it would be quiet, and then it would move again. Maybe an owl, or maybe some little harmless animal. I couldn't find it with the light.

I had been there I suppose half an hour, when a new noise came from the direction of the car. It sounded like something heavy bumping against it. I turned the light that way, and at first saw nothing because I was looking too close to the ground, and then saw quite plainly, edging out from the front fender, a fold of material that looked like part of a coat, maybe a sleeve. I opened my mouth to sing out, but abruptly shut it again and turned off the light and slid from the fence and sidestepped. It was just barely possible that the Guernsey League had one or two tough guys on the roll, or even that Clyde Osgood himself was tough or thought he was. I stepped along the grass to the back of the car, moved around it keeping close to the side, reached over the front fender for what was huddled there, grabbed, and got a shoulder.

There was a squeal and a wiggle, and a protest: "Say! That hurts!" I flashed the light and then turned loose and stepped back.

"For God's sake," I grumbled, "don't tell me you're sentimental about that bull too."

Lily Rowan stood up, a dark wrap covering the dress she had worn at dinner, and rubbed at her shoulder. "If I hadn't stumbled against the fender," she declared, "I'd have got right up against you before you knew I was there, and I'd have scared you half to death."

"Goody. What for?"

"Darn it, you hurt my shoulder."

"I'm a brute. How did you get here?"

"Walked. I came out for a walk. I didn't realize it was so dark; I thought my eyes would get used to it. I have eyes like a cat, but I don't think I ever saw it so dark. Is that your face? Hold still."

She put a hand out, her fingers on my cheek. For a second I thought she was going to claw, but the touch was soft, and when I realized it was going to linger I stepped back a pace and told her, "Don't do that, I'm ticklish."

She laughed. "I was just making sure it was your face. Are you going to have lunch with me tomorrow?"

"Yes."

"You are?" She sounded surprised.

"Sure. That is, you can have lunch with me. Why not? I think you're amusing. You'll do fine to pass away some time, just a pretty toy to be enjoyed for an idle moment and then tossed away. That's all any woman can ever mean to me, because all the serious side of me is concentrated on my career. I want to be a policeman."

"Goodness. I suppose we ought to be grateful that you're willing to bother with us at all. Let's get in your car and sit down and be comfortable."

"It's locked and I haven't got the key. Anyhow, if I sat down I might go to sleep and I mustn't because I'm guarding the bull. You'd better run along. I promised to be on the alert."

"Nonsense." She moved around the fender, brushing against

me, and planted herself on the running board. "Come here and give me a cigarette. Clyde Osgood lost his head and made a fool of himself. How could anyone possibly do anything about that bull, with only the two gates, and one of them on the side towards the house and the other one right there? And you can't do any work on your career, here on a lonely road at night. Come and play with one of your toys."

I flashed the light on the gate, a hundred feet away, then switched it off and turned to join her on the running board. Stepping on an uneven spot, I got off balance and plumped down right against her. She jerked away.

"Don't sit so close," she said in an entirely new tone. "It gives me the shivers."

I reached for cigarettes, grinning in the dark. "That had the element of surprise," I said, getting out the matches, "but it's only fair to warn you that tactics bore me, and any you would be apt to know about would be too obvious. Besides, it was bad timing. The dangle-it-then-jerk-it-away is no good until after you're positive you've got the right lure, and you have by no means reached that point . . ."

I stopped because she was on her feet and moving off. I told the dark, where her form was dim, "The lunch is off. I doubt if you have anything new to contribute."

She came back, sat down again on the running board about a foot from me, and ran the tips of her fingers down my sleeve from shoulder to elbow. "Give me a cigarette, Escamillo." I lit for her and she inhaled. "Thanks. Let's get acquainted, shall we? Tell me something."

"For instance."

"Oh . . . tell me about your first woman."

"With pleasure." I took a draw and exhaled. "I was going up the Amazon in a canoe. I was alone because I had fed all our provisions to the alligators in a spirit of fun and my natives, whom I called boys, had fled into the jungle. For two months I had had nothing to eat but fish, then an enormous tarpon had gone off with my tackle and I was helpless. Doggedly I kept on up the river, and had resigned myself to the pangs of starvation when, on the fifth day, I came to a small but beautiful island with a woman standing on it about eight feet tall. She was an Amazon. I beached the canoe and she picked me up and carried me into a sort of bower she had, saying that what I needed was a woman's care. However, there did not appear to be anything on the island to eat, and she looked as if she wouldn't need to eat again for weeks. So I adopted the only course that was left to me, laid my plans and set a trap, and by sundown I had her stewing merrily in an enormous iron pot which she had apparently been using for making lemon butter. She was delicious. As well as I can remember, that was my first woman. Of course since then—"

She stopped me at that point and asked me to tell her about something else. Her wrap had fallen open in front, and she drew it to her again. We sat there for two more cigarettes, and might have finished the rest of my shift there on the running board, if it hadn't been for a noise I heard from the pasture. It sounded like a dull thud, very faint through the concert of the crickets and katydids, and there was no reason to suppose it was anything alarming, but it served to remind me that the nearby gate wasn't the only possible entry to the pasture, and I decided to take a look. I stood up and said I was going to do a patrol around to the other side. Lily protested that it was all foolishness, but I started off and she came too. The bull wasn't within range of my light.

She hung onto my arm to keep from stumbling, she said, though it didn't appear she had done any to speak of when she had been sneaking up on me. I forgot about the briar patch along the stretch at the far end, and she got entangled and I had to work her loose. After we turned the next corner we were in the orchard, fairly close to the house, and I told her she might as well scoot, but she said she was enjoying it. I hadn't found the bull, but he had seemed to have a preference for the other end anyhow. We kept on along the fence, left the orchard, and reached the other gate, and still no bull. I stood still and listened, and heard a noise, or thought I did, like someone dragging something, and then went ahead, with Lily trotting along behind, flashing the light into the pasture. The noise, I suppose it was, had made me uneasy, and I was relieved when I saw the bull on ahead, only ten yards or so from the fence. Then I saw he was standing on his head, at least that was what it looked like at that distance in the dim ray of light. I broke into a jog. When I stopped again to direct the light over the top of the fence, I could see he was fussing with something on the ground, with his horns. I went on until I was even with him, and aimed the light at him again, and after one look I felt my wrist going limp and had to stiffen it by clamping my fingers tight on the cylinder of the flash. I heard Lily's gasp behind me and then her hoarse whisper:

"It's a . . . it's for God's sake make him stop!"

I supposed there was a chance he was still alive, and if so there was no time to go hunt somebody who knew how to handle a bull. I climbed the fence, slid off inside the pasture, switched the light to my left hand and with my right pulled my automatic from the holster, and slowly advanced. I figured that if he made a sudden rush it would be for the light, so I held my left arm extended full length to the side, keeping the light spotted on his face. He didn't rush. When I was ten feet off he lifted his head and blinked at the light, and I jerked up the pistol to aim at the sky and let fly with three shots. The bull tossed his head and pivoted like lightning, and danced off sideways, shaking the ground. He didn't stop. I took three strides and aimed the light at the thing on the ground. One glance was plenty. Alive hell, I thought. I felt something inside of me start to turn, and tightened the muscles there. I was sorry I had aimed at the sky, and lifted the light to look for the bull, gripping the butt of the pistol, then I realized there was no sense in making a fool of myself, and walked over and leaned on the fence. Lily was making half hysterical requests for information, and I growled, "It's Clyde Osgood. Dead. Very dead. Beat it or shut up or something." Then I heard shouts from the direction of the house and headed the light that way and yelled:

"This way! Down beyond the pit!"

More shouts, and in a few seconds a couple of flashlights showed, one dancing on the lawn and one coming along the fence. Within three minutes after I had fired the pistol four of them were on the scene: Pratt, Jimmy, Caroline and McMillan. I didn't have much explaining to do, since they had lights and there it was on the ground. After one look Caroline turned her back and stood there. Pratt pushed his chest against the fence and pulled at his lower lip, looking. Jimmy climbed up on the fence and then climbed down again.

Pratt said, "Get him out. We have to get him out of there. Where's Bert? Where the hell is Bert?"

McMillan had walked over to the remains to inspect, and now came back and asked me, "What did you shoot at? Did you shoot at Caesar? Where is he?" I said I didn't know. Bert came trotting up with a big electric lantern. Dave appeared out of the darkness, with overalls on top of a night-shirt, carrying the shotgun. McMillan came back from somewhere and said the bull was up along the fence and should be tied up before the rest of us entered the pasture, and he couldn't find the tie-rope that had been left hanging on the fence and had I seen it or anyone else. We said no, and

McMillan said any strong rope would do, and Dave volunteered to bring one. I climbed up on the fence and sat there, and Caroline asked me something, I don't know what, and I shook my head at her.

It was after Dave had returned with some rope, and McMillan had gone off with it and come back in a few minutes and said the bull was tied up and we could go ahead, that I became aware that Nero Wolfe had joined us. I heard my name, and turned my head in surprise, and there he was, with his hat on and carrying his applewood stick, peering up at me where I was still sitting on the fence.

"You're not using that flashlight," he said. "May I borrow it?"

I demanded, "How did you get here without a light?"

"I walked. I heard shots and wondered about you. As I passed by, Mr. McMillan was tying the bull to the fence and he told me what had happened—or at least, what had been found. By the way, perhaps I should warn you once again to control the exuberance of your professional instincts. It would be inconvenient to get involved here."

"What would I be doing with professional instincts?"

"Oh. You've had a shock. When you regain your senses, be sure you regain your discretion also." He stuck out a hand. "May I have the light?"

I handed it to him, and he turned and went, along the fence. Then I heard McMillan calling to me to come and help, so I slid into the pasture on stiff knees and made myself walk back over there. Dave had brought a roll of canvas, and Jimmy and McMillan were spreading it on the ground while Pratt and Dave and Bert stood and looked on, Bert holding the electrice lantern.

Pratt said in a shaky voice, "We shouldn't . . . if there's any chance . . . are you sure he's dead?"

McMillan, jerking at the canvas, answered him. "You got any eyes? Look at him." He sounded as if someone had hurt his feelings. "Give us some help, will you, Goodwin? Take his feet. We'll ease him onto the canvas and then we can all get hold. We'd better go through the gate."

I tightened my belly muscles again and moved.

We all helped with the carrying except Dave, who went on ahead to get the gate open. As we passed where the bull was tied he twisted his head around to look at us. Outside the pasture we put it down a minute to change holds and then picked it up again and went on. On the terrace there was hesitation and discussion of where to put it, when

Caroline suddenly appeared and directed us to the room off of the living room that had a piano in it, and we saw that she had spread some sheets over the divan at one end. We got it deposited and stretched out, but left the flaps of the canvas covering it, and then stood back and stretched our fingers, nobody looking at anybody.

Dave said, "I never seen such a sight." He looked incomplete without the shotgun. "Godalmighty, I never seen anything like it."

"Shut up," Pratt told him. Pratt looked sick. He began pulling at his lower lip again. "Now we'll have to telephone . . . we'll have to notify the Osgoods. All right. A doctor too. We have to notify a doctor anyway. Don't we?"

Jimmy took hold of his uncle's elbow. "Brace up, Uncle Tom. It wasn't your fault. What the hell was he doing in that pasture? Go get yourself a drink. I'll do the phoning."

Bert bustled out as soon as he heard the word "drink." Caroline had disappeared again. The others shuffled their feet. I left them and went upstairs.

In our room Wolfe was in the comfortable upholstered chair, under a reading lamp, with one of the books we had brought along. Knowing my step, he didn't bother to glance up as I entered and crossed to the bathroom—we might have been at home in the office. I took off my shirt to scrub my hands and splash cold water over my face, then put it on again, and my necktie and coat, and went out and sat on the edge of a straight-backed chair.

Wolfe let his eyes leave the page long enough to ask, "Not going to bed? You should. Relax. I'll stop reading shortly. It's eleven o'clock."

"Yeah, I know it is. There'll be a doctor coming, and before he gives a certificate he'll probably want to see me. I was first on the scene."

He grunted and returned to his reading. I stayed on the edge of the chair and returned to my thoughts. I don't know when I began it, since it was unconscious, or how long I kept it up, but when Wolfe spoke again I became aware that I had been rubbing the back of my left hand with the finger tips of my right as I sat staring at various spots on the floor.

"You should realize, Archie, that that is very irritating. Rubbing your hand indefinitely like that."

I said offensively, "You'll get used to it in time."

He finished a paragraph before he dog-eared a page and closed the book, and sighed. "What is it, temperament? It was a shock, of course, but you have seen violence before, and the poor monstrosity life leaves behind when it departs—"

"I can stand the monstrosity. Go ahead and read your book. At present I'm low, but I'll snap out of it by morning. Down there you mentioned professional instinct. I may be short on that, but you'll allow me my share of professional pride. I was supposed to be keeping an eye on that bull, wasn't I? That was my job, wasn't it? And I sat over by the roadside smoking cigarettes while he killed a man."

"You were guarding the bull, not the man. The bull is intact."

"Much obliged for nothing. Phooey. You're accustomed to feeling pleased because you're Nero Wolfe, aren't you? All right, on my modest scale I permit myself a similar feeling about Archie Goodwin. When did you ever give me an errand that you seriously expected me to perform and I didn't perform it? I've got a right to expect that when Archie Goodwin is told to watch a pasture and see that nothing happens to a bull, nothing will happen. And you tell me that nothing happened to the bull, the bull's all right, he just killed a man . . . what do you call that kind of suds?"

"Sophistry. Casuistry. *Ignoratio elenchi.*"

"Okay, I'll take all three."

"It's the feeling that you should have prevented the bull from killing a man that has reduced you to savagery."

"Yes. It was my job to keep things from happening in that pasture."

"Well." He sighed. "To begin with, will you never learn to make exact statements? You said that I told you the bull killed a man. I didn't say that. If I did say that, it wouldn't be true. Mr. Osgood was almost certainly murdered, but not by a bull."

I goggled at him. "You're crazy. I saw it."

"Suppose you tell me what you did see. I've had no details from you, but I'll wager you didn't see the bull impale Mr. Osgood, alive, on his horns. Did you?"

"No. When I got there he was pushing at him on the ground. Not very hard. Playing with him. I didn't know whether he was dead or not, so I climbed the fence and walked over and when I was ten feet away—"

Wolfe frowned. "You were in danger. Unnecessarily. The man was dead."

"I couldn't tell. I fired in the air, and the bull beat it, and I took a look. I didn't have to apply any tests. And now you have the nerve to say the bull didn't kill him. What are you trying to do, work up a case because business has been bad?"

"No. I'm trying to make you stop rubbing the back of your hand so I can finish this chapter before going to bed. I'm explaining that Mr. Osgood's death was not due to your negligence and would have occurred no matter where you were, only I presume the circumstances would have been differently arranged. I was not guilty of sophistry. I might suggest a thousand dangers to your self-respect, but a failure on the job tonight would not be one. You didn't fail. You were told to prevent the removal of the bull from the pasture. You had no reason to suspect an attempt to harm the bull, since the enemy's purpose was to defend him from harm, and certainly no reason to suspect an effort to frame him on a charge of murder. I do hope you won't begin—"

He stopped on account of footsteps in the hall. They stopped by our door. There was a knock and I said come in and Bert entered.

He looked at me. "Could you come downstairs? Mr. Osgood is down there and wants to see you."

I told him I'd be right down. After he had gone and his footsteps had faded away Wolfe said, "You might confine yourself to direct evidence. That you rubbed your hand and I endeavored to make you stop is our affair."

I told him that I regarded it as such and left him to his book.

5

AT THE FOOT of the stairs I was met by Pratt,
standing with his hands stuck deep in his pockets
and his wide jaw clamped tight. He made a motion with
his head without saying anything, and led me into the big
living room and to where a long-legged gentleman sat on a
chair biting his lip, and letting it go, and biting it again.
This latter barked at me when I was still five paces short of
him, without waiting for Pratt or me to arrange contact:

"Your name's Goodwin, is it?"

It stuck out all over him, one of those born-to-command
guys. I never invite them to parties. But I turned on the
control and told him quietly, "Yep. Archie Goodwin."

"It was you that drove the bull off and fired the shots?"

"Yes, doctor."

"I'm not a doctor! I'm Frederick Osgood. My son has
been killed. My only son."

"Excuse me, I thought you looked like a doctor."

Pratt, who had backed off and stood facing us with his
hands still in his pockets, spoke: "The doctor hasn't got here
yet. Mr. Osgood lives only a mile away and came in a few
minutes."

Osgood demanded, "Tell your story. I want to hear it."

"Yes, sir." I told him. I know how to make a brief but
complete report and did so, up to the point where the others
had arrived, and ended by saying that I presumed he had had
the rest of it from Mr. Pratt.

"Never mind Pratt. Your story is that you weren't there
when my son entered the pasture."

"My story is just as I've told it."

"You're a New York detective."

I nodded. "Private."

"You work for Nero Wolfe and came here with him."

"Right. Mr. Wolfe is upstairs."

"What are you and Wolfe doing here?"

I said conversationally, "If you want a good sock in the
jaw, stand up."

He started to lift. "Why, damn you—"

I showed him a palm. "Now hold it. I know your son has just been killed and I'll make all allowances within reason, but you're just making a damn fool of yourself. What's the matter with you, anyway? Are you hysterical?"

He bit his lip. In a second he said, with his tone off a shade, "No, I'm not hysterical. I'm trying to avoid making a fool of myself. I'm trying to decide whether to get the sheriff and the police here. I can't understand what happened. I don't believe it happened the way you say it did."

"That's too bad." I looked him in the eye. "Because for my part of it I have a witness. Someone was with me all the time. A . . . a young lady."

"Where is she? What's her name?"

"Lily Rowan."

He stared at me, stared at Pratt, and came back to me. He was beyond biting his lip. "Is *she* here?"

"Yes. I'll give you this free: Mr. Wolfe and I had an accident to our car and walked to this house to telephone. Everyone here was a stranger to us, including Lily Rowan. After dinner she went for a walk and found me guarding the pasture and stayed to keep me company. She was with me when I found the bull and drove him off. If you get the police and they honor me with any attention they'll be wasting their time. I've told you what I saw and did, and everything I saw and did."

Osgood's fingers were fastened onto his knees like claws digging for a hold. He demanded, "Was my son with this Lily Rowan?"

"Not while she was with me. She joined me on the far side of the pasture around nine-thirty. I hadn't seen your son since he left here in the afternoon. I don't know whether she had or not. Ask her."

"I'd rather wring her neck, damn her. What do you know about a bet my son made today with Pratt?"

A rumble came from Pratt: "I've told you all about that, Osgood. For God's sake give yourself a chance to cool down a little."

"I'd like to hear what this man has to say. What about it, Goodwin? Did you hear them making the bet?"

"Sure, we all heard it, including your daughter and your son's friend—name of Bronson." I surveyed him with decent compassion. "Take some advice from an old hand, mister, from one who has had the advantage of watching Nero

Wolfe at work. You're rotten at this, terrible. You remind me of a second-grade dick harassing a dip. I've seen lots of people knocked dizzy by sudden death, and if that's all that's wrong with you there's nothing anyone can give you except sympathy, but if you're really working on an idea the best thing you can do is turn it over to professionals. Have you got a suspicion you can communicate?"

"I have."

"Suspicion of what?"

"I don't know, but I don't understand what happened. I don't believe my son walked into that pasture alone, for any purpose whatever. Pratt says he was there to get the bull. That's an idiotic supposition. My son wasn't an idiot. He wasn't a greenhorn with cattle, either. Is it likely he would go up to a loose bull, and if the bull showed temper, just stand there in the dark and let it come?"

Another rumble from Pratt: "You heard what McMillan said. He might have slipped or stumbled, and the bull was too close—"

"I don't believe it! What was he there for?"

"To win ten thousand dollars."

Osgood got to his feet. He was broad-shouldered, and a little taller than Pratt, but a bit paunchy. He advanced on Pratt with fists hanging and spoke through his teeth. "You damn skunk. I warned you not to say that again . . ."

I slipped in between them, being more at home there than I was with bulls. I allotted the face to Osgood: "And when the doctor comes his duty would be to get you two bandaged up. That would be nice. If Pratt thinks your son was trying to win a bet that's what he thinks, and you asked for his opinion and you got it. Cut out the playing. Either wait till morning and get some daylight on it, or go ahead and send for the sheriff and see what he thinks of Pratt's opinion. Then the papers will print it, along with Dave's opinion and Lily Rowan's opinion and so forth, and we'll see what the public thinks. Then some intelligent reporters from New York will print an interview with the bull—"

"Well, Mr. Pratt! I'm sorry I couldn't make it sooner . . ."

We turned. It was a stocky little man with no neck, carrying a black bag.

"I was out when the call . . . oh, Mr. Osgood. This is terrible. A very terrible thing. Terrible."

I followed the trio into the next room, where the piano was, and the divan. There was no sense in Osgood going in there again, but he went. Jimmy Pratt, who had been sitting on the piano stool, got up and left. The doctor trotted over to the divan and put his bag down on a chair. Osgood crossed to a window and stood with his back to the room. When the sound came of the canvas being opened, and the doctor's voice saying "My God!" quite loud, involuntarily, Osgood turned his head half around and then turned it back again.

Thirty minutes later I went upstairs and reported to Wolfe, who, in yellow pajamas, was in the bathroom brushing his teeth:

"Doc Sackett certified accidental death from a wound inflicted by a bull. Frederick Osgood, bereaved father, who would be a duke if we had dukes or know the reason why, suspects a fly in the soup, whether for the same reason as yours or not I can't say, because you haven't told me your reason if any. I didn't know your wishes in regard to goading him with innuendo . . ."

Wolfe rinsed his mouth and spat. "I requested you merely to give direct evidence."

"There was no merely about it. I tell you Osgood is in the peerage and he doesn't believe it happened the way it did happen, his chief reason being that Clyde was too smart to fall for a bull in the dark and that there is no acceptable reason to account for Clyde being in the pasture at all. He offered those observations to Doc Sackett, along with others, but Sackett thought he was just under stress and shock, which he was, and refused to delay the certification, and arranged for an undertaker to come in the morning. Whereupon Osgood, without even asking permission to use the telephone, called up the sheriff and the state police."

"Indeed." Wolfe hung the towel on the rack. "Remind me to wire Theodore tomorrow. I found a mealy bug on one of the plants."

6

AT ELEVEN o'clock Tuesday morning I stood
working on a bottle of milk which I had
brought in from a dairy booth, one of hundreds lining the
enormous rotunda of the main exhibits building at the Crowfield exposition grounds, and watching Nero Wolfe being
gracious to an enemy. I was good and weary. On account of
the arrival of the officers of the law at Pratt's around midnight, and their subsequent antics, I hadn't got to bed until
after two. Wolfe had growled me out again before seven.
Pratt and Caroline had been with us at breakfast, but not
Lily Rowan or Jimmy. Pratt, looking as if he hadn't slept at
all, reported that McMillan had insisted on guarding the bull
the remainder of the night and was now upstairs in bed.
Jimmy had gone to Crowfield with a list of names which
probably wasn't complete, to send telegrams cancelling the
invitations to the barbecue. It seemed likely that Hickory
Caesar Grindon's carcass would never inspire a rustic festivity,
but his destiny was uncertain. All that had been decided
about him was that he wouldn't be eaten on Thursday. He
had been convicted by the sheriff and the state police, who
had found lying in the pasture, near the spot where Clyde
Osgood had died, a tie-rope with a snap at one end, which
had been identified as the one which had been left hanging
on the fence. Even that had not satisfied Frederick Osgood,
but it had satisfied the police, and they had dismissed Osgood's suspicions as vague, unsupported, and imaginary.
When, back upstairs packing, I had asked Wolfe if he was
satisfied too, he had grunted and said, "I told you last night
that Mr. Osgood was not killed by the bull. My infernal
curiosity led me to discover that much, and the weapon
that was used, but I refuse to let the minor details of the
problem take possession of my mind, so we won't discuss it."

"You might just mention who did it—"

"Please, Archie."

I put it away with moth balls and went on with the luggage.

We were decamping for a Crowfield hotel. The contract for bull-nursing was cancelled, and though Pratt mumbled something about our staying on to be polite, the atmosphere of the house said go. So the packing, and lugging to the car, and spraying the orchids and getting them on board too, and the drive to Crowfield with Caroline as chauffeur, and the fight for a hotel room which was a pippin—I mean the fight, not the room—and getting both Wolfe and the crates out to the exposition grounds and finding our space and getting the plants from the crates without injury . . . It was in fact quite a morning.

Now, at eleven o'clock, I was providing for replacement of my incinerated tissue by filling up with milk. The orchids had been sprayed and straightened and manicured and were on the display benches in the space which had been allotted to us. The above-mentioned enemy that Wolfe was being gracious to was a short fat person in a dirty unpressed mohair suit with keen little black eyes and two chins, by name Charles E. Shanks. I watched them and listened to them as I sipped the milk, because it was instructive. Shanks knew that the reason Wolfe had busted precedent and come to Crowfield to exhibit albinos which he had got by three new crosses with Paphiopedilum lawrenceanum hyeanum was to get an award over one Shanks had produced by crossing P. callosum sanderae with a new species from Burma; that Wolfe desired and intended to make a monkey of Shanks because Shanks had fought shy of the metropolitan show and had also twice refused Wolfe's offers to trade albinos; and that one good look at the entries in direct comparison made it practically certain that the judges' decision would render Shanks not only a monkey but even a baboon. Furthermore, Wolfe knew that Shanks knew that they both knew; but hearing them gabbing away you might have thought that when a floriculturist wipes his brow it is to remove not sweat but his excess of brotherly love; which is why, knowing the stage of vindictiveness Wolfe had had to arrive at before he decided on that trip, I say it was instructive to listen to them.

I had been subjected to a few minor vexations in connection with the pasture affair. During the battle for a room at the hotel I had been approached by a bright-eyed boy with big ears and a notebook who grabbed me by the lapel and said he wanted, not only for the local Journal but also for the Associated Press, as lurid an account as possible of the carnage and gore. I traded him a few swift details for his help on the room problem. A couple of other news retrievers, in town to cover the exposition I suppose, also came sniffing around; and while I had been helping Wolfe get the orchids primped up I had been accosted by a tall skinny guy in a pin-check suit, as young as me or younger, wearing a smile that I would recognize if I saw it in Siam—the smile of an elected person who expects to run again, or a novice in training to join the elected person class at the first opportunity. He looked around to make sure no spies were sneaking up on us at the moment, introduced himself as Mr. Whosis, Assistant District Attorney of Crowfield County, and told me at the bottom of his voice, shifting from the smile to Expression 9B, which is used when speaking of the death of a voter, that he would like to have my version of the unfortunate occurrence at the estate of Mr. Pratt the preceding evening.

Feeling pestered, I raised my voice instead of lowering it. "District Attorney, huh? Working up a charge of murder against the bull?"

That confused him, because he had to show that he appreciated my wit without sacrificing Expression 9B; also I attracted the attention of passers-by and a few of them stopped in the aisle to look at us. He did it pretty well. No, he said, not a charge of murder, nothing like that, not even against the bull; but certain inquiries had been made and it was felt desirable to supplement the reports of the sheriff and police by firsthand information so there could be no complaint of laxity. . . .

I drew the picture for him without any retouching or painting out, and he asked a few fairly intelligent questions. When he had gone I told Wolfe about him, but Wolfe had orchids and Charles E. Shanks on his mind and showed no sign of comprehension. A little later Shanks himself appeared on the scene and that was when I went for the bottle of milk.

There was an ethical question troubling me which couldn't be definitely settled until one o'clock. In view of what had happened at Pratt's place I had no idea that Lily Rowan would show up for the lunch date, and if she didn't what was the status of the two dollars Caroline had paid me? Anyhow, I had decided that if the fee wasn't earned it wouldn't be my fault, and luckily my intentions fitted in with Wolfe's plans which he presently arranged, namely to have lunch with Shanks. I wouldn't have eaten with them anyway, since I had heard enough about stored pollen and nutritive solutions and fungus inoculation for a while, so a little before one I left the main exhibits building and headed down the avenue to the right in the direction of the tent which

covered the eatery operated by the ladies of the First Methodist Church. That struck me as an incongruous spot to pick
for being undone by a predatory blonde, but she had said
the food there was the best available at the exposition
grounds, and Caroline's reply to an inquiry during the morning ride to Crowfield had verified it, so I smothered my con-
science and went ahead.

It was another fine day and the crowd was kicking up
quite a dust. Banners, balloons, booby booths and bingo games
were all doing a rushing business, not to mention hot dogs,
orange drinks, popcorn, snake charmers, lucky wheels, shoot-
ing galleries, take a slam and win a ham, two-bit fountain
pens and Madam Shasta who reads the future and will let
you in on it for one thin dime. I passed a platform whereon
stood a girl wearing a grin and a pure gold brassière and a
Fuller brush skirt eleven inches long, and beside her a hoarse
guy in a black derby yelling that the mystic secret Dingaroola
Dance would start inside the tent in eight minutes. Fifty
people stood gazing up at her and listening to him, the men
looking as if they might be willing to take one more crack at
the mystic, and the women looking cool and contemptuous. I
moseyed along. The crowd got thicker, that being the main
avenue leading to the grandstand entrance. I got tripped up
by a kid diving between my legs in an effort to resume
contact with mamma, was glared at by a hefty milkmaid, not
bad-looking, who got her toe caught under my shoe, wriggled
away from the tip of a toy parasol which a sweet little girl
kept digging into my ribs with, and finally left the worst of
the happy throng behind and made it to the Methodist grub-
tent, having passed by the Baptists with the snooty feeling
of a man-about-town who is in the know.

Believe it or not, she was there, at a table against the canvas wall toward the rear. I pranced across the sawdust, concealing my amazement. Dressed in a light tan jersey thing,
with a blue scarf and a little blue hat, among those hearty
country folk she looked like an antelope in a herd of Guernseys. I sat down across the table from her and told her so.
She yawned and said that what she had seen of antelopes'
legs made it seem necessary to return the compliment for re-
pairs, and before I could arrange a comeback we were interrupted by a Methodist lady in white apron who wanted to
know what we would have.

Lily Rowan said, "Two chicken fricassee with dumplings."

"Wait a minute," I protested. "It says there they have
beef pot roast and veal—"

"No." Lily was firm. "The fricassee with dumplings is made by a Mrs. Miller whose husband has left her four times on account of her disposition and returned four times on account of her cooking and is still there. So I was told yesterday by Jimmy Pratt."

The Methodist bustled off. Lily looked at me with a corner of her mouth curled up and remarked as if it didn't matter much, "The chief reason I came was to see how surprised you would look when you found me here, and you don't look surprised at all and you begin by telling me I have legs like an antelope."

I shrugged. "Go ahead and nag. I admit I'm glad you came, because if you hadn't I wouldn't have known about the fricassee. Your harping on legs is childish. Your legs are unusually good and you know it and so do I. Legs are made to be walked with or looked at, not talked about, especially not in a Methodist stronghold. Are you a Catholic? What's the difference between a Catholic and a river that runs uphill?"

She didn't know and I told her, and we babbled on. The fricassee came, and the first bite, together with dumpling and gravy, made me marvel at the hellishness of Mrs. Miller's disposition, to drive a man away from that. It gave me an idea, and a few minutes later, when I saw Wolfe and Charles E. Shanks enter the tent and get settled at a table on the other side, I excused myself and went over and told him about the fricassee, and he nodded gravely.

I was corralling the last of my rice when Lily asked me when I was going back to New York. I told her it depended on what time the orchids were judged on Wednesday; we would leave either Wednesday afternoon or Thursday morning.

"Of course," she said, "we'll see each other in New York."

"Yeah?" I swallowed the rice. "What for?"

"Nothing in particular. Only I'm sure we'll see each other, because if you weren't curious about me you wouldn't be so rude, and I was curious about you before I ever saw your face, when I saw you walking across that pasture. You have a distinctive way of walking. You move very . . . I don't know . . ."

"Distinctive will do. Maybe you noticed I have a distinctive way of getting over a fence too, in case of a bull. Speaking of bulls, I understand the barbecue is off."

"Yes." She shivered a little. "Naturally. I'm thinking of leaving this afternoon. When I came away at noon there was a string of people gawking along the fence, there where your car had been . . . where we were last night. They would have crossed the pasture and swarmed all over the place if there hadn't been a state trooper there."

"With the bull in it?"

"The bull was at the far end. That what's-his-name—McMillan—took him there and tied him up again." She shivered. "I never saw anything like last night . . . I had to sit on the ground to keep from fainting. What were they asking questions for? Why did they ask if I was with you all the time? What did that have to do with him getting killed by the bull?"

"Oh, they always do that in cases of accidental death. Eye-witnesses. By the way, you won't be leaving for New York today if they hold an inquest, only I don't suppose they will. Did they ask if you had seen Clyde Osgood around there after dinner, before you went for your walk and ran onto me?"

"Yes. Of course I hadn't. Why did they ask?"

"Search me." I put sugar in my coffee and stirred. "Maybe they thought you had deprived him of all hope or something and he climbed into the pasture to commit suicide. All kinds of romantic ideas, those birds get. Did they ask if Clyde had come to Pratt's place to see you?"

"Yes." Her eyes lifted up at me and then dropped back to her coffee cup. "I didn't understand that either. Why should they think he had come to see me?"

"Oh, possibly Clyde's father sicked them on. I know when I mentioned your name to him last night and said you were there, he nearly popped open. I got the impression he had seen you once in a nightmare. Not that I think you belong in a nightmare, with your complexion and so on, but that was the impression I got."

"He's just a pain." She shrugged indifferently. "He has no right to be talking about me. Anyway, not to you." Her eyes moved up me and over me, up from my chest over my face to the top of my head, and then slowly traveled down again. "Not to you, Escamillo," she said. I wanted to slap her, because her tone, and the look in her eyes going over me, made me feel like a potato she was peeling. She asked, "What did he say?"

"Not much." I controlled myself. "Only his expression was suggestive. He spoke of wringing your neck. I gathered that you and his son Clyde had once been friends. I suppose he told the police and sheriff that, or maybe they knew it already, and that's why they asked if Clyde came to see you last night."

"Well, he didn't. He would have been more apt to come to see Caroline than me."

That was turning a new page for me, but I covered my surprise and inquired idly, "You mean Miss Pratt? Why, did they have dealings?"

"They used to have." She opened the mirror of her compact to study nature with an eye to improvement. "I guess they were engaged, or about to be. Of course you don't know about the Osgood-Pratt situation. The Osgoods have been rich for generations, they go back to a revolutionary general I think it was—their relatives in New York think the Social Register is vulgar. To me that's all a bore . . . my mother was a waitress and my father was an immigrant and made his money building sewers."

"Yet look at you. I heard Pratt say yesterday that he was born in an old shack on the spot where his new house stands."

"Yes. His father worked as a stablehand for Osgood's father. Clyde told me about it. A farmer had a beautiful daughter named Marcia and young Pratt got himself engaged to her and Frederick Osgood came back from college and saw her and married her. So she became Clyde Osgood's mother, and Nancy's. Pratt went to New York and soon began to make money. He didn't marry, and as soon as he had time to spare he started to find ways to annoy Osgood. When he bought land up here and started to build, it looked as if the annoyance might become really serious."

"And Clyde read up on family feuds and found that the best way to cure it would be for him to marry Pratt's niece. A daughter is better in such cases, but a niece will do."

"No, it wasn't Clyde's idea, it was his sister's. Nancy's." Lily closed her compact. "She was staying in New York for the winter, studying rhythm at the best night clubs, and met Jimmy and Caroline, and thought it might be helpful for the four of them to know each other, and when Clyde came down for a visit she arranged it. It made a sort of a situation, and she and Jimmy got really friendly, and so did Clyde and Caroline. Then Clyde happened to get interested in me, and I guess that reacted on Nancy and Jimmy."

"Did you and Clyde get engaged?"

"No." She looked at me, and the corner of her mouth turned up, and I saw her breasts gently putting the weave of the jersey to more strain as she breathed a deep one. "No,

Escamillo." She peeled her potato again. "I don't suppose I'll marry. Because marriage is really nothing but an economic arrangement, and I'm lucky because I don't have to let the economic part enter into it. The man would be lucky too—I mean if a man attracted me and I attracted him."

"He sure would." I was wondering which would be more satisfactory, to slap her and then kiss her, or to kiss her and then slap her. "Did Clyde attract you much?"

"He did for a while." She shivered delicately. "You know how tiresome it is when someone you found exciting gets to be nothing but a nuisance? He wanted me to marry him, too. You mustn't think I'm heartless, because I'm not. Caroline would have been a swell wife for him, and I told him so. I rather thought they would make it up, and I hoped they would, and that's why I said he would have been more apt to come to see Caroline than me last night."

"Maybe he did. Have you asked her?"

"Good lord no. Me ask Caroline anything about Clyde? I wouldn't dare mention his name to her. She hates me."

"She invited you up for the barbecue, didn't she?"

"Yes, but that was because she was being clever. Her brother Jimmy and I were beginning to be friendly, and she thought if he saw me out here in the country, a lot of me, he would realize how superficial and unhealthy I am."

"Oh. So you're unhealthy?"

"Terribly." The corner of her mouth went up another sixteenth of an inch. "Because I'm frank and simple. Because I never offer anything I don't give, and I never give anything and then expect to get paid for it. I'm frightfully unhealthy. But I guess I was wrong to say superficial. I doubt if Caroline thinks I'm superficial."

"Excuse me a minute," I said, and stood up.

Even in the midst of being ruined I had had Wolfe's table across the tent in the corner of my eye, partly to note his reaction to the fricassee, which had appeared to be satisfactory since he had ordered a second portion, and my interrupting my despoiler was on account of a sign from him. A man was standing by Wolfe's chair talking to him, and Wolfe had glanced in my direction with a lift to his brow which I considered significant. So I excused myself to Lily and got up and ambled over. As I arrived the man turned his head and I saw it was Lew Bennett, the secretary of the National Guernsey League.

"Archie, I must thank you." Wolfe put his napkin down. "For suggesting the fricassee. It is superb. Only female

Americans can make good dumplings, and not many of them."

"Yes, sir."

"You have met Mr. Bennett."

"Yes, sir."

"Can you conveniently extricate yourself from that . . ." He turned a thumb in the direction I had come from.

"You mean right now?"

"As soon as may be. Now if you are not too involved. Mr. Bennett has been looking for me at the request of Mr. Osgood, who is waiting in the exposition office and wishes to see me. Mr. Shanks and I shall have finished our lunch in ten minutes."

"Okay. I'm badly involved but I'll manage it."

I went back to my table and told Lily we must part, and summoned the Methodist to give me a check. The damage proved to be $1.60, and, having relinquished a pair of dimes for the missionaries, I reflected with pride that the firm had cleaned up 20 cents net on the deal.

Lily said in a tone of real disappointment without any petulance that I could detect, "I had supposed we would spend the afternoon together, watching the races and riding on the merry-go-round and throwing balls at things . . ."

"Not ever," I said firmly. "Not the afternoon. Whatever the future may have in store for us, whatever may betide, I work afternoons. Understand once and for all that I am a workingman and I only play with toys at odd moments. I am working when you would least expect it. Throughout this delightful lunch with you, I have been working and earning money."

"I suppose while you were paying me all those charming compliments one part of your brain, the most important part, was busy on some difficult problem."

"That's the idea."

"Dear Escamillo. Darling Escamillo. But the afternoon comes to an end, doesn't it? What will you be doing this evening?"

"God knows. I work for Nero Wolfe."

7

THE ROOM in the exposition offices, to which
Bennett led us, on a kind of mezzanine in the
Administration Building, was large and lofty, with two dusty
windows in the board wall and plain board partitions for the
other three sides. The only furniture were three big rough
tables and a dozen wooden chairs. On one table were a pile
of faded bunting and a bushel basket half-full of apples;
the other two were bare. Three of the chairs were occupied.
Sidney Darth, Chairman of the North Atlantic Exposition
Board, was on the edge of one but jumped up as we entered;
Frederick Osgood, the upstate duke, had sagging shoulders
and a tired and bitter but determined expression; and Nancy
Osgood sat with her spine curved and looked miserable
all over.

Bennett did the introductions. Darth mumbled something
about people waiting for him and loped off. Wolfe's eyes
traveled over the furniture with a hopeless look, ending at
me, meaning couldn't I for God's sake rustle a chair somewhere that would hold all of him, but I shook my head in-
flexibly, knowing how useless it was. He compressed his lips,
heaved a sigh, and sat down.

Bennett said, "I can stay if you want . . . if I can be
of any help . . ." Wolfe looked at Osgood and Osgood shook
his head: "No thanks, Lew. You run along." Bennett hesitated
a second, looking as if he wouldn't mind staying a bit, and
then beat it. After the door had closed behind him I requisitioned a chair for myself and sat down.

Osgood surveyed Wolfe with an aristocratic scowl. "So
you're Nero Wolfe. I understand you came to Crowfield to
exhibit orchids."

Wolfe snapped at him, "Who told you so?"

The scowl got half startled away, but came right back
again. "Does it matter who told me?"

"No. Nor does it matter why I came to Crowfield. Mr.

Bennett said you wished to consult me, but surely not about orchids."

I restrained a grin, knowing that Wolfe was not only establishing control, which was practical and desirable, but was also relieving his resentment at having been sent for and having come, even if it was on his way anyhow.

"I don't give a damn about the orchids." Osgood preserved the scowl. "The purpose of your presence here is relevant because I need to know if you are a friend of Tom Pratt's, or are being employed by him, or have been. You were at his house last night."

"Relevant to what, sir?" Wolfe sounded patient with distress. "Either you want to consult me or you don't. If you do, and I find that I am in any way committed to a conflicting interest, I shall tell you so. You have started badly and offensively. Why the devil should I account to you for my presence here in Crowfield or anywhere else? If you need me, here I am. What can I do for you?"

"Are you a friend of Tom Pratt's?"

Wolfe grunted with exasperation, got himself raised, and took a step. "Come, Archie."

Osgood raised his voice: "Where you going? Damn it, haven't I got a right to ask—"

"No, sir." Wolfe glared down at him. "You have no right to ask me anything whatever. I am a professional detective in good standing. If I accept a commission I perform it. If for any reason I can't undertake it in good faith, I refuse it. Come, Archie."

I arose with reluctance. Not only did I hate to walk out on what might develop into a nice piece of business, but also my curiosity had been aroused by the expression on Nancy Osgood's face. When Wolfe had got up and started to go she had looked relieved, and when after Osgood's protest he had started off again her relief had been even more evident. Little contrary things like that disturbed my peace of mind, so it suited me fine when Osgood surrendered.

"All right," he growled. "I apologize. Come back and sit down. Of course I've heard about you and your damned independence. I'll have to swallow it because I need you and I can't help it. These damn fools here . . . in the first place they have no brains and in the second place they're a pack of cowards. I want you to investigate the death of my son Clyde."

Sure enough, as Wolfe accepted the apology by returning

to sit down, Nancy quit looking relieved and her hands on her lap, having relaxed a little, were clasped tight again.

Wolfe asked, "What aspect of your son's death do you want investigated?"

Osgood said savagely, "I want to know how he was killed."

"By a bull. Wasn't he? Isn't that the verdict of the legal and medical authorities?"

"Verdict hell. I don't believe it. My son knew cattle. What was he in the pasture at night for? Pratt's idea that he went there to get the bull is ridiculous. And he certainly wasn't ass enough to let himself be gored like that in the pitch-dark."

"Still he was gored." Wolfe shifted on the measly chair. "If not by the bull, then how and by what?"

"I don't know. I don't pretend to know. You're an expert and that's what I want you to find out. You're supposed to have intelligence above the average . . . what do you think? You were at Pratt's place. Knowing the circumstances as you do, do you think he was killed by the bull?"

Wolfe sighed. "Expert opinions cost money, Mr. Osgood. Especially mine. I charge high fees. I doubt if I can accept a commission to investigate your son's death. My intention is to leave for New York Thursday morning, and I shouldn't care to be delayed much beyond that. I like to stay at home, and when I am away I like to get back. Without committing myself to an investigation, my fee for an opinion, now, will be a thousand dollars."

Osgood stared. "A thousand dollars just to say what you think?"

"To say what I have deduced and decided, yes. I doubt if it's worth it to you."

"Then why the devil do you ask it?"

Nancy's voice came in, a husky protest, "Dad. I told you. It's foolish . . . it's all so foolish . . ."

Wolfe glanced at her, and back at her father, and shrugged. "That's the price, sir."

"For one man's guess."

"Oh, no. For the truth."

"Truth? You're prepared to prove it?"

"No. I sell it as an opinion. But I don't sell guesses."

"All right. I'll pay for it. What is it?"

"Well." Wolfe pursed his lips and half shut his eyes. "Clyde Osgood did not enter the pasture voluntarily. He was unconscious, though still alive, when he was placed in the pasture. He was not gored, and therefore not killed, by the bull. He was murdered, probably by a man, possibly by two men, barely possibly by a woman or a man and a woman."

Nancy had straightened up with a gasp and then sat stiff. Osgood was gazing at Wolfe with his clamped jaw working a little from side to side.

"That . . ." He stopped and clamped his jaw again. "You say that's the truth? That my son was murdered?"

"Yes. Without a guaranty. I sell it as an opinion."

"How good is it? Where did you get it? Damn you, if you're playing me—"

"Mr. Osgood! Really. I'm not playing, I'm working. I assure you my opinion is a good one. Whether it's worth what you're paying for it depends on what you do with it."

Osgood got up, took two steps, and was looking down at his daughter. "You hear that, Nancy?" he demanded, as if he was accusing her of something. "You hear what he says? I knew it, I tell you, I knew it." He jerked his head up. "Good God . . . my son dead . . . murdered . . ." He whirled to Wolfe, opened his mouth and closed it again, and went back to his chair and let himself down.

Nancy looked at Wolfe and asked indignantly, "Why do you say that? How can you know . . . Clyde was murdered? Why do you say it as if . . . as if you could know . . ."

"Because I had arrived at that opinion, Miss Osgood."

"But how? Why?"

"Be quiet, Nancy." Osgood turned to Wolfe. "All right, I've got your opinion. Now I want to know what you base it on."

"My deductions. I was there last night, with a flashlight."

"Deductions from what?"

"From the facts." Wolfe wiggled a finger at him. "You may have them if you want them, but see here. You spoke of 'these damn fools here' and called them a pack of cowards. Referring to the legal authorities?"

"Yes. The District Attorney and the sheriff."

"Do you call them cowards because they hesitate to institute an investigation of your son's death?"

"They don't merely hesitate, they refuse. They say my suspicions are arbitrary and unfounded. They don't use those words, but that's what they mean. They simply don't want to pick up something they're afraid they can't handle."

"But you have position, power, political influence—"

"No. Especially not with Waddell, the District Attorney. I opposed him in '36, and it was chiefly Tom Pratt's money that elected him. But this is murder! You say yourself it was murder!"

"They may be convinced it wasn't. That's quite plausible under the circumstances. Do you suggest they would bottle up a murder to save Pratt annoyance?"

"No. Or yes. I don't care a damn which. I only know they won't listen to reason and I'm helpless, and I intend that whoever killed my son shall suffer for it. That's why I came to you."

"Precisely." Wolfe shifted in his chair again. "The fact is, you haven't given them much reason to listen to. You have told them your son wouldn't have entered the pasture, but he was there; and that he wasn't fool enough to let a bull kill him in the dark, which is conjectural and by no means a demonstrated fact. You have asked me to investigate your son's death, but I couldn't undertake it unless the police exert themselves simultaneously. There will be a lot of work to do, and I have no assistance here except Mr. Goodwin; and I can't commandeer evidence. If I move in the affair at all, the first stop must be to enlist the authorities. Is the District Attorney's office in Crowfield?"

"Yes."

"Is he there now?"

"Yes."

"Then I suggest that we see him. I engage to persuade him to start an investigation immediately. That of course will call for an additional fee, but I shall try not to make it extravagant. After that is done we can reconsider your request that I undertake an investigation myself. You may decide it isn't necessary, or I may regard it as impractical. Do you have a car there? May Mr. Goodwin drive it? He ran mine into a tree."

"I do my own driving. Or my daughter does. I don't like going back to that jackass Waddell."

"I'm afraid it's unavoidable." Wolfe elevated his bulk. "Certain things must be done without delay, and they will need authority behind them."

It turned out that the daughter drove. We found Osgood's big black sedan parked in a privileged and exclusive space at one side of the Administration Building, and piled in. I sat in front with Nancy. For the two miles into Crowfield the highway and streets were cluttered with the exposition traffic, and although she was impulsive with the wheel and jerky on the gas pedal, she did it pretty well. I glanced around once and saw Wolfe hanging onto the strap for dear life. We finally rolled up to the curb in front of a stretch of lawn and a big old stone building with its status carved above the entrance: CROWFIELD COUNTY COURT HOUSE.

Osgood, climbing out, spoke to his daughter: "You go on home, Nancy, to your mother. There was no sense in your coming anyway. I'll phone when there is anything to say."

Wolfe intervened, "It would be better for her to wait for us here. In case I take this job I shall need to talk with her without delay."

"With my daughter?" Osgood scowled. "What for? Nonsense!"

"As you please, sir." Wolfe shrugged. "It's fairly certain I won't want the job. For one thing, you're too infernally combative for a client."

"But why the devil should you need to talk to my daughter?"

"To get information. I offer you advice, Mr. Osgood: go home with your daughter and forget this quest for vengeance. There is no other form of human activity quite so impertinent as a competent murder investigation, and I fear you're not equipped to tolerate it. Abandon the idea. You can mail me a check at your convenience—"

"I'm going on with it."

"Then prepare yourself for annoyance, intrusion, plague, the insolence of publicity—"

"I'm going on with it."

"Indeed." Wolfe inclined his head an inch toward the lovely but miserable face of the daughter at the steering wheel. "Then you will please wait here, Miss Osgood."

8

In all ordinary circumstances Wolfe's cocky and unlimited conceit prevents the development of any of the tender sentiments, such as compassion for instance, but that afternoon I felt sorry for him. He was being compelled to break some of his most ironclad rules. He was riding behind strange drivers, walking in crowds, obeying a summons from a prospective client, and calling upon a public official, urged on by his desperate desire to find a decent place to sit down. The hotel room we had managed to get—since we hadn't arrived Monday evening to claim the one we had reserved—was small, dark and noisy, and had one window which overlooked a building operation where a concrete mixer was raising cain. If you opened the window, cement dust entered in clouds. There was nowhere at all to sit near our space in the exhibits building. At the Methodist tent they had folding chairs. The ones at the room where we had gone to meet Osgood, where Wolfe had probably expected something fairly tolerable, had been little better; and obviously Wolfe regarded the District Attorney's office as a sort of forlorn last hope. I never saw him move faster than when we entered and a swift glance showed him there was just one upholstered, in dingy black leather, with arms. You might almost have called it a swoop. He stood in front of it for the introduction and then sank.

Carter Waddell, the District Attorney, was pudgy and middle-aged and inclined to bubble. I suppose he did special bubbling for Osgood, on account of sympathy for bereavement and to show that the 1936 election had left no hard feelings, not to mention his love for his country of which Osgood owned 2000 acres. He said he was perfectly willing to reopen the discussion they had had earlier in the day, though his own opinion was unaltered. Osgood said he didn't intend to discuss it himself, that would be a waste of time and effort, but that Mr. Nero Wolfe had something to say.

"By all means," Waddell bubbled. "Certainly. Mr. Wolfe's

reputation is well known, of course. Doubtless we poor rustics could learn a great deal from him. Couldn't we, Mr. Wolfe?"

Wolfe murmured, "I don't know your capacity, Mr. Waddell. But I do think I have something pertinent to offer regarding the murder of Clyde Osgood."

"Murder?" Waddell stretched his eyes wide. "Now I don't know. *Petitio principii* isn't a good way to begin. Is it?"

"Of course not." Wolfe wriggled himself comfortable, and sighed. "I offer the word as something to be established, not as a postulate. Did you ever see a bull kill a man, or injure one with his horn?"

"No, I can't say I have."

"Did you ever see a bull who had just gored a man or a horse or any animal? Immediately after the goring?"

"No."

"Well, I have . . . long ago . . . a dozen times or more, at bullfights. Horses killed, and men injured . . . one man killed." Wolfe wiggled a finger. "Whether you've seen it or not, surely you can imagine what happens when a bull thrusts his horn deep into a living body, and tosses, and tears the wound. While the heart of the victim is still furiously pumping. Blood spurts all over the bull's face and head, and often clear to his shoulders and beyond. The bleeding of a man killed in that manner is frightful; the instant such a wound is made a torrent gushes forth. It was so in the case of Clyde Osgood. His clothing was saturated. I am told that the police report that where he was killed there is an enormous caked pool of it. Is that correct? You acknowledge it Last night Mr. Goodwin, my assistant, found the bull turning Clyde Osgood's body over on the ground, with his horns, without much force or enthusiasm. The natural supposition was that the bull had killed him. Not more than fifteen minutes later, when the bull had been tied to the fence, I examined him at close range with a flashlight. He has a white face, and there was only one smudge of blood on it, and his horns were bloody only a few inches down from the tips. Was that fact included in the police report?"

Waddell said slowly, "I don't remember . . . no."

"Then I advise that the bull be inspected at once, provided he hasn't been already washed off. I assure you that my report is reliable." Wolfe wiggled a finger again. "I didn't come here to offer a conjecture, Mr. Waddell. I don't intend to argue it with you. Often in considering phenomena we encounter a suspicious circumstance which requires study and permits debate, but the appearance of the bull's face and head last night is not that, it is much more. It is conclusive proof that the bull didn't kill Clyde Osgood. You spoke of my reputation; I stake it on this."

"By God," Clyde Osgood's father muttered. "Well, by God. I looked at that bull myself, and I never thought . . ."

"I'm afraid you weren't doing much thinking last night," Wolfe told him. "It couldn't be expected of you. But it might have been expected of the police by the sanguine . . . particularly the rustic police."

The District Attorney, without any sign of bubbling, said, "You've made a point, I grant that. Of course you have. But I'd like to have a doctor's opinion about the bleeding—"

"It was all over his clothes and the grass. Great quantities. If you consult a doctor, let it be the one who saw the wound. In the meantime, it would be well to act, and act soon, on the assumption that the bull didn't do it, because that's the fact."

"You're very positive, Mr. Wolfe. Very."

"I am."

"Isn't it possible that the bull withdrew his horn so quickly that he escaped the spurt of blood?"

"No. The spurt is instantaneous, and bulls don't gore like that anyway. They stay in to tear. Has the wound been described to you?"

Waddell nodded. I noticed that he wasn't looking at Osgood. "That's another thing," he said. "That wound. If it wasn't made by the bull, what could possibly have done it? What kind of weapon?"

"The weapon is right there, not thirty yards from the pasture fence. Or was. I examined it."

I thought, uh-huh, see the bright little fat boy with all the pretty skyrockets! But I stared at him, and so did the others. Osgood ejaculated something, and Waddell's voice had a crack in it as he demanded, "You what?"

"I said, I examined it."

"The weapon that killed him?"

"Yes. I borrowed a flashlight from Mr. Goodwin, because of a slight difficulty in believing that Clyde Osgood would let himself be gored by a bull in the dark. I had heard him remark, in the afternoon, that he knew cattle. Later his father experienced the same difficulty, but didn't know how to resolve it. I did so by borrowing the light and inspecting the bull, and perceived at once that the supposition which already prevailed was false. The bull hadn't killed him. Then what had?"

Wolfe squirmed in his chair, which was after all eight

inches too narrow, and continued, "It is an interesting question whether rapid and accurate brain work results from superior equipment or from good training. In my case, whatever my original equipment may have been, it has certainly had the advantage of prolonged and severe training. One result, not always pleasant and rarely profitable, is that I am likely to forget myself and concentrate on problems which are none of my business. I did so last night. Within thirty seconds after inspecting the bull's clean face, I had guessed at a possible weapon. Knowing where it was, I went and inspected it, and verified my guess. I then returned to the house. By the time I arrived there I had reached a conclusion as to how the crime had been committed—and I have not altered it since."

"What was the weapon? Where was it?"

"It was rustic too. An ordinary pick for digging. In the afternoon, in an emergency created by the bull—preceded by Mr. Goodwin's destruction of my car—I had been conveyed from the pasture by Miss Pratt in an automobile. We had passed by an excavation—the barbecue pit as I learned afterwards—with freshly dug earth and picks and shovels lying there. My guess was that a pick might have been used. I went with a flashlight to see, and found confirmation. There were two picks. One of them was perfectly dry, with bits of dried soil clinging to it, and the other was damp. Even the metal itself was still damp on the under side, and the wooden handle was positively wet. There was no particle of soil clinging to the metal. Obviously the thing had been thoroughly and recently washed, not more than an hour previously at the outside. Not far away I found the end of a piece of garden hose. It was connected somewhere, for when I turned the nozzle a little, water came. Around where the nozzle lay the grass was quite wet when I pressed my palm into it. It was more than a surmise, it was close to a certainty, that the pick had done the goring, got deluged with blood, been carefully washed with the garden hose and replaced on the pile of excavated soil where I found it."

"You mean—" Frederick Osgood stopped with his jaw clamped. His clenched fists, resting on his hams, showed white knuckles. He went on, harshly, "My son . . . was killed like that . . . dug at with a pick?"

Waddell was looking decomposed. He tried to bluster. "If all this is true—you knew it last night, didn't you? Why the hell didn't you spill it when the sheriff was there? When the cops were there on the spot?"

"I represented no interest last night, sir."

"What about the interest of justice? You're a citizen, aren't you? Did you ever hear of withholding evidence—"

"Nonsense. I didn't withhold the bull's face or the pick. You must know you're being silly. My cerebral processes, and the conclusions they lead me to, belong to me."

"You say the pick handle was wet and there was no dirt sticking to the metal. Couldn't it have been washed for some legitimate reason? Did you inquire about that?"

"I made no inquiries of anybody. At eleven o'clock at night the pick handle was wet. If you regard it as a rational project to find a legitimate nocturnal pick-washer, go ahead. The time might be better spent, if you need confirmation, in looking for blood residue in the grass around the hose nozzle and examining the pick handle with a microscope. It is hard to remove all vestige of blood from a piece of wood. Those steps are of course obvious, and others as well."

"You're telling me." The District Attorney sent a glance, half a glare, at Osgood, and away again, back at Wolfe. "Now look here, don't get me wrong . . . you neither, Fred Osgood. I'm the prosecutor for this county and I know my duty and I intend to do it and I try to do it. If there's been a crime I don't want to back off from it and neither does Sam Lake, but I'm not going to raise a stink just for the hell of it and you can't blame me for that. The people who elected me wouldn't want it and nobody ought to want it. And the way it looks to me—in spite of no blood on the bull and whether I find a legitimate nocturnal pick-washer or not—it still strikes me as cuckoo. Did he climb into the pasture carrying the pick—where the bull was—and then Clyde Osgood climbed in after him and obligingly stood there while he swung the pick? Or was Clyde already in the pasture, and he climbed in with the pick and let him have it? Can you imagine aiming anything as clumsy and heavy as a pick at a man in the dark, and him still being there when it landed? And wouldn't the blood spurt all over you too? Who is he and where did he go to, covered with blood?"

Osgood snarled, "I told you, Wolfe. Listen to the damn fool.—Look here, Carter Waddell! Now I'll tell you something—"

"Please, gentlemen!" Wolfe had a palm up. "We're wasting a lot of time." He regarded the District Attorney and said patiently, "You're going about it wrong. You should stop squirming and struggling. Finding yourself confronted by an unpleasant fact . . . you're like a woman who conceals a stain on a table cover by putting an ash tray over it. Ineffectual, because someone is sure to move the ash tray. The fact is that Clyde Osgood was murdered by someone with that pick, and unhappily your function is to establish the fact and reveal its mechanism; you can't obliterate it merely by inventing unlikely corollaries."

"I didn't invent anything, I only—"

"Pardon me. You assumed the fictions that Clyde climbed the fence into the pasture and obligingly stood in the dark and permitted himself to be fatally pierced by a clumsy pick. I admit that the first is unlikely and the second next to incredible. Those considerations occurred to me last night on the spot. As I said, by the time I reached the house I had satisfied myself as to how the crime was committed, and I am still satisfied. I don't believe Clyde Osgood climbed the fence. He was first rendered unconscious, probably by a blow on the head. He was then dragged or carried to the fence, and pushed under it or lifted over it, and further dragged or carried ten or fifteen yards into the pasture, and left lying on his side. The murderer then stood behind him with the pick and swung it powerfully in the natural and ordinary manner, only instead of piercing and tearing the ground it pierced and tore his victim. The wound would perfectly resemble the goring of a bull. The blood-spurt would of course soil the pick, but not the man who wielded it. He got the tie-rope from where it was hanging on the fence and tossed it on the ground near the body, to make it appear that Clyde had entered the pasture with it; then he took the pick to the convenient hose nozzle, washed it off, returned it where he had got it, and went—" Wolfe shrugged "—went somewhere."

"The bull," Waddell said. "Did the bull just stand and look on and wait for the murderer to leave, and then push the body around so as to have bloody horns? Even a rustic sheriff might have noticed it if he had had no blood on him at all."

"I couldn't say. It was dark. A bull may or may not attack in the dark. But I suggest (1) the murderer, knowing how to handle a bull in the dark, before performing with the pick, approached the bull, snapped the tie-rope onto the nose ring, and led him to the fence and tied him. Later, before releasing him, he smeared blood on his horns. Or (2), after the pick had been used the murderer enticed the bull to the spot and left him there, knowing that the smell of blood would lead him to investigate. Or (3), the murderer acted when the bull was in another part of the pasture and made no effort to manufacture the evidence of bloody horns, thinking that in the excitement and with the weight of other circumstances as arranged, it wouldn't matter. It was his good luck that Mr. Goodwin happened to arrive while the bull was satisfying his curiosity . . . and his bad luck that I happened to arrive at all."

Waddell sat frowning, his mouth screwed up. After a moment he blurted, "Fingerprints on the pick handle."

Wolfe shook his head. "A handkerchief or a tuft of grass, to carry it after washing it. I doubt if the murderer was an idiot."

Waddell frowned some more. "Your idea about tying the bull to the fence and smearing blood on his horns. That would be getting pretty familiar with a bull, even in the dark. I don't suppose anyone could have done it except Monte Mc-Millan . . . he was Monte's bull, or he had been. Maybe you're ready to explain why Monte McMillan would want to kill Clyde Osgood?"

"Good heavens, no. There are at least two other alternatives. Mr. McMillan may be capable of murder, I don't know, and he was certainly resolved to protect the bull from molestation—but don't get things confused. Remember that the murder was no part of an effort to guard the bull; Clyde was knocked unconscious not in the pasture, but somewhere else."

"That's your guess."

"It's my opinion. I am careful with my opinions, sir; they are my bread and butter and the main source of my self-esteem."

Waddell sat with his mouth screwed up. Suddenly Osgood barked at him ferociously:

"Well, what about it?"

Waddell nodded at him, and then unscrewed his mouth to mutter, "Of course." He got up and kicked his chair back, stuck his hands in his pockets, stood and gazed at Wolfe a minute, and then backed up and sat down again. "Goddam it," he said in a pained voice. "Of course. We've got to get on it as quick and hard as we can. Jesus, what a mess. At Tom Pratt's place. Clyde Osgood. Your son, Fred. And you know the kind of material I have to work with—for instance Sam Lake—on a thing like this . . . I'll have to pull them away from the exposition . . . I'll go out and see Pratt myself, now . . ."

He jerked himself forward and reached for the telephone.

Osgood said to Wolfe, bitterly, "You see the prospect."

Wolfe nodded, and sighed. "It's an extraordinarily difficult situation, Mr. Osgood."

"I know damn well it is. I may have missed the significance

of the bull's face, but I'm not a fool. The devil had brains and nerve and luck. I have two things to say to you. First, I apologize again for the way I tackled you this afternoon. I didn't know you had really earned your reputation, so many people haven't, but I see now you have. Second, you can see for yourself that you'll have to do this. You'll have to go on with it."

Wolfe shook his head. "I expect to leave for New York Thursday morning. Day after tomorrow."

"But my God, man! This is what you do, isn't it? Isn't this your job? What's the difference whether you work at it in New York or here?"

"Enormous; the difference, I mean. In New York I have my home, my office in it, my cook, my accustomed surroundings—"

"Do you mean . . ." Osgood was up, spluttering. "Do you mean to say you have the gall to plead your personal comfort, your petty convenience, to a man in the position I'm in?"

"I do." Wolfe was serene. "I'm not responsible for the position you're in. Mr. Goodwin will tell you: I have a deep aversion to leaving my home or remaining long away from it. Another thing, you might not think me so petty if you could see and hear and smell the hotel room in which I shall have to sleep tonight and tomorrow night . . . and heavens knows how many more nights if I accepted your commission."

"What's wrong with it?"

"Everything imaginable."

"Then leave it. Come to my house. It's only sixteen miles out, and you can have a car until yours is repaired, and your man here can drive it . . ."

"I don't know." Wolfe looked doubtful. "Of course, if I undertake it I shall need immediately a good deal of information from you and your daughter, and your own home would be a good place for that . . ."

I stood up with my heels together and saluted him, and he glared at me. Naturally he knew I was on to him. Machiavelli was a simple little shepherd lad by comparison. Not that I disapproved by any means, for the chances were that I would get a fairly good bed myself, but it was one more proof that under no circumstances could you ever really trust him.

9

WITH NANCY still chauffering, we drove to the hotel for our luggage, and then had to leave town by way of the exposition grounds in order to give the orchids a look and another spraying. Shanks wasn't around, and Wolfe made arrangements with a skinny woman who sat on an upturned box by a table full of dahlias, to keep an eye on our pots.

Driving into Crowfield that morning, Caroline Pratt had pointed out the Osgood demesne, the main entrance of which was only a mile from Pratt's place. It was rolling farm land, a lot of it looking like pasture, with three or four wooded knolls. The stock barns and other outbuildings were in plain view, but the dwelling, which was all of half a mile from the highway, was out of sight among the trees until the private drive straightened out at the beginning of a wide expanse of lawn. It was a big old rambling white house, with an old-fashioned portico, with pillars, extending along the middle portion of the front. It looked as if it had probably once been George Washington's headquarters, provided he ever got that far north.

There was an encounter before we got into the house. As we crossed the portico, a man approached from the other end, wiping his brow with his handkerchief and looking dusty and sweaty. Mr. Bronson had on a different shirt and tie from the day before, and another suit, but was no more appropriate to his surroundings than he had been when I first saw him on Pratt's terrace. Osgood tossed a nod at him, then, seeing that he intended to speak, stopped and said, "Hullo."

Bronson came up to us. I hadn't noticed him much the day before, with my attention elsewhere, but I remarked now that he was around thirty, of good height and well-built, with a wide full mouth and a blunt nose and clever gray eyes. I didn't like the eyes, as they took us in with a quick glance. He said deferentially, "I hope you won't mind, Mr. Osgood. I've been over there."

"Over where?" Osgood demanded.

"Pratt's place. I walked across the fields. I knew I had offended you by disagreeing this morning with your ideas about the . . . accident. I wanted to look it over. I met young Pratt, but not his father, and that man McMillan—"

"What did you expect to accomplish by that?"

"Nothing, I suppose. I'm sorry if I've offended again. But I didn't . . . I was discreet. I suppose I shouldn't be here, I should have left this morning, but with this terrible . . .with Clyde dead, and I'm the only one of his New York friends here . . . it seemed . . ."

"It doesn't matter," said Osgood roughly. "Stay. I said so."

"I know you did, but frankly . . . I feel very much de trop . . . I'll leave now if you prefer it . . ."

"Excuse me." It was Wolfe's quiet murmur. "You had better stay, Mr. Bronson. Much better. We may need you."

The clever eyes flickered at him. "Oh. If Nero Wolfe says stay . . ." He lifted his shoulders and let them down. "But I don't need to stay here. I can go to a Crowfield hotel—"

"Nonsense." Osgood scowled at him. "Stay here. You were Clyde's guest, weren't you? Stay here. But if you want to walk in the fields, there's plenty of directions besides the one leading to Pratt's."

Abruptly he started off, and we followed, as Bronson again lifted his handkerchief to his sweaty brow.

A few minutes later we were seated in a large room with French windows, lined with books and furnished for comfort, and were being waited on by a lassie with a pug nose who had manners far superior to Bert's but was way beneath him in speed and spirit as a drink-slinger. Nancy had disappeared but was understood to be on call. Osgood was scowling at a highball, Wolfe was gulping beer which, judging from his expression, was too warm, and I had plain water.

Wolfe was saying testily, "My own method is the only one available to me. I either use that or none at all. I may be only clearing away rubbish, but that's my affair. The plain fact is, sir, that last night, in Mr. Goodwin's presence, you behaved in an astonishing manner to him and Mr. Pratt. You were rude, arrogant and unreasonable. I need to know whether that was due to the emotional shock you had had, or to your belief that Mr. Pratt was somehow involved in the death of your son, or was merely your normal conduct."

"I was under a strain, of course," Osgood snapped. "I suppose I'm inclined to arrogance, if you want to call it that. I wouldn't like to think I'm habitually rude, but I would be rude to Pratt on sight if the circumstances were such that I couldn't ignore him. Last night I couldn't ignore him. Call it normal conduct and forget it."

"Why do you dislike and despise Mr. Pratt?"

"Damn it, I tell you that has nothing to do with it! It's an old story. It had no bearing—"

"It wouldn't account for a reciprocal hatred from Mr. Pratt that might have led him to murder?"

"No." Osgood stirred impatiently and put down his highball. "No."

"Can you suggest any other motive Mr. Pratt might have had for murdering your son? Make it plausible."

"I can't make it plausible or implausible. Pratt's vindictive and tricky, and in his youth he had fits of violence. His father worked for my father as a stablehand. In a fit of temper he might have murdered, yes."

Wolfe shook his head. "That won't do. The murder was carefully planned and executed. The plan may have been rapid and extempore, but it was cold and thorough. Besides, your son was not discovered in an effort to molest the bull, remember that. You insisted on that point yourself before you had my demonstration of it. What could have got Mr. Pratt into a murderous temper toward your son if he didn't find him trying to molest the bull?"

"I don't know. Nothing that I know of."

"I ask the same question regarding Jimmy Pratt."

"I don't know him. I've never seen him."

"Actually never seen him?"

"Well . . . seen him perhaps. I don't know him."

"Did Clyde know him?"

"I believe they were acquainted. They met in New York."

"Do you know of any motive Jimmy Pratt might have had for killing your son?"

"No."

"I ask the same question regarding Caroline Pratt."

"The same answer. They too met in New York, but the acquaintance was slight."

"Excuse me, boss," I put in. "Do I release cats in public?"

"Certainly." Wolfe shot me a glance. "We're talking of Mr. Osgood's son, who is dead."

"Okay. Clyde and Caroline Pratt were engaged to be married, but the clutch slipped."

"Indeed," Wolfe murmured. Osgood glared at me and said, "Ridiculous. Who the devil told you that?"

I disregarded him and told Wolfe, "Guaranteed. They were

engaged for quite a while, only apparently Clyde didn't want
his father to know that he had been hooked by a female Pratt
who was also an athlete. Then Clyde saw something else
and made a dive for it, and the Osgood-Pratt axis got multiple
fracture. The something else was the young lady who was
outdoors with me last night, named Lily Rowan. Later . . .
we're up to last spring now . . . she skidded again and Clyde
fell off. Since then he has been hanging around New York
trying to get back on. One guess is that he came up here because he knew she would be here, but that's not in the guarantee. I haven't had a chance—"

Osgood was boiling. "This is insufferable! Preposterous
gossip! If this is your idea—"

I growled at Wolfe, "Ask him why he wants to wring Lily
Rowan's neck."

"Mr. Osgood, please." Wolfe keyed it up. "I warned you
that a murder investigation is of necessity intrusive and impertinent. Either bear it or abandon it. If you resent the vul-
garity of Mr. Goodwin's jargon I don't blame you, but nothing can be done about it. If you resent his disclosure of facts,
nothing can be done about that either except to drop the
inquiry. We have to know things. What about your son's engagement to marry Miss Pratt?"

"I never heard of it. He never mentioned it. Neither did
my daughter, and she would have known of it; she and Clyde
were very close to each other. I don't believe it."

"You may, I think, now. My assistant is careful about facts.
What about the entanglement with Miss Rowan?"

"That . . . yes." As badly as Osgood's head needed a rest,
it was a struggle for him to remove the ducal coronet. "You
understand this is absolutely confidential."

"I doubt it. I suspect that at least a hundred people in
New York know more about it than you do. But what do
you know?"

"I know that about a year ago my son became infatuated
with the woman. He wanted to marry her. She's wealthy, or
her father is. She's a sex maniac. She wouldn't marry him. If
she had she would have ruined him, but she did that anyway,
or she was doing it. She got tired of him, but her claws were
in him so deep he couldn't get them out, and there was no
way of persuading him to act like a man. He wouldn't come
home; he stayed in New York because she was there. He
wasted a lot of my money and I cut off his income entirely,
but that didn't help. I don't know what he has been living on
the past four months, but I suspect my daughter has been

helping him, though I decreased her allowance and forbade it. I went to New York in May and went to see the Rowan woman, and humiliated myself, but it did no good. She's a damned strumpet."

"Not by definition. A strumpet takes money. However . . . I see, at this point, no incentive for Miss Rowan to murder him. Miss Pratt . . . it might be. She was jilted, and she is muscular. Mortification could simmer in a woman's breast a long time, though she doesn't look it. When did your son arrive here from New York?"

"Sunday evening. My daughter and his friend Bronson rode up with him."

"Had you expected him?"

"Yes. He phoned from New York Saturday night."

"Was Miss Rowan already at Mr. Pratt's place?"

"I don't know. I didn't know she was there until your man told me last night, when I went over there."

"Was she, Archie?"

I shook my head. "No sale. I was working on another case at lunch."

"It doesn't matter. I'm only clearing away rubbish, and I doubt if it amounts to more than that." Back at Osgood: "Why did your son come after so long an absence? What did he say?"

"He came—" Osgood stopped. Then he went on, "They came to be here for the exposition."

"Why did he come, really?"

Osgood glared and said, "Damn it."

"I know, Mr. Osgood. We don't usually hang our linen on the line till it has been washed, but you've hired me to sort it out. Why did your son come to see you? To get money?"

"How did you know that?"

"I didn't. But men so often need money; and you had stopped your son's income. Was his need general or specific?"

"Specific as to the sum. He wanted $10,000."

"Oh." Wolfe's brows went up a trifle. "What for?"

"He wouldn't tell me. He said he would be in trouble if he didn't get it." Osgood looked as if it hurt where the coronet had been. "I may as well . . . he had used up a lot of money during his affair with that woman. I found out in May that he had taken to gambling, and that was one reason I cut him off. When he asked for $10,000 I suspected it was for a gambling debt, but he denied it and said it was something more urgent. He wouldn't tell me what."

"Did you let him have it?"

"No. I absolutely refused."

"He was insistent?"

"Very. We . . . there was a scene. Not violent, but damned unpleasant. Now . . ." Osgood set his jaw, and looked at space. He muttered with his teeth clamped, "Now he's dead. Good God, if I thought that $10,000 had anything to do—"

"Please, sir. Please. Let's work. I call your attention to a coincidence which you have probably already noticed: the bet your son made yesterday afternoon with Mr. Pratt was for $10,000. That raises a question. Mr. Pratt declined to make a so-called gentleman's wager with your son unless it was underwritten by you. I understand that he telephoned you to explain the difficulty, and you guaranteed payment by your son if he lost. Is that correct?"

"Yes."

"Well." Wolfe frowned at his two empty bottles. "It seems a little inconsistent . . . first you refuse to advance $10,000 needed urgently by your son to keep him out of trouble, and then you casually agree on the telephone to underwrite a bet he makes for that precise sum."

"There was nothing casual about it."

"Did you have any particular reason to assume that your son would win the bet?"

"How the hell could I? I didn't know what he was betting on."

"You didn't know that he had wagered that Mr. Pratt would not barbecue Hickory Caesar Grindon this week?"

"No. Not then. Not until my daughter told me afterwards . . . after Clyde was dead."

"Didn't Mr. Pratt tell you on the phone?"

"I didn't give him a chance. When I learned that Clyde had been to Tom Pratt's place and made a bet with him, and that Pratt had the insolence to ask me to stand good for my son—what do you think? Was I going to ask the dog for details? I told him that any debt my son might ever owe him, for a bet or anything else, or for $10,000 or ten times that would be instantly paid, and I hung up."

"Didn't your son tell you what the bet was about when he got home a little later?"

"No. There was another scene. Since you have . . . you might as well have all of it. When Clyde appeared I was furious, and I demanded . . . I was in a temper, and that roused his, and he started to walk out. I accused him of betraying me. I accused him of arranging a fake bet with Pratt and getting Pratt to phone me, so that I would have to pay it, and then Pratt would hand him the money. Then he did walk out. As I said, I didn't find out until afterwards what the bet was about or how it was made. I left the house and got in a car and drove over the other side of Crowfield to the place of an old friend of mine. I didn't want to eat dinner at home. Clyde's friend, this Bronson, was here, and my daughter and my wife . . . and my presence wouldn't make it a pleasant meal. It was already unpleasant enough. When I got back, after ten o'clock, there was no one around but my wife, and she was in her room crying. About half an hour later the phone call came from Pratt's—his nephew. I went. That was where I had to go to find my son dead."

Wolfe sat looking at him, and after a moment sighed. "That's too bad," he said. "I mean it's too bad that you were away from home, and weren't on speaking terms with your son. I had hoped to learn from you what time he left the house, and under what circumstances, and what he may have said of his destination and purpose. You can't tell me that."

"Yes, I can. My daughter and Bronson have told me—"

"Pardon me. If you don't mind, I'd rather hear it from them. What time is it, Archie?"

I told him, ten after five.

"Thank you. —You realize, Mr. Osgood, that we're fishing in a big stream. This is your son's home, hundreds of people in this county know him, one or more of them may have hated or feared him enough to want him dead, and almost anyone could have got to the far end of the pasture without detection, despite the fact that my assistant had the pasture under surveillance. It was a dark night. But we'll extend our field only if we're compelled to; let's finish with those known to be present. Regarding motive, what about Mr. McMillan?"

"None that I know of. I've known Monte McMillan all my life; his place is up at the north end of the county. Even if he had caught Clyde trying some fool trick with the bull— my God, Monte wouldn't murder him . . . and you say yourself—"

"I know. Clyde wasn't caught doing that." Wolfe sighed. "That seems to cover it. Pratt, McMillan, the nephew, the niece, Miss Rowan . . . and on motive you offer no indictment. I suppose, since this place is at a distance of only a mile or so from Mr. Pratt's, which might fairly be called propinquity, we should include those who were here. What about Mr. Bronson?"

"I don't know him. He came with Clyde and was introduced as a friend."

"An old friend?"

"I don't know."

"You never saw him or heard of him before?"

"No."

"What about the people employed here? There must be quite a few. Anyone with a grudge against your son?"

"No. Absolutely not. For three years he more or less supervised things here for me, and he was competent and had their respect, and they all liked him. Except—" Osgood stopped abruptly, and was silent, suspended, with his mouth open. Then he said, "Good God, I've just remembered . . . but no, that's ridiculous . . ."

"What is?"

"Oh . . . a man who used to work here. Two years ago one of our best cows lost her calf and Clyde blamed this man and fired him. The man has done a lot of talking ever since, denying it was his fault, and making some wild threats I've been told about. The reason I think of it now . . . he's over at Pratt's place. Pratt hired him last spring. His name is Dave Smalley."

"Was he there last night?"

"I presume so. You can find out."

I put in an oar: "Sure he was. You remember Dave, don't you? How he resented your using that rock as a waiting room?"

Wolfe surveyed me. "Do you mean the idiot who waved the gun and jumped down from the fence?"

"Yep. That was Dave."

"Pfui." Wolfe almost spat. "It won't do, Mr. Osgood. You remarked, correctly, that the murderer had brains and nerve and luck. Dave is innocent."

"He's done a lot of talking."

"Thank God I didn't have to listen to it." Wolfe stirred in the big comfortable chair. "We must get on. I offer an observation or two before seeing your daughter. First, I must warn you of the practical certainty that the official theory will be that your son did enter the pasture to molest the bull, in spite of my demonstration to Mr. Waddell. They will learn that Clyde bet Mr. Pratt that he would not barbecue Hickory Caesar Grindon *this week*. They will argue that all Clyde had to do to win the bet was to force a postponement of the feast for five days, and he might have tried that. They will be fascinated by the qualification *this week*. It is true that there is something highly significant in the way the terms of the bet were stated, but they'll miss that."

"What's significant about it? It was a damned silly—"

"No. Permit me. I doubt if it was silly. I'll point it out to you when I'm ready to interpret it. Second, whatever line Mr. Waddell takes should have our respectful attention. If he offends, don't in your arrogance send him to limbo, for we can use his facts. Many of them. We shall want, for instance, to know what the various persons at Mr. Pratt's house were doing last night between 9 o'clock and 10:30. I don't know, because at 9 o'clock I felt like being alone and went up to my room to read. We shall want to know what the doctor says about the probable time of your son's death. The presumption is that it was not more than, say 15 minutes, before Mr. Goodwin arrived on the spot, but the doctor may be helpful. We shall want to know whether my conclusions have been supported by such details as the discovery of blood residue in the grass by the hose nozzle, and on the pick handle, et cetera. Third, I'd like to repeat a question which you evaded a while ago. Why do you hate Mr. Pratt?"

"I didn't evade it. I merely said it has no bearing on this."

"Tell me anyway. Of course I'm impertinent, but I'll have to decide if I'm also irrelevant."

Osgood shrugged. "It's no secret. This whole end of the state knows it. I don't hate him, I only feel contempt for him. As I told you, his father was one of my father's stablehands. As a boy Tom was wild, and aggressive, but he had ambition, if you want to call it that. He courted a young woman in the neighborhood and persuaded her to agree to marry him. I came home from college, and she and I were mutually attracted, and I married her. Tom went to New York and never made an appearance around here. Apparently he was nursing a grievance all the time, for about eight years ago he began to make a nuisance of himself. He had made a lot of money, and he used some of it and all his ingenuity concocting schemes to pester and injure me. Then two years ago he bought that land next to mine, and built on it, and that made it worse."

"Have you tried retaliation?"

"If I ever tried retaliation it would be with a horsewhip. I ignore him."

"Not a democratic weapon, the whip. Yesterday afternoon your son accused him of projecting the barbecue as an offense to you. The idea seemed to be that it would humiliate you and make you ridiculous if a bull better than your best bull was cooked and eaten. It struck me as farfetched. Mr. Pratt maintained that the barbecue was to advertise his business."

"I don't care a damn. What's the difference?"

"None, I suppose. But the fact remains that the bull is a central character in our problem, and it would be a mistake to lose sight of him. So is Mr. Pratt, of course. You reject the possibility that his festering grievance might have impelled him to murder."

"Yes. That's fantastic. He's not insane . . . at least I don't think he is."

"Well." Wolfe sighed. "Will you send for your daughter?"

Osgood scowled. "She's with her mother. Do you insist on speaking to her? I know you're supposed to be competent, but it seems to me the people to ask questions of are at Pratt's, not here."

"It's my competence you're hiring, sir. Your daughter comes next. Mr. Waddell is at Pratt's, where he belongs, since he has authority." Wolfe wiggled a finger. "If you please."

Osgood got up and went to a table to push a button, and then came back and downed his highball, which must have been as warm as Wolfe's beer by that time, in three gulps. The pug-nosed lassie appeared and was instructed to ask Miss Osgood to join us. Osgood sat down again and said:

"I don't see what you're accomplishing, Wolfe. If you think by questioning me you've eliminated everybody at Pratt's—"

"By no means. I've eliminated no one." Wolfe sounded faintly exasperated, and I perceived that it was up to me to arrange with Pug-nose for more and colder beer. "Elimination, as such, is tommyrot. Innocence is a negative and can never be established; you can only establish guilt. The only way I can apodictically eliminate any individual from consideration as the possible murderer is to find out who did it. You can't be expected to see what I am accomplishing; if you could do that, you could do the job yourself. Let me give you a conjecture for you to try your hand on: for example, is Miss Rowan an accomplice? Did she join Mr. Goodwin last night and sit with him for an hour on the running board of my car, which he had steered into a tree, to distract him while the crime was being committed? Or if you would prefer another sort of problem . . ."

He stopped with a grimace and began preparations to arise. I got up too, and Osgood started across the room toward the door which had opened to admit his daughter, and with her an older woman in a dark blue dress with her hair piled on top of her head. Osgood made an effort to head off the latter, and protested, but she advanced toward us anyhow. He submitted enough to introduce us:

"This is Mr. Nero Wolfe, Marcia. His assistant, Mr. Goodwin. My wife. Now dear, there's no sense in this, it won't help any . . ."

While he remonstrated with her I took a polite look. The farmer's beautiful daughter who, according to one school of thought, was responsible for Tom Pratt's unlucky idea of making beefsteak out of Hickory Caesar Grindon, was still beautiful I suppose; it's hard for me to tell when they're around fifty, on account of my tendency to concentrate on details which can't be expected to last that long. Anyway, with her eyes red and swollen from crying and her skin blotchy, it wasn't fair to judge.

She told her husband, "No, Fred, really, I'll be all right. Nancy has told me what you've decided. I suppose you're right . . . you always are right . . . now you don't need to look like that . . . you're perfectly right to want to find out about it, but I don't want just to shut myself away . . . you know Clyde always said it wasn't a pie if I didn't have my finger in it . . ." her lip quivered ". . . and if it is to be discussed with Nancy I want to be here . . ."

"It's foolish, Marcia, there's no sense in it." Osgood had hold of her arm. "If you'll just—"

"Permit me." Wolfe was frowning, and made his tone crisp. "Neither of you will stay. I wish to speak with Miss Osgood alone.—Confound it, sir, I am working, and for you! However I may want to sympathize with grief, I can't afford to let it interfere with my job. The job you want done. If you want it done."

Osgood glared at him, but said to his wife, "Come, Marcia." I followed them three steps and halted him: "Excuse me. It would be to everyone's advantage if he had more beer, say three bottles, and make it colder."

10

NANCY, sitting in the chair Osgood had vacated, looked more adamant than the situation seemed to call for, considering that Wolfe's client was her father. You might have thought she was confronted by hostile forces. Of course her brother had just been killed and she couldn't be expected to beam with cheerful eagerness, but her stiffness as she sat looked not only tense but antagonistic, and her lips, which only 24 hours before had struck me as being warm and trembly, now formed a thin rigid colorless line.

Wolfe leaned back and regarded her with half-closed eyes. "We'll be as brief as we can with this, Miss Osgood," he said, with honey in his mouth. "I thought we might reach our objective a little sooner with your father and mother absent."

She nodded, her head tilted forward once and back again, and said nothing. Wolfe resumed:

"We must manage to accompany your brother yesterday afternoon as continuously as possible from the time he left Mr. Pratt's terrace. Were you and Mr. Bronson and he riding in one car?"

Her voice was low and firm: "Yes."

"Tell me briefly your movements after leaving the terrace."

"We walked across the lawn and back to the car and got in and came—no, Clyde got out again because Mr. McMillan called to him and wanted to speak to him. Clyde went over to him and they talked a few minutes and then Clyde came back and we drove home."

"Did you hear his conversation with Mr. McMillan?"

"No."

"Was it apparently an altercation?"

"It didn't look like it."

Wolfe nodded. "Mr. McMillan left the terrace with the announced intention of advising your brother not to do anything foolish. He did it quietly then."

"They just talked a few minutes, that was all."

"So. You returned home, and Clyde had a talk with your father."

"Did he?"

"Please, Miss Osgood." Wolfe wiggled a finger. "Discretion will only delay us. Your father has described the . . . unpleasant scene, he called it . . . he had with his son. Was that immediately after you got home?"

"Yes. Dad was waiting for us at the veranda steps."

"Infuriated by the phone call from Mr. Pratt. Were you present during the scene?"

"No. They went into the library . . . this room. I went upstairs to clean up . . . we had been at Crowfield nearly all day."

"When did you see your brother again?"

"At dinnertime."

"Who was at table?"

"Mother and I, and Mr. Bronson and Clyde. Dad had gone somewhere."

"What time was dinner over?"

"A little after eight. We eat early in the country, and we sort of rushed through it because it wasn't very gay. Mother was angry . . . Dad had told her about the bet Clyde had made with Monte Cris—with Mr. Pratt, and Clyde was glum—"

"You called Mr. Pratt Monte Cristo?"

"That was a slip of the tongue."

"Obviously. Don't be perturbed, it wasn't traitorous, your father has told me of Mr. Pratt's rancor. You called him Monte Cristo?"

"Yes, Clyde and I did, and . . ." Her lip started to quiver, and she controlled it. "We thought it was funny when we started it."

"It may have been so. Now for your movements after dinner, please."

"I went to mother's room with her and we talked a while, and then I went to my room. Later I came downstairs and sat on the veranda and listened to the katydids. I was there when Dad came home."

"And Clyde?"

"I don't know. I didn't see him after I went upstairs with mother after dinner."

She wasn't much good as a liar; she didn't know how to relax for it. Wolfe has taught me that one of the most important requirements for successful lying is relaxed vocal cords and throat muscles; otherwise you are forced to put on extra pressure to push the lie through, and the result is that you talk faster and raise the pitch and the blood shows in your face. Nancy Osgood betrayed all of those signs. I moved my eyes for a glance at Wolfe, but he merely murmured a question:

"So you don't know when your brother left the house? Left here to go to Pratt's?"

"No." She stirred a little, and was still again, and repeated, "No."

"That's a pity. Didn't he tell you or your mother that he was going to Pratt's?"

"So far as I know, he told no one."

There was an interruption, a knock at the door. I went to it and took from Pug-nose a tray with three bottles of beer, felt one and approved of the temperature, and taxied them across to Wolfe. He, opening and pouring, asked Nancy if she would have, and she declined with thanks. He drank, put down the empty glass, and wiped his lips with his handkerchief.

"Now Miss Osgood," he said in a new tone. "I have more questions to ask of you, but this next is probably the most material of all. When did your brother tell you how and why he expected to win his bet with Mr. Pratt?"

She stared a second and said, "He didn't tell me at all. What makes you think he did?" It sounded straight to me.

"I thought it likely. Your father says that you and your brother were very close to each other."

"We were."

"But he told you nothing of that wager?"

"He didn't have to tell me he made it, I heard him. He didn't tell me how or why he expected to win it."

"What was discussed as you rode home from Pratt's yesterday?"

"I don't know. Nothing in particular."

"Remarkable. The bizarre wager which had just been made wasn't mentioned?"

"No. Mr. Bronson was . . . well, it only takes a couple of minutes to drive here from Pratt's—"

"Mr. Bronson was what?"

"Nothing. He was there, that's all."

"Is he an old friend of your brother's?"

"He's not—no. Not an old friend."

"But a friend, I presume, since you and your brother brought him here?"

"Yes." She clipped it. She was terrible.

"Is he a friend of yours too?"

"No." She raised her voice a little. "Why should you ask me about Mr. Bronson?"

"My dear child." Wolfe compressed his lips. "For heaven's sake don't start that. I am a hired instrument of vengeance . . . . hired by your father. Nowadays an Erinys wears a coat and trousers and drinks beer and works for pay, but the function is unaltered and should still be performed, if at all, mercilessly. I am going to find out who killed your brother. A part of the operation is to prick all available facts. I intend to look into Mr. Bronson as well as everyone else unlucky enough to be within range. For example, take Miss Pratt. Did you approve of your brother's engagement to marry Miss Caroline Pratt?"

She stared in consternation, opened her mouth, and closed it.

Wolfe shook his head at her. "I'm not being wily, to disconcert you and corner you. I don't think I need to; you have made yourself too vulnerable. To give you an idea, here are some questions I shall expect you to answer: Why, since you regard Mr. Bronson with loathing, do you permit him to remain as a guest in this house? I know you loathe him, because when he happened to brush against you yesterday on Mr. Pratt's terrace you drew away as if slime had touched your dress. Why would you prefer to have the mystery of your brother's death unsolved and to leave the onus to the bull? I know you would, from the relief on your face this afternoon when your father's incivility started me for the door. Why did you tell me that you didn't see your brother after dinner last evening? I know it was a lie, because I was hearing and seeing you when you said it. You see how you have exposed yourself?"

Nancy was standing up, and the line of her mouth was thinner than ever. She took a step and said, "My father . . . I'll see if he wants—"

"Nonsense," Wolfe snapped. "Please sit down. Why do you think I had your father leave? Shall I send for him? He intends to learn who murdered his son, and for the moment all other considerations surrender to that, even his daughter's dignity and peace of mind. You won't get peace of mind by concealing things, anyway. You must give satisfactory and complete answers to those questions, and the easiest way is here, to me, at once."

"You can't do this." She fluttered a hand. Her chin trembled, and she steadied it. "Really you can't. You can't do this." She was beauty in distress if I ever saw it, and if the guy harassing her had been anybody else I would have smacked him cold and flung her behind my saddle.

Wolfe told her impatiently, "You see how it is. Sit down. Confound it, do you want to turn it into a brawl, with your father here too and both of us shouting at you? You'll have to tell these things, for we need to know them, whether they prove useful or not. You can't bury them. For example, your dislike for Mr. Bronson. I can pick up that telephone and call a man in New York named Saul Panzer, an able and industrious man, and tell him I want to know all he can discover about Bronson and you and your brother. You see how silly it would be to force us to spend that time and money. What about Mr. Bronson? Who is he?"

"If I told you about Bronson—" She stopped to control her voice. "I can't. I promised Clyde I wouldn't."

"Clyde is dead. Come, Miss Osgood. We'll learn it anyhow, I assure you we will. You know that."

"I suppose . . . you will." She sat down abruptly, buried her face in her hands, and was rigid. Her muffled voice came: "Clyde! Clyde!"

"Come." Wolfe was sharp. "Who is Bronson?"

She uncovered her face slowly, and lifted it. "He's a crook."

"A professional? What's his specialty?"

"I don't know. I don't know him. I only met him a few days ago. I only know what Clyde—"

She stopped, and gazed at Wolfe's face as if she was hoping that something would blot it out but knew that nothing would. "All right," she said. "I thought I had enough guts, but apparently I haven't. What good will it do? What good will it do you or Dad or anyone to know that Bronson killed him?"

"Do you know it?"

"Yes."

"Bronson murdered your brother?"

"Yes."

"Indeed. Did you see it done?"

"No."

"What was his motive?"

"I don't know. It couldn't have been to get the money, because Clyde didn't have it."

Wolfe leaned back and heaved a sigh. "Well," he murmured. "I guess we must have it out. What money would Mr. Bronson have wanted to get, and why?"

"Money that Clyde owed him."

"The amount being, I presume, $10,000. Don't ask me how I know that, please. And Bronson was insisting on payment?"

"Yes. That was why he came up here. It was why Clyde came, too, to try to get the money from Father. He had to pay it this week or—" She stopped, and stretched out a hand, and let it fall again. "Please," she said, pleading. "*Please*. That's what I promised Clyde I wouldn't tell."

"The promise died with him," Wolfe told her. "Believe me, Miss Osgood, if you weren't bewildered by shock and grief you wouldn't get values confused like this. Was it money that Clyde had borrowed from Mr. Bronson?"

"No. It was money that Bronson had paid him."

"What had he paid it for?"

He pulled it out of her, patiently, in pieces. The gist of the story was short and not very sweet. Clyde had shot his wad on Lily Rowan, and had followed it with various other wads, pried loose from his father, requisitioned from his sister, borrowed from friends. Then he had invited luck to contribute to the good cause, by sundry methods from crackaloo to 10-cent bridge, and learned too late that luck's clock was slow. At a time when he was in up to his nose, a Mr. Howard Bronson permitted him to inspect a fistful of real money and expressed a desire to be introduced into certain circles, including the two most exclusive bridge clubs in New York; Clyde, with his family connections, having the entree to about everything from the aquarium up. But Clyde had needed the dough not some time tomorrow, but now, and Bronson had given it to him; whereupon Clyde had mollified a few debts and slid the rest down his favorite chute, before dawn. Following a lifelong habit, he had confided in his sister, and her horror added to his own belated reflections had shown him that in his desperation he had taken an order which no Osgood could possibly fill. He had so notified Bronson, with regret and the expressed intention of repaying the ten grand at the earliest opportunity, but Bronson had revealed a nasty streak. He wanted the order filled, or the cash returned, forthwith; and a complication was that Clyde had rashly signed a receipt for the money which included specifications of what Bronson was to get for it. Bronson threatened to show the receipt to the family connections. Bad all around. When Clyde decided, as a last resort, on a trip to Crowfield for an appeal to his father, Bronson's distrust of him had got so deplorable that he insisted on going along and he couldn't be ditched; and Nancy had accompanied them for the purpose of helping out with father. But father had been obdurate, and Monday it was beginning to look as if Clyde would have to confess all in order to get the money, which would be worse than bad, when on Pratt's terrace luck reared its pretty head again and Clyde made a bet.

Wolfe got all that out of her, patiently, with various details and dates, and then observed, having finished the second bottle of beer, that while it seemed to establish Bronson as a man of disreputable motives it didn't seem to include one for murder.

"I know it," Nancy said. "I told you he couldn't have done it to get the money, because Clyde didn't have it, and anyway if he had had it he would have given it to him."

"Still you say he did it?"

"Yes."

"Why?"

"Because I saw Bronson follow Clyde over to Pratt's place."

"Indeed. Last night?"

"Yes."

"Tell me about it."

The bag was open now, and most of the beans gone. She dumped the rest: "It was around 9 o'clock, maybe a little later. When I left mother's room I came downstairs to look for Clyde, to ask him why he had made the bet with Pratt. I was afraid he was going to try something wild. I found him out by the tennis court, talking with Bronson, and they shut up when they heard me coming. I said I wanted to ask him something and he came away with me, but he wouldn't tell me anything. I told him I was pretty sure I would be able to get the money through mother, and reminded him that he had sworn to me he would stop acting like a fool, and said if he did something else foolish it might be the finish of him. I told him things like that. He said that for once I was wrong and he was right, that what he was doing wasn't foolish, that he had turned over a new leaf and was being sensible and practical and I would agree with him when I found out about it, but he wouldn't tell me then. I insisted, but he was always stubborner than I was."

"You got no inkling of what he had in mind."

Nancy shook her head. "Not the slightest. He said something about not interfering with the barbecue."

"Give me his exact words, if you can."

"Well, he said, 'I'm not going to harm anyone, not even Monte Cristo, except to win his money. I'll even let him have his damn pot roast, and he won't know the difference until after it's over, if I can fix it that way.' That's about it."

"Anything else about the barbecue or the bull or anyone at Mr. Pratt's place?"

"No, nothing."

"You left him outdoors?"

"I did then. I came back to the house and ran up to my room and changed to a dark-colored sweater and skirt. Then I came down and left by the west wing because the veranda lights were on in front and I didn't want to be seen. I didn't know whether Clyde intended to go anywhere or do anything, but I was going to find out. I couldn't find him. Beyond the range of the veranda lights it was pitch-dark, but I made a tour and looked as well as I could, and listened, and there wasn't a sign of him. The cars were in the garage, and anyway if he had taken a car or one of the farm trucks I would have heard it. If he was up to anything it could only be at Pratt's, so I decided to try that. I went past the kennels and the grove and through a gate into the meadow, which was the shortest cut, and across another field to the end of the row of pines, the windbreak—"

"All this in the dark?" Wolfe demanded.

"Of course. I know every foot of it, this is where I was born. I can find my way in the dark all right. I was about halfway along the windbreak when I saw a glimmer of a flashlight ahead, and I got careless and started to trot, because I wanted to get closer to find out if it was Clyde, and I stepped into a hole and tumbled and made a lot of noise. The flashlight was turned towards me, and Clyde's voice called, and I saw it was no use and answered him. He came back to me, and Bronson was with him, carrying a club, a length of sapling. Clyde was furious. I demanded to know what he was going to do, and that made him more furious. He said . . . oh, it doesn't matter what he said. He made me promise to go back home and go to bed—"

"Again without divulging his campaign."

"Yes. He wouldn't tell me. I came back home as I had promised I would. If only I hadn't! If only—"

"I doubt if it would have mattered. You have enough distress, Miss Osgood, without trying to borrow. But you haven't told me yet why you think Mr. Bronson murdered your brother."

"Why . . . he was there. He went to Pratt's with him. He's the kind of man who would do anything vile—"

"Nonsense. You had no sleep last night. Your mind isn't

working even on the lowest level. Do you know when Bronson got back here?"

"No. I was on the veranda until Dad came—"

"Then there's a job for you. You'll be better doing something. Find out from the servants if anyone saw him return, and let me know. It may save some time." Wolfe pushed his lips out, and in again. "I should think Mr. Bronson would be a little apprehensive about your disclosing his presence at Pratt's last night. Have you any idea why he isn't?"

"Yes I have. He . . . he spoke to me this morning. He said he had left Clyde at the end of the windbreak, where the fence is that bounds our property, and come back here and sat out by the tennis court and smoked. He said he thought my father was mistaken, that the bull had killed Clyde, and that everyone else would think so. He showed me the receipt Clyde had signed and given him, and said he supposed I wouldn't want Clyde's memory blackened by such a thing coming out, and that he was willing to give me a chance to repay him the money before going to my father about it, provided I would save him the annoyance of being questioned about last night by forgetting that I had seen him with Clyde."

"And even when further developments gave you the notion that he was the murderer, you decided to withhold all this to protect your brother's memory."

"Yes. And I wish I had stuck to it." She leaned forward at Wolfe, and a flush of determination showed faintly on her cheeks. "You got it out of me," she said. "But what Clyde wanted most was that Dad shouldn't know about it. Does Dad have to know? Why does he? What good will it do?"

Wolfe grimaced. "Can you pay Bronson the $10,000?"

"Not now. But I've been trying to think of a way ever since Bronson spoke to me this morning . . . didn't Clyde win his bet with Pratt? Surely he won't have that barbecue now, will he? Won't he owe the money?"

"My dear child." Wolfe opened his eyes at her. "What a remarkable calculation. Amazing. It deserves to bear fruit, and we must see what can be done. I underestimated you, for which I apologize. Also I think you deserve to be humored. If it is feasible, and it should be, your promise to your brother shall be kept. I have undertaken a specific commission from your father, to expose the murderer of his son, and I should think that can be managed without disclosing his contract with Bronson. That's a superb idea, to collect from Pratt to pay Bronson. I like it. By winning his last wager your brother vindicated, as far as he could, all his previous sacrifices in the shabby temple of luck. Magnificent and neat . . . and fine of you, very fine, to perceive the necessity of completing the gesture for him . . . I assure you I'll do all I can—"

He broke off and glanced at me because a knock sounded at the door. I lifted from my chair and started across, but it opened before I got there and two men entered. I halted, slightly popeyed, when I saw it was Tom Pratt himself and McMillan. Behind them, catching up with them, hustled a middle-aged woman in a black dress, looking indignant, calling to them something about Mr. Osgood not being in there, they should wait for him in the hall. . . .

Then affairs began to get simultaneous and confused. I caught a glimpse of Mr. Howard Bronson standing at one of the French windows, looking in, and saw that Wolfe had spotted him too. At the same time a purposeful tread sounded from the hall, and then Mr. Frederick Osgood was among us, wearing a scowl that beat all his previous records. He directed it at Pratt, ignoring inessentials. He stood solid and enraged three feet in front of him, glaring at him, and spoke like an irate duke:

"Out!"

McMillan started to say something, but Osgood exploded at him: "Damn you, Monte, did you bring this man here? Get him away at once! I don't want his foot on my place—"

"Now wait a second, Fred." McMillan sounded as if he wasn't brooking anything much either. "Just a second and give us a chance. I didn't bring him; no, but we came. There's hell to pay around here, and Pratt doesn't like it any better than you do, and neither do I. Waddell, and Sam Lake with a bunch of deputies, and a herd of state police, are tearing things apart over there, and if there's anything to be found we hope they find it. At least I do; Pratt can do his own talking. But in my opinion there's going to have to be some talking. Not only on account of Clyde, but on account of what happened an hour ago."

McMillan paused, returning Osgood's gaze, and then said heavily, "Caesar's dead. My bull Caesar."

Pratt growled, "My bull."

"Okay, Pratt, your bull." McMillan didn't look at him. "But he's dead. I bred him and he was mine. Now he's lying there on the ground dead."

11

Osgood's scowl had got adulterated by a touch of bewilderment. But he exploded again: "What the devil do I care about your bull?" He transferred to Pratt: "You get out of here. Get!"

He was turned, and so were the others, by Wolfe's voice booming across the room. "Mr. Osgood! Please!"

Wolfe had left the comfortable chair and was approaching. I saw by the look on his face, knowing it as I did, that something had jolted and irritated him almost to the limit, and wondered what it could be. He joined the circle. "How do you do, gentlemen. Mr. Pratt, it is a poor return for your hospitality if I've offended you by renting my services to Mr. Osgood, and I hope you don't feel that way about it. Mr. Osgood, this is your house, but however you may resent Mr. Pratt's entering it, surely you can bottle your hostility for the present crisis. I assure you it's highly desirable. He seems to have brought vital news, with Mr. McMillan—"

Osgood, glaring at Pratt, rumbled, "You dirty abominable mud lark!"

Pratt, returning the glare, growled, "You goddam stuffed shirt!"

Fair enough, I thought, for a duke and a millionaire. Wolfe said, "Pfui. What if you are both right? —Mr. McMillan, please. What's this about the bull?"

"He's dead."

"What killed him?"

"Anthrax."

"Indeed. That's a disease, isn't it?"

"No. It's sudden and terrible death. Technically it's a disease, of course, but it's so swift and deadly that it's more like a snake or a stroke of lightning." The stockman snapped his fingers. "Like that."

Wolfe nodded. "I knew of it, vaguely, in my boyhood in Europe. But wasn't Caesar healthy this morning? When did you observe symptoms?"

"With anthrax you don't observe symptoms. Not often. You go to the pasture in the morning and find dead cattle. That's what happened at my place a month ago. It's what happened with Caesar at 5 o'clock this afternoon. One of Sam Lake's deputies went down to the far end of the pasture, where I had him tied behind a clump of birch, and found him keeled over dead. I had gone to Crowfield to see Lew Bennett. They phoned me and I came back out, and Pratt and I decided to come over here."

Osgood's scowl had got adulterated some more. I didn't know then that the sound of the word "anthrax," with the news that it had struck within a mile of his own herd, was enough to adulterate any man's scowl, no matter what had happened to him. Wolfe turned and said brusquely:

"Mr. Pratt. I'd like to buy the bull's carcass. What will you take for it?"

I stared at him, wondering if whatever had jolted him had thrown him off balance. Pratt stared too.

Osgood blurted, "You can't buy an anthrax carcass. The state takes it."

Pratt demanded, "What in the name of God do you want it for?"

McMillan said sourly, "They're already there. A member of the State Board was at Crowfield, and he got there as soon as I did, with a dozen men. Why, what did you expect to do with it?"

Wolfe sighed. "I suppose Mr. Waddell has told you of my demonstration of the fact that Clyde Osgood wasn't killed by the bull. The absence of blood on his face. I wanted the hide. Juries like visual evidence. What is the member of the State Board doing with his men? Carting it away?"

"No. You don't cart it away. You don't want the hide either. You don't touch it, because it's dangerous. You don't bury it, because the spores live in the soil for years. You don't even go close to it. What the state men are doing is collecting wood to pile it around the carcass for a fire." McMillan slowly shook his head. "He'll burn all night, Caesar will."

"How did he get it? I understand you delivered him to Mr. Pratt last Friday. Did he bring it with him from your place?"

"He couldn't have. It doesn't wait that long to kill. The question of how he got it . . . that's one thing we came over here to discuss." McMillan faced Osgood. He hesitated a second and said, "Look here, Fred, say we sit down. I'm about played out. We want to ask you something."

Osgood said curtly, "Come to the veranda."

I controlled a grin. By gum, he wasn't going to have a mud lark sitting within his walls. They all moved, Wolfe followed, and I brought up the rear, after a glance to see that Nancy was just getting up from her chair and Bronson was no longer visible through the French window. I requested her not to forget to ask the servants what Wolfe had told her, and she nodded.

When I got to the veranda they were seated in a group in the wicker chairs and McMillan was telling Osgood, "We all want it cleared up and that's why Pratt and I came over here. Waddell will be along pretty soon. Someone had an idea, it doesn't matter who, after Caesar was found dead, and we thought it was only fair to tell you about it before it is followed up. If you want to know why I came to tell you . . . I came because everybody else was afraid to. It's Waddell's job, or Sam Lake's, not mine, and it will be up to them to investigate it if they decide to, but they asked me to come and discuss it with you first. Pratt offered to come, but we knew how far that would get and it might even lead to some more violence of which we've had plenty, so I came, and he came along with what I would call good intentions . . . he can tell you—"

Pratt began, "The fact is, Fred—"

"My name's Osgood, damn you!"

"All right. Take your name and stick it up your chimney and go to hell."

Osgood ignored him and demanded, "What do you want to discuss, Monte?"

"About Clyde," McMillan said. "You're going to be sore naturally, but it won't help any to fly off the handle. The fact is that Clyde was in that pasture. What for? Waddell and Sam Lake, and Captain Barrow of the state police, admit that Nero Wolfe's reconstruction of it is possible, but it's hard to believe, and one reason it's hard is that if somebody did all that, who was it? That's chiefly what has them stumped."

"Not unique," murmured Wolfe.

"Do you claim the bull killed him?" Osgood demanded.

"I don't claim anything." McMillan lifted his sagging shoulders. "Don't get me wrong, Fred. I told you I came to see you because the others, except Pratt, were afraid to. I don't claim anything. What they say is this, that the main difficulty with supposing that Clyde climbed into the pasture himself was to try to figure what for. I said myself this morning that it was dumb as hell for anybody to imagine that he went in there to get the bull, because that would have been plain crazy and Clyde wasn't a lunatic. What could he have intended to do with him? You can't hide a bull in a barrel. But when Caesar was found dead of anthrax . . . it was Captain Barrow who suggested it first as a possibility . . . that might account for Clyde entering the pasture. As you know, anthrax can be communicated subcutaneously, or by contact, or by ingestion. If Caesar was fed something last night, something that had been activated . . . well . . ."

Involuntarily I hunched forward and drew my feet under me, ready to move. Frederick Osgood was stiff, and his eyes glassy, with cold rage. His chronic scowl had been merely funny, but he didn't look funny now. He said in a composed and icy tone:

"Look out, Monte. By God, look out. If you're suggesting that my son deliberately poisoned that bull . . ."

McMillan said gruffly, "I'm not suggesting anything. I've told you I came here as a messenger. The fact is, I wanted to come, because I thought you ought to be warned by a friend. Waddell's attitude, and Captain Barrow's, is that it was you who insisted on an investigation, and if there is any part of it you don't like you've got yourself to thank for it. Anyhow, they'll be here any minute now, with the idea of finding out where Clyde had been the past few days and whether he had access, or could have had access, to any source of anthrax."

"Anybody who comes here—" Osgood had to stop to control his voice "—with that idea can go away again. So can you. It . . . it's infamous." He began to tremble. "By God—"

"Mr. Osgood!" It was Wolfe, using his sharpest tone. "Didn't I warn you? I said annoyance, intrusion, plague. Mr. McMillan is perfectly correct, you have yourself to thank for it."

"But I don't have to tolerate—"

"Oh yes you do. Anything from inanity to malevolence, though I doubt if we're dealing with the latter in this instance. I don't know Captain Barrow, but I can see Mr. Waddell, like a befuddled trout, leaping for such a fly as this in all innocence. It is amazing with what frivolity a mind like his can disregard a basic fact—in this case the fact that Clyde was not killed by the bull. I entreat you to remember what I said about our needing Mr. Waddell. It is really fortunate he's coming here, for now we can get information that we need without delay. If first you must submit to an inquiry which you regard as monstrous, you will do so because it is necessary. They represent authority . . . and here they are, I suppose . . ."

There was a sound of wheels crunching gravel, and a car swung into view on the drive and rolled to a stop at the foot of the veranda steps. First out was a state cossack in uniform, a captain, looking grim and unflinching, and following him appeared the district attorney, trying to look the same. They came up the steps and headed for the group.

I missed that battle. Wolfe got up from his chair and started off, and, seeing that he had his handkerchief in his hand, I arose and followed him. With a nod to Waddell as we passed he went on, entered the house, stopped in the main hall, turned to me and told me to wait there for him, and disappeared in the direction of the library. I stood and wondered what was causing all his violent commotion.

In a few minutes he came back looking disgruntled. He frowned at me and muttered, "Entirely too fast for us, Archie. We are being made to look silly. We may even have been outwitted. I got Mr. Bennett on the telephone, but drew a blank. Did you bring a camera along?"

"No."

"After this always have one. Take a car and get over there. Someone there must have a camera—the niece or nephew or Miss Rowan. Borrow it and take pictures of the carcass from all angles . . . a dozen or more, as many as you can get. Hurry, before they get that fire started."

I made myself scarce. It sounded fairly loco. As I trotted out to where Osgood's sedan was still parked, and got in and got it going, my mind was toying with theories that would account for Wolfe's sudden passion for photography, but I couldn't concoct one that wasn't full of holes. For instance, if all he wanted was to have it on record that the bull's face was comparatively clean, why pictures from all angles? I devised others, wilder and more elaborate, during the four minutes it took to drive to the highway and along it for a mile to Pratt's place, but none was any good. At the entrance to the drive a state cop stopped me and I told him I was sent by Waddell.

I parked in the space in front of the garage, alongside the yellow Wethersill standing there, and jumped out and headed for the house. But I was only halfway there when I heard a call:

"Hey! Escamillo!"

I turned and saw Lily Rowan horizontal, lifted onto an elbow, on a canvas couch under a maple tree. I trotted over to her, telling her on the way:

"Hullo, plaything. I want to borrow a camera."

"My lord," she demanded, "am I such a pretty sight that you just have to—"

"No. This is serious and urgent. Have you got a camera?"

"Oh, I see. You came from the Osgoods. Oh, I knew you were there. It's that yellow-eyed Nancy—"

"Cut it. I tell you I'm serious. I want to take a picture of the bull before they get their—"

"What bull?"

"*The* bull."

"Good heavens. What a funny job you have. No one will ever take another picture of *that* bull. They've started the fire."

"Goddam it! Where?"

"Down at the other end . . ."

I was off on the lope, which may have been dumb, but I was in the throes of emotion. I heard her clamoring, "Wait! Escamillo! I'm coming along!" but I kept going. Leaving the lawn, as I passed the partly dug pit for the barbecue, I could smell the smoke, and soon I could see it, above the clump of birches towards the far end of the pasture. I slowed to a trot and cussed out loud as I went.

There was quite a group there, 15 or 20 besides the ones tending the fire. I joined them unnoticed. A length of the fence had been torn down and we stood back of the gap. Apparently Hickory Caesar Grindon had had a ring built around him of good dry wood, in ample quantity, for there was so much blaze that you could only catch an occasional glimpse of what was left of him between the tongues of flame. It was hot as the devil, even at the distance we were standing. Four or five men in shirt sleeves, with sweat pouring from them, were throwing on more wood from nearby piles. The group of spectators stood, some silent, some talking. I heard a voice beside me:

"I thought maybe you might get around."

I turned for a look. "Oh, hello, Dave. What made you think I'd be here?"

"Nothin' particular, only you seem like a feller that likes to be around where things is goin' on." He pinched at his nose. "I'll be derned if it don't smell like a barbecue. Same smell exactly. You might close your eyes and think he was bein' et."

"Well, he's not. He won't be."

"He sure won't." Silence, while we watched the flames. In a little he resumed, "You know, it gets you thinkin', a sight like that, derned if it don't. A champion bull like that Caesar bein' burnt up with scorn. It's ignominious. Ain't it?"

"Absolutely."

"Yes it is." He pinched his nose again. "Do you read pohtry?"

"No. Neither do you."

"The hell I don't. A book my daughter give me one Christmas I've read twenty times, parts of it more. In one place it says 'I sometimes think that never grows so red the rose as where some buried Caesar bled.' Of course this Caesar's bein' burnt instead of buried, but there's a connection if you can see it."

I made a fitting reply and shoved off. There was no percentage in standing there getting my face roasted and I wasn't in a mood to listen to Dave recite poetry.

Up a ways, near the gate through which we had carried the canvas with its burden the night before, Lily Rowan sat on the grass holding her nose. I had a notion to stop and tell her with a sneer that it was only a pose to show how sensitive and feminine she was, since Dave's olfactory judgment had been correct, but I didn't even feel like sneering. I had been sent there on the hop with my first chance to get a lick in, and had arrived too late, and I knew that Nero Wolfe wouldn't be demanding a snapshot of a bull just to put it in his album.

Lily held her hands out. "Help me up."

I grabbed hold, gave a healthy jerk, and she popped up and landed flat against me; and I enclosed her with both arms and planted a thorough one, of medium duration, on her mouth, and let her go.

"Well," she said, with her eyes shining. "You cad."

"Don't count on that as a precedent," I warned her. "I'm overwrought. I may never feel like that again. I'm sore as the devil and had to relieve the tension somehow. May I use your telephone? Mr. Pratt's telephone."

"Go climb a tree," she said, and got her arm through mine, and we went to the house that way, though it is a form of intimacy I don't care for, since I have a tendency to fight shy of bonds. Nor did I respond to the melting quality that seemed to be creeping into her tone, but kept strictly to persiflage.

Caroline was on the terrace, reading, looking even more under the weather than she had that morning, and I paused for a greeting. I didn't see Jimmy anywhere. Lily went with me to the phone in an alcove of the living room, and sat and looked at me with a corner of her mouth turned up, as she had the day before. I got the number of Osgood's place, and was answered by a maid, and asked for Wolfe.

His familiar grunt came: "Hello, Archie."

"Hello. Hell all haywire. They already had the fire started and it's like an inferno. What can I do?"

"Confound it. Nothing. Return."

"Nothing at all I can do here?"

"No. Come and help me admire stupidity."

I hung up and turned to Lily: "Listen, bauble. What good would it do if you told anyone that I came here to take a picture of the bull?"

"None whatever." She smiled and ran the tips of her fingers down my arm. "Trust me, Escamillo."

12

AN HOUR later, after eight o'clock, Wolfe and I sat in the room that had been assigned to him upstairs, eating off of trays, which he hated to do except at breakfast. But he wasn't complaining. He never talked business at meals, and was glad to escape from his client. Osgood had explained that his wife wouldn't appear, and his daughter would remain with her, and that perhaps it would be as well to forego service in the dining room altogether, and Wolfe had politely assented. His room was commodious and comfortable. It was a little chintzy, but one of its chairs was adequate for his bulk, and the bed would have held two of him. It might have been supposed that the kitchen would be sharing in the general household derangement, but the covered dishes of broiled lamb chops with stuffed tomatoes were hot and tasty, the salad was way below Fritz's standard but edible, and the squash pie was towards the top.

Osgood's collision with Waddell and Captain Barrow had been brief, for it had ended by the time I got back. The captain was collecting fingerprints from everyone who had been at Pratt's place the night before, without disclosing how dire his intent might be, and since Wolfe had already obliged I figured I might as well. After he had got my ten specimens collected and marked and put away in his little case, he had announced that he was ready for a call on the foreman of the stock barns, and at Wolfe's suggestion Osgood and McMillan had accompanied him, and Pratt had departed for home, which left Wolfe and me alone with District Attorney Waddell.

Waddell was glad to cooperate, he said, with Fred Osgood's representative. More than willing. He had pursued, and intended to pursue, the investigation without fear or favor. No one had a supported alibi except Lily Rowan and me. They had left the dinner table before 9 o'clock. Wolfe had gone upstairs to read. Pratt had gone to his desk in the room next to the living room to look over some business papers. McMillan had been shown to a room upstairs by Bert, and had lain down with his shoes off for a nap until 1 o'clock, at which time he was to relieve me on guard duty. He had slept lightly and the sound of the shots had awakened him. Caroline had sat on the terrace for a while and had then gone to the living room and looked at magazines. Jimmy had been on the terrace with his sister, and when she left he had remained there, and sat and smoked. He had heard our voices, Lily's and mine, as we had followed the pasture fence on our tour, especially as we encountered the briar patch, but remembered no other sounds above the noise of the crickets and katydids. Bert had helped with the dinner dishes until 10 o'clock and had then sat in the kitchen and listened to the radio, with his ear glued to it because it had to be kept pianissimo. Dave Smalley—Waddell knew all about his having been fired by Clyde Osgood—Dave, on parting from me at a quarter to 9, had gone to his room in a wing of the garage building, shaved himself, and retired. Wolfe demanded, "Shaved?" in incredulity, and got the explanation Dave had given, that he always shaved at bedtime because he was too hungry to do it before breakfast, and after breakfast there was no time.

So far as that went, Waddell conceded, anyone could have done it. When you went on and asked why anyone would have done it, that was different. There was no one there with anything like a decent known motive to murder Clyde Osgood unless you wanted to make an exception of Dave Smalley, but Dave was harmless and always had been. Say someone had caught Clyde sneaking in there after the bull. If it had been Pratt, he would have simply ordered him off. If it had been Jimmy, he would have socked him. If it had been McMillan, he would have picked him up and thrown him over the fence. If it had been Dave, he would have yelled for help. If it had been Goodwin, who was guarding the bull, of course he didn't know. . . .

"I've explained," said Wolfe patiently, "that the murder was planned. Did you examine the bull?"

"I looked at him, and so did Sam Lake and the police. There was one splotch on his face and a little caked on his horns, but not much, he had rubbed most of that off. A bull likes to keep his horns clean."

"What about the grass around the hose and the pick handle?"

"We sent the pick to Albany for laboratory inspection.

There were a few, kind of clots, we found in the grass, and we sent them too. We won't know until tomorrow."

"They'll report human blood, and then what? Will you still waste time blathering about Clyde approaching the bull with a meal of anthrax, and the bull, after consuming it, becoming resentful and goring him?"

"If they report human blood that will add weight to your theory, of course. I said I'd cooperate, Wolfe, I didn't agree to lap up your sarcasm."

"Pfui." Wolfe shrugged. "Don't think I don't understand your position, sir. You are fairly sure there has been a murder, but you want to leave a path open to a public pretense that there was none, in case you fail to solve it. You have made no progress whatever toward a solution and see no prospect of any, and you would abandon the attempt now and announce it as accidental death as a result of malicious trespass, but for me. You know I am employed by Mr. Osgood, who may be obstructed but not ignored, and you further know that I have the knack of arranging, when I do make a fool of myself, that no one shall know it but me."

"You make . . ." Waddell sputtered with anger. "You accuse me of obstructing justice? I'm the law officer of this county—"

"Bah! Swallow it, sir! You know perfectly well Clyde Osgood was murdered, and you descend to that gibberish about him poisoning that bull!" Wolfe halted abruptly, and sighed. "But there, I beg your pardon. I have forfeited the right to reproach even gibberish. I had this case like that, complete—" he showed a clenched fist "—and I let it go." The fist popped open.

"You don't mean you know the mur—"

"I mean I was lazy and conceited. You may quote that. Forget my dispraise, it was beside the point; you do your best. So do I. That's the devil of it: my best wasn't good enough this afternoon. But it will be. Drop all notion of filing it as an accident, Mr. Waddell; you may as well close that path, for you won't be allowed to return by it . . ."

Soon after that McMillan and Captain Barrow had returned, and they had all left, after Wolfe had arranged for McMillan to pay us a visit at 9 o'clock that evening.

During dinner Wolfe wasn't talkative, and I made no special effort at conversation because he didn't deserve it. If he wanted to be charitable enough to concede Waddell a right to live, I wouldn't have objected to that, but he might have kept within bounds. Decorum is decorum. If he wanted to admit he had made a boob of himself and prattle about forfeiting rights, that was okay, but the person to admit it too wasn't a half-witted crime buzzard from the upstate sticks, but me. That's what a confidential assistant is for. The only thing that restrained me from letting my indignation burst into speech was the fact that I didn't know why the hell he was talking about.

McMillan was punctual. It was 9 on the dot, and we were sipping coffee, when a maid came to say he was below. I went down and told him that Wolfe calculated there might be more privacy if he didn't object to coming upstairs, and he said certainly not. On the upper landing we ran into Nancy and he stopped for a couple of words with her, having, as he had observed the day before, known the Osgood youngsters since they were babies.

Wolfe greeted him. He sat down and declined coffee. Wolfe looked at him and sighed. I sipped coffee and watched them over the rim of the cup.

Wolfe said, "You look tired."

The stockman nodded. "I'm about all in. I guess I'm getting old. Scores of times I've stayed up all night with a cow dropping a calf . . . but of course this wasn't exactly the same as a cow dropping a calf."

"No. Its antithesis. Death instead of birth. It was obliging of you to come over here; I dislike expeditions at night. In my capacity as an investigator for your friend Mr. Osgood, may I ask you some questions?"

"That's what I came for."

"Good. Then first, you left Mr. Pratt's terrace yesterday afternoon with the announced intention of telling Clyde not to do anything foolish. Miss Osgood has told me that you called Clyde from the car and conversed with him a few minutes. What was said?"

"Just that. I knew Clyde had a streak of recklessness in him—not bad, he wasn't a bad boy, just a little reckless sometimes—and after what he had said to Pratt I thought he might need a little quieting down. I sort of made a joke of it and told him I hoped he wasn't going to try to pull any Halloween stunt. He said he was going to win his bet with Pratt. I told him there was no way he could do it and the sensible thing was to let me go and arrange with Pratt to call the bet off. He refused, and I asked him how he expected to win it, and of course he wouldn't tell me. That was all there was to it. I couldn't get anything out of him, and he went and got in his car."

"Without giving you the slightest hint of his intentions."

"Right."

Wolfe grimaced. "I hoped you would be able to tell me a little more than that."

"I can't tell you more than what happened."

"Of course not. But I had that much, which is nothing, from Mr. Waddell, as you told it to him. He is the district attorney. I represent your friend Mr. Osgood. I had rather counted on your willingness to disclose things to me which you might choose to withhold from him."

McMillan frowned. "Maybe you'd better say that again. It sounds to me as if you meant I'm lying about it."

"I do. —Now please!" Wolfe showed a palm. "Don't let's be childish about the depravity of lying. Victor Hugo wrote a whole book to prove that a lie can be sublime. I strongly suspect you're lying, and I'd like to explain why. Briefly, because Clyde Osgood wasn't an imbecile. I suppose you have heard from Mr. Waddell of my theory that Clyde didn't climb into the pasture, but was put there. I still incline to that, but whether he voluntarily entered the pasture or not, he certainly went voluntarily from his home to Pratt's place. What for?"

He paused to empty his coffee cup. McMillan, still frowning, sat and looked at him.

Wolfe resumed, "I risk the assumption that he wasn't merely out for a stroll. He had a purpose, to do something or see somebody. I counted Dave out. Miss Rowan was with Mr. Goodwin. Mr. Waddell tells me that the others, including you, profess complete ignorance of Clyde's presence on the premises. I find it next to impossible to believe that; the reason being, as I said, that Clyde was not an imbecile; for if he didn't go there to see someone I must assume that his object was some sort of design, singlehanded, against the bull, and that's preposterous. What design? Remove the bull from the pasture, lead him away and keep him hid somewhere until the week was up? Feed him anthrax to kill him and render him inedible? Glue wings on him and ride him, a bovine Pegasus, to the moon? The last surmise is no more unlikely than the first two."

"You're not arguing with me," McMillan said drily. "If I set out to try to prove anything I wouldn't know where to start. But about my lying—"

"I'm coming to it." Wolfe pushed at his tray, with a glance at me, and I got up and moved it out of his way. He went on, "Frankly, I am not now dealing with the murder. I haven't got that far. I must first find a reasonable hypothesis to account for Clyde's going there . . . or rather, let me go back still further and put it this way: I must find a reasonable hypothesis for his evident expectation of winning that bet. Didn't he tell you he expected to win the bet?"

"Yes."

"And he wouldn't tell you how?"

"No."

"Well." Wolfe compressed his lips. "That's what I can't believe. I can't believe that, because he could expect to win the bet only with your assistance."

McMillan stared, with his heavy brows down. "Now," he said finally, "I don't think you want to start talking like that. Not to me. I don't believe so."

"Oh yes I do," Wolfe assured him. "It's my one form of prowess. I do talk. But I mean no offense, I'm speaking only of Clyde's expectations. I must account for his expecting to win that bet before I can approach the murder at all. I have considered, thoroughly, all the possible schemes, as well as the impossible, he might have had in mind, and there is one which appears neat, not too atrocious, and practicable though perhaps difficult. I have said he couldn't have expected simply to remove the bull from the pasture, because he couldn't have hid him from the resulting search. But why couldn't he remove Caesar and put another bull in his place?"

The stockman snorted. "A good grade Holstein maybe."

"No. Humor me, sir. Take my question as serious and answer it. Why couldn't he?"

"Because he couldn't."

"But why not? There were, I don't know how many, Guernsey bulls at the exposition, only seventeen miles away, and cattle trucks there to haul them in. There were some much closer, here at his father's place, within leading distance. Might not one of them, though vastly inferior to the champion Caesar in the finer qualities which I don't know about, resemble him sufficiently in size and coloring to pass as a substitute? A substitute for only one day, since the butcher was to come on Wednesday? Who would have known the difference?"

McMillan snorted again. "I would."

"Granted. You could have mistaken no other bull for your Caesar. But everyone else might easily have been fooled. At the very least there was an excellent sporting chance of it. It is obvious at what point such a scheme might have entered Clyde's mind. Yesterday afternoon he was sitting on the pasture fence, looking at Hickory Caesar Grindon through his binoculars. It occurred to him that there was a bull of similar general appearance, size and markings, either in his father's herd or among the collection at the exposition, which he had just come from; and that accidental reflection blossomed into an idea. Chased away from the pasture, he went to the house and made the wager with Mr. Pratt. Followed from the terrace to his car by you, he called you aside and made a proposal."

Wolfe sighed. "At least he might have. Let's say his proposal was that he should, with your consent, remove Caesar and put another bull in his place. He would take Caesar to the Osgood barns. You would, during Tuesday, help to guard the substitute so that no one who would be at all likely to notice the deception would be permitted to approach too closely. With the substitute once butchered, on Wednesday, the danger would of course be over. On Thursday Mr. Pratt and his guests, with trumpets of publicity, would eat the barbecued bull. On Sunday, with the week expired, Clyde would present Mr. Pratt with irrefutable evidence that it was not Caesar who had been sacrificed and that he had therefore won the bet. Mr. Pratt would of course explode with rage, but in the end he would have to compose himself and admit his helplessness and pay the $10,000, for if the facts were made public the roar of laughter would obliterate him. Customers in a pratteria would say, 'Do you suppose this is really beef? It may be woodchuck.' Mr. Pratt would have to pay and keep his mouth shut. He couldn't even take Caesar back, for what would he do with him? Clyde Osgood would get the $10,000, and doubtless a part of his proposal would be that you would get Caesar. I don't know how that would work out, since officially Caesar would be dead, but there might be a way around that difficulty, and as a minimum benefit you could breed his exceptional qualities into your herd."

Wolfe intertwined his fingers at his abdominal peak. "That, of course, is merely the outline of the proposal. Clyde had probably developed it in detail, including the time and manner of shuffling the bulls. The most auspicious time for that would have been after 1 o'clock, when you would be the one on guard, but you might have refused to involve yourself to that extent; and therefore one possibility is that the shuffling was set for earlier and had actually taken place. Caesar may be alive at this moment. The bull who died of anthrax may have been only a substitute. I offer that only as a conjecture; obviously it is tenable only on the supposition that you agreed to Clyde's proposal and entered into his scheme . . . and you know more about that than I do. But leaving that entirely aside, what do you think of the scheme itself? Do you detect any flaws?"

McMillan was eying him with a grim smile. He said calmly, "You're slick, aren't you?"

"Moderately." Wolfe's eyes closed and came half open again. "But don't make the mistake of supposing that I'm trying to waylay you. I may be passably slick, but my favorite weapon is candor. Here is my position, sir. I can account satisfactorily for Clyde's expectation of winning that bet only by assuming that he concocted such plan as I have outlined. If he did so, you either acceded or refused. In either case, I would like to know what he said. Don't think I am insulting you by reckoning that you might have withheld facts from Mr. Waddell. I would myself be reluctant to trust him with a fact of any delicacy. I appeal to you, did Clyde make you a proposal, and did you accept or decline?"

McMillan still wore the grim smile. "You're slick all right. Maybe the next thing is, did I murder him? Maybe I murdered him because he insulted me?"

"I'm never facetious about murder. Besides, I haven't got to the murder yet. I need first to justify Clyde's optimism about his bet, and establish what he came here to do or whom to see. Did he make you a proposal?"

"No." McMillan abruptly stood up.

Wolfe lifted his brows. "Going?"

"I don't see much point in staying. I came as a favor to Fred Osgood."

"And as a favor to him, you have no information at all that might help? Nothing that might explain—"

"No. I can't explain a damn thing." The stockman took three heavy steps and turned. "Neither can you," he declared, "by trying to smear any of the mess on me."

He strode to the door and opened it, and it closed after him.

Wolfe sighed, shut his eyes, and sat. I stood and looked at him a minute, detecting none of the subtle signs of glee or triumph on his map, and then treated myself to a healthy sigh and got busy with the trays. Not being sure whether a maid was supposed to be available at 10 o'clock at night, and not liking to dump the trays in the hall, I got them perched on my arms and sought the back stairs. That was a blunder, because the stairs were a little narrow and I nearly got stuck on a turn. But I navigated to the kitchen without disaster, unloaded, and proceeded via the pantry and dining room to the main hall. There was a light in the library, and through the open door I saw Howard Bronson reading a newspaper. No one else was visible, and I completed the circuit back to Wolfe's room by way of the main stair.

He was still dormant. I sat down and yawned, and said: "It is in the bag. Lily killed him, thinking that by erasing evidence of her past she could purify herself and perhaps some day be worthy of me. Caroline killed him to practise her follow-through. Jimmy killed him to erase Lily's past, making twice for that one motive. Pratt killed him to annoy Mr. Osgood. McMillan killed him because the substitute he brought for Caesar proved to be a cow. Dave killed him—"

"Confound it, Archie, shut up."

"Yes, sir. I'll close it forever and seal the crack with rubber cement the minute you explain at what time and by what process you got this nice little case like that." I doubled my fist, but the gesture was wasted because he didn't open his eyes.

He was in bad shape, for he muttered mildly, "I did have it like that."

"What became of it?"

"It went up in fire and smoke."

"The bull motif again. Phooey. Try and persuade me . . . and incidentally, why don't you stop telling people that I steered your car into a tree and demolished it? What good do you expect to accomplish by puerile paroxysms like that? To go back to this case you've dragged us into through your absolute frenzy to find an adequate chair to sit on, I suppose now it's hopeless? I suppose these hicks are going to enjoy the refreshing sight of Nero Wolfe heading south Thursday morning with his tail between his legs? Or shall I go on with the list until I offer one that strikes your fancy? Dave killed him because he missed breakfast the day he was fired two years ago and has never caught up. Bronson killed him . . . by the way, I just saw Mr. Bronson—"

"Bronson?"

"Yep. In the library reading a newspaper as if he owned the place."

"Go and get him." Wolfe stirred and his eyes threatened to open. "Bring him here."

"Now?"

"Now."

I arose and sallied forth. But on my way downstairs it occurred to me that I might as well make arrangements in case of a prolonged session, so I went to the kitchen first and abducted a pitcher of Advanced Register Guernsey milk from the refrigerator. With that in my hand, I strutted on to the library and told Bronson I hated to interrupt him but that Mr. Wolfe had expressed a desire for his company.

He looked amused and put down his newspaper and said he had begun to fear he was going to be slighted.

"No sirree," I said. "He'll banish that fear easy."

13

HE SAT in the chair McMillan had vacated and continued to look tolerably amused. Wolfe, immovable, with his eyes nearly shut, appeared to be more than half asleep, which may or may not have deceived Bronson but didn't deceive me. I yawned. With the angle of the light striking Bronson as it did, his nose looked blunter than it had on the veranda, as if it had at some time been permanently pushed, and his clever gray eyes looked smaller.

Finally he said in a cultivated tone, "I understood you wanted to ask me something."

Wolfe nodded. "Yes, sir. Were you able to overhear much of my conversation with Miss Osgood this afternoon?"

"Not a great deal. In fact, very little." Bronson smiled. "What was that for, to see if I would make an effort at indignation? Let me suggest . . . we won't really need finesse. I know a little something about you, I'm aware of your resources, but I have a few myself. Why don't we just agree that you're not a fool and neither am I?"

"Indeed." Wolfe's lids had lifted so that his eyes were more than slits. "Are you really a coolheaded man? There are so few."

"I'm fairly intelligent."

"Then thank heaven we can discuss facts calmly, without a lot of useless pother . . . facts which I have got from Miss Osgood. For instance, that you are what Mr. Osgood—and many other people—would call an unscrupulous blackguard."

"I don't . . ." Bronson flipped a hand. "Oh, well. Calling names . . ."

"Just so. I can excoriate stupidity, and often do, because it riles me, but moral indignation is a dangerous indulgence. Ethology is a chaos. Financial banditry, for example . . . I either condemn it or I don't; and if I do, without prejudice, where will I find jailers? No. My only excuse for labeling you an unscrupulous blackguard is the dictionary, and I do it to clarify our positions. I'm in the detective business, and you're in the blackguard business . . . and I want to consult with you about both. I am counting on you to help me in my investigation of a murder, and I also have a suggestion to make regarding one of your projects—the one that brought you here. Regarding the murder—"

"Perhaps we'd better take the last one first and get it out of the way. I'm always open to a reasonable suggestion."

"As you please, sir." Wolfe's lips pushed out, and in again. "You have a paper signed by Clyde Osgood. You showed it to Miss Osgood this morning."

"A receipt for money I paid him."

"Specifying the services he was to perform in return."

"Yes."

"The performance of which would render him likewise a blackguard . . . in the estimation of his father."

"That's right."

Wolfe stirred. "I want that paper. Now wait. I offer no challenge to your right to expect your money back. I concede that right. But I don't like your methods of collection. You may have a right to them too, but I do not like them. Miss Osgood aroused my admiration this afternoon, which is rare for a woman, and I want to relieve the pressure on her. I propose that you hand the paper to Mr. Goodwin; it will be safe in his custody. Within 10 days at the outside I shall either pay you the $10,000, or have it paid, or return the paper to you. I make that pledge without reservation." Wolfe aimed a thumb at me. "Give it to him."

The blackguard shook his head, slowly and positively. "I said a reasonable suggestion."

"You won't do it?"

"No."

"The security is superlative. I rarely offer pledges, because I would redeem one, tritely, with my life."

"I couldn't use your life. The security you offer may be good, but the paper signed by Osgood is better, and it belongs to me. Why the deuce should I give it up?"

I looked at Wolfe inquiringly. "I'd be glad to undertake—"

"No, thanks, Archie. We'll pass it, at least for the present. —I hope, Mr. Bronson, that your antagonism will find—"

"I'm not antagonistic," Bronson interrupted. "Don't get me wrong. I said I'm not a fool, and I would be a fool to antagonize you. I know very well I'm vulnerable, and I know what you can do. If I make an enemy of you I might as well leave New York. I've only been there two months, but if you wanted to take the trouble to trace me back I don't deny you could do it. You wouldn't find that a cell is waiting for me anywhere, but you could collect enough to make it damned hard going . . . too hard. I've had a bad break on this Clyde Osgood thing, but I can try again and expect better luck, and God knows I don't want you hounding me, and you wouldn't go to the expense and trouble just for the fun of it. Believe me, I'm not antagonistic. You have no right to get sore about my not surrendering that paper, because it's mine, but otherwise I'm for you. If I can help any I will."

"No finesse, Mr. Bronson?"

"None."

"Good. Then tell me first, where were you born?"

Bronson shook his head. "I said help you, not satisfy your curiosity."

"You've admitted I can trace you back if I care to take the trouble."

"Then take the trouble."

"Very well, I'll be more direct. Have you ever handled cattle?"

Bronson stared, then let out a short laugh and said, "My God, must I take it back about your not being a fool? Do you mean to say you're trying to fit me in that thing?"

"Have you ever handled cattle?"

"I've never had the slightest association with cattle. I know where milk and beef come from only because I read it somewhere."

"Where is the club you were carrying last night when you accompanied Clyde Osgood to Pratt's place?"

"Club?"

"Yes. A rough club, a length of sapling."

"Why . . . I don't think . . . Oh yes. Sure, I remember. It was leaning up against a shed as we went by, and I just—"

"Where is it?"

"You mean now? After all—"

"Where did you leave it?"

"Why . . . I don't . . . Oh! Sure. When we got to the fence, where the trees ended, Clyde went on and I came back. He took the club with him."

"What for?"

Bronson shrugged. He had himself collected again. "Just to have it, I suppose. I notice you carry a heavy walking stick. What for?"

"Not to knock myself unconscious with. Did Clyde ask for the club? Did you offer it to him?"

"I don't know. It was quite casual, one way or the other.

Why, was he knocked on the head? I thought he was killed with a pick, according to your—"

"You're supposed to be helping, sir, not chattering. I need the truth about that club."

"You've had it."

"Nonsense. You were obviously disconcerted, and you stalled." Wolfe wiggled a finger at him. "If you don't want my antagonism, beware. This is the most favorable chance you'll have to tell the truth, here privately with me in comparative amity. Isn't it a fact that you yourself carried the club to Mr. Pratt's place?"

"No. I didn't go there."

"You stick to that?"

"It's the truth."

"I warn you again, beware. But say we take that, for the moment, for truth, tell me this: why was Clyde going to Pratt's? What was he going to do there?"

"I don't know."

"What did he say he was going to do?"

"He didn't say."

Wolfe shut his eyes and was silent. I saw the tip of his index finger making little circles on the arm of his chair, and knew he was speechless with fury. After a minute Bronson began:

"I may as well—"

"Shut up!" Wolfe's lids quivered as he opened his eyes. "You're making a mistake. A bad one. Listen to this. You were demanding immediate repayment of your money. Clyde, unable to raise the sum in New York, came here to appeal to his father, and you were in such a hurry, or mistrusted him so greatly, or both, that you came along. You wouldn't let him out of your sight. His father refused his appeal, since Clyde wouldn't tell him what the money was needed for—to save the Osgood honor would be correct phrasing—and you were ready to disclose the facts to the father and collect your debt direct from him. Then Clyde, in desperation, made a bet. He couldn't possibly win the bet and pay you for 6 days, until the week expired, and what acceptable assurance could he give you that he would win it at all? Only one assurance could have induced you to wait: a satisfactory explanation of the method by which he expected to win. So he gave it to you. Don't try to tell me he didn't; I'm not a gull. He told you how he expected to win, and the steps he proposed to take. Very well, you tell me."

Bronson shook his head. "All I can say is, you're wrong. He didn't tell—"

"Pfui. I'm right. I know when I'm right. Beware, sir."

Bronson shrugged. "It won't get you anywhere to keep telling me to beware. I can't tell you what I don't know."

"Did Clyde Osgood tell you how and why he expected to win the bet?"

"No."

"Or what he intended to do at Pratt's or whom he expected to see there?"

"No."

"Did he make any remark, drop any hint, that led you to guess?"

"No."

"You're making a bad blunder."

"No, I'm not. I may be getting in bad with you, but I can't help it. For God's sake—"

"Shut up. You're a fool after all." Wolfe turned and snapped at me: "Archie, get that paper."

He might have prepared me by one swift glance before putting it into words, but when I complained to him about such things he always said that my speed and wit required no preparation, and I retorted that I could put up with less sarcastic flattery and more regard for my convenience.

On this occasion it didn't matter much. Bronson was about my size but I doubted if he was tough. However, it was a murder case, and Wolfe had just been insinuating that this gentleman had been on the scene of hostilities with a club in his hand, so I got upright and across to his neighborhood quick enough to forestall any foolish motions he might make. I stuck my hand out and said:

"Gimme."

He shook his head and got up without haste, kicking his chair back without looking at it, looking instead at me with his eyes still steady and clever.

"This is silly," he said. "Damned silly. You can't bluff me like this."

I asked without turning my head, "Do you want it, Mr. Wolfe?"

"Get it."

"Okay. —Reach for the moon. I'll help myself."

"No you won't." His eyes didn't flicker. "If you try taking it away from me, I won't fight. I'm not much of a coward, but I'm not in condition and I'd be meat for you. Instead,

I'll yell, and Osgood will come, and of course he'll want a look at the paper that's causing the trouble." He smiled.

"You will?"

"I will."

"Back at you. If you do, I'll show you how I make sausage. I warn you, one bleat and I'll quit only when the ambulance comes. After Osgood reads the paper he'll offer to pay me to do it again. Hold that pose."

I started to reach, and I'll be damned if he didn't try a dive with his knee up, and without flashing a flag. He was fairly quick, but I side-stepped in time. It wasn't absolutely essential to punch him, but a guy as tricky as he was needed a lesson anyway, so I let him have it, a good stiff hook that lifted him out of his dive and turned him over. I was beside him, bending over him, by the time he got his eyes open again.

"Stay there," I told him. "I don't know which pocket it's in. Do you think you can remember that? If so, gimme."

His hand started for his inside breast pocket, and I reached in ahead of him and pulled out something that proved to be a handsome brown leather wallet with a monogram on it in platinum or maybe tin. He grabbed for it and I jerked away and told him to get up and sit down, and backed off a little to examine the loot.

"My word." I whistled. "Here's an accumulation of currency out of all proportion. A couple of thousand or more. Pipe down, you. I don't steal from blackguards. But I don't see . . . ah, here we are. Secret compartments you might say." I unfolded it and ran my eye over it, and handed it to Wolfe. "Return the balance?"

He nodded, reading. I handed the wallet back to Bronson, who was back on his feet. He looked a little disarranged, but he met my eye as he took the wallet from me, and I had to admit there was something to him, although misplaced; it isn't usual to meet the eye of a bird who has just knocked you down and made you like it. Wolfe said, "Here, Archie," and handed me the paper, and from my own breast pocket I took the brown ostrich cardcase, gold-tooled, given to me by Wolfe on a birthday, in which I carried my police and fire cards and operator's license. I slipped the folded paper inside and returned it to my pocket.

Wolfe said, "Mr. Bronson. There are other questions I meant to ask, such as the purpose of your trip to Mr. Pratt's place this afternoon, but it would be futile. I am even beginning to suspect that you are now engaged in an enterprise which may prove to be a bigger blunder than your conduct here with me. As for the paper Mr. Goodwin took from you, I guarantee that within 10 days you will get it back, or your money. Don't try any stratagems. I'm mad enough already. Good night, sir."

"I repeat . . . I've told you . . ."

"I don't want to hear it. You're a fool. Good night."

Bronson went.

Wolfe heaved a deep sigh. I poured out a glass of milk, and sipped, and saw that he had an eye cocked at me. In a minute he murmured:

"Archie. Where did you get that milk?"

"Refrigerator."

"In the kitchen?"

"Yes, sir."

"Well?"

"Yes, sir. There's 5 or 6 bottles in there. Shall I bring you one?"

"You might have saved yourself a trip." His hand dived into his side coat pocket and came out clutching a flock of beer bottle caps. He opened his fist and counted them, frowning, and told me, "Bring two."

14

At 10 o'clock the next morning, Wednesday, a motley group piled into Osgood's sedan, bound for Crowfield. All except Nero Wolfe looked the worse for wear—I couldn't say about me. Osgood was seedy and silent, and during a brief talk with Wolfe had shown an inclination to bite. Bronson no longer looked disarranged, having again donned the Crawnley suit he had worn Monday, but the right side of his jaw was swollen and he was sullen and not amused. Nancy, who took the wheel again, was pale and had blood-shot eyes and moved in jerks. She had already made one trip to Crowfield and back, for a couple of relatives at the railroad station. The funeral was to be Thursday afternoon, and the major influx of kin would be 24 hours later. Apparently Wolfe had changed his mind about immediately relieving the pressure on the woman he admired, for I had been instructed that there was no hurry about telling Miss Osgood that the paper her brother had signed was in my possession. Which, considering how I had got it, was in my judgment just as well.

During the 30-minute drive to Crowfield no one said a word, except for a brief discussion between Osgood and Nancy to arrange for meeting later in the day, after errands had been performed. First we dropped Osgood on Main Street in front of an establishment with palms and ferns in the window and a small sign painted down in a corner which said Somebody or other, MORTICIAN. Our next stop was two blocks down, at the hotel, where Bronson left us, in a dismal all-around silence and unfriendly atmosphere that is probably the chief occupational hazard of the blackguard business.

Nancy muttered at me, "Thompson's Garage, isn't it?" and I told her yes, and three minutes later she let me out there, around on a side street, the idea being that since there might be a delay about the car she would proceed to deliver Wolfe at the exposition grounds, for which I was grateful, not wanting him muttering around underfoot.

The bill was $66.20, which was plenty, even including

the towing in. Of course there was no use beefing, so I contented myself with a thorough inspection to make sure everything was okay, filled up with gas and oil; paid in real money, and departed.

Then I was supposed to find Lew Bennett, secretary of the National Guernsey League. I tried the hotel and drew a blank, and wasted 20 minutes in a phone booth, being met with busy lines, wrong numbers, and general ignorance. There seemed to be an impression that he was somewhere at the exposition, so I drove out there and after a battle got the car parked in one of the spaces reserved for exhibitors. I plunged into the crowd, deciding to start at the exposition offices, where I learned that this was a big cattle day and Bennett was in up to his ears. He would be around the exhibition sheds, which were at the other end of the grounds. Back in the crowd again, I fought through men, women, children, balloons, horns, popcorn and bedlam, to my objective.

I hadn't seen this part before. There was a city of enormous sheds, in a row, each one 50 yards long or more and half as wide. There weren't many people around. I popped into the first shed. It smelled like cows, which wasn't surprising, because it was full of them. A partition 5 feet high ran down the middle of the shed its entire length, and facing it, tied to it, were cattle, on both sides. Bulls and cows and calves. Two more rows of them faced the walls. But none of them looked like the breed I was most familiar with after my association with Hickory Caesar Grindon. A few spectators straggled down the long aisle, and I moseyed along to where a little squirt in overalls was combing tangles out of a cow's tail, and told him I was looking for Lew Bennett of the Guernsey League.

"Guernsey?" He looked contemptuous. "I wouldn't know. I'm a Jersey man."

"Oh. Excuse me. Personally, I fancy Guernseys. Is there a shed where they allow Guernseys?"

"Sure. Down beyond the judging lot. He might be at the lot. They're judging Ayrshires and Belted Swiss this morning, but they begin on Guernseys at 1 o'clock."

I thanked him and proceeded. After I had passed three sheds there was a large vacant space, roped off into divisions, and that was where the crowd was, several hundred of them, up against the ropes. Inside were groups of cattle, black with belts of white around their middles, held by men and boys with tie-ropes. Other men walked or stood around, frowning at the cattle, accompanied by still others armed with foun-

tain pens and sheets of cardboard. One guy was kneeling
down, inspecting an udder as if he expected to find the Clue
of the Month on it. I couldn't see Bennett anywhere.

I found him in the second shed ahead, which was devoted
to Guernseys. It was full of activity and worriment—brushing
coats, washing hoofs and faces, combing tails, discussing and
arguing. Bennett was rushing back and forth. He didn't recognize me, and I nearly had to wrestle him to stop him. I reminded him of our acquaintance and said that Nero Wolfe
wanted to see him at the main exhibits building, or some
more convenient spot, as soon as possible. Urgent.

"Out of the question," he declared, looking fierce. "I haven't
even got time to eat. They're judging us at 1 o'clock."

"Mr. Wolfe's solving a murder for Mr. Frederick Osgood.
He needs important information from you."

"I haven't got any."

"He wants to ask you."

"I can't see him now. I just can't do it. After 1 o'clock . . .
when they start judging . . . you say he's at the main exhibits
building? I'll see him or let him know . . ."

"He'll lunch at the Methodist tent. Make it soon. Huh?"

He said just as soon as possible.

It was noon by the time I got to our space in the main exhibits building. It was judgment day for more than Guernseys,
as 4 o'clock that afternoon was zero hour for the orchids.
Wolfe was there spraying and manicuring. The sprayer was
a pippin, made specially to his order, holding two gallons,
with a compression chamber and a little electric motor, weighing only 11 pounds empty. His rival and enemy, Shanks, was
with him admiring the sprayer when I joined them. I told
him the car was okay and named the extent of the damage,
and described the plight of Mr. Bennett.

He grimaced. "Then I must wait here."

"Standing is good for you."

"And the delay. It is Wednesday noon. We have nothing
left but shreds. I telephoned Mr. Waddell. The club carried
to Mr. Pratt's place has not been found, and the police took
no photographs of the bull. Pfui. Inspector Cramer's inde-
fatigable routine has its advantages. Miss Osgood reports
that none of the servants saw Bronson return. Our next move
depends on Mr. Bennett."

"He says he has no information."

"But he has. He is ignorant of its application. Perhaps if
you went back and explained? . . ."

"Not without using force. He says he hasn't got time to eat."

That of course silenced him. He grunted and returned to Shanks.

I propped myself against the edge of the dahlia table across the aisle and yawned. Dissatisfaction filled my breast. I had failed to bring what I had been sent for, which was infrequent and irritating. I had been relieved of $66.20 of Wolfe's money. We were going to dine and sleep that night in a house where family and relatives were preparing for a funeral. Wolfe had just stated that in the murder case we were supposed to be solving we had nothing left but shreds. Altogether, the outlook was not rosy. Wolfe and Shanks went on chewing the rag, paying no attention to the visitors passing up and down the aisle, and I stood propped, with no enthusiasm for any effort to combat the gloom. I must have shut my eyes for the first I knew there was a tug at my sleeve and a voice:

"Wake up, Escamillo, and show me the flowers."

I let the lids up. "How do you do, Miss Rowan. Go away. I'm in seclusion."

"Kiss me."

I bent and deposited a peck on her brow. "There. Thank you for calling. Nice to see you."

"You're a lout."

"I have at no time asked you to submit bids."

The corner of her mouth went up. "This is a public exposition. I paid my way in. You're an exhibitor. Go ahead and exhibit. Show me."

"Not exhibitionist. Exhibitor. Anyway, I'm only an employee." I took her elbow and eased her across the aisle. "Mr. Wolfe, you know Miss Rowan. She wants to be shown the orchids."

He bowed. "That is one compliment I always surrender to."

She looked him in the eye. "I want you to like me, Mr. Wolfe. Or not dislike me. Mr. Goodwin and I are probably going to be friends. Will you give me an orchid?"

"I rarely dislike women, and never like them, Miss Rowan. I have only albinos here. I'll give you orchids at 5 o'clock, after the judging, if you'll tell me where to send them."

"I'll come and get them."

The upshot of that was that she went to lunch with us.

The Methodist tent was fuller than the day before, probably because we got there earlier. Apparently Mrs. Miller had no off days, for the fricassee with dumplings was as good as the memory of it, and, thinking it might be my last appearance among the devout, I permitted myself to run the meal in two sections, as did Wolfe. He, as always in the company of good food, was sociable and expansive. Discovering that Lily had been in Egypt, he told about his house in Cairo, and they chatted away like a pair of camels, going on to Arabia and making quite a trip of it. She let him do most of the talking but made him chuckle a couple of times, and I began to suspect she wasn't very obvious and might even be smooth.

As I put down my empty coffee cup Wolfe said, "Still no Bennett. It's 1:30. Is it far to the cattle sheds?"

I told him not very.

"Then if you will please find out about him. Confound it, I must see him. If he can't come at once, tell him I'll be here until 3 o'clock, and after that at the exhibit."

"Right."

I got up. Lily arose too, saying that she was supposed to be with Mr. Pratt and Caroline and they were probably looking for her. She left the tent with me, whereupon I informed her that it was now working hours and I would be moving through the throngs too energetically for pleasant companionship. She stated that up to date she had failed to detect any taint of pleasantness in my make-up and would see me at 5 o'clock, and departed in the direction of the grandstand. My errand was the other way.

They were going strong at the judging lot. I was pleased to note that Guernseys were evidently a more popular breed than Belted Swiss or Ayrshires, as the crowd was much larger than it had been 2 hours earlier. Bennett was within the enclosure, along with judges, scorekeepers and cattle with attendants. For a second my heart stopped, as I caught sight of a bull I would have sworn was Hickory Caesar Grindon; then I saw he was a lighter shade of tan and had a much smaller white spot on his face. I maneuvered around to the other side where the crowd wasn't so thick, and stood there, and when I felt a pull at my sleeve I thought for an instant that Lily Rowan had tailed me.

But it was Dave, dressed up in coat and pants and shirt and tie, and a shiny straw hat. He cackled: "Didn't I say you like to be around where things is goin' on? First I seen you. Was you here when them derned fools put down Bella Grassleigh for that Silverville cow? Her with a barrel more like a deer than any good milker I ever saw."

"Good God," I said, "that's the worst I ever heard. I just got here. I don't suppose . . . well, I'll be derned. There's our friend Monte McMillan."

"Yep, I drove him in this morning." Dave shook his head. "Poor old Monte, got to start practically all over again. He's got it in mind to do some buyin' if prices is right, to build up another foundation. You wouldn't have thought a year ago . . ."

I missed the rest because I was diving under the rope. Bennett was momentarily disengaged, standing mopping his forehead, and I made for him. He blinked at me in the sunlight and said he was sorry, he hadn't been able to make it. I told him okay, that was forgiven, but couldn't he come to the Methodist tent right now. Impossible, he said, they were judging Produce of Dam and Breeders' Young Herd simultaneously. There was nothing he could tell Nero Wolfe anyway. And I didn't belong there in the enclosure—

I got a little peremptory: "Wolfe's working on a murder, and he says he needs to see you and can't make another move until he does. Are you primarily a citizen and a friend of Fred Osgood's, or a sergeant at arms in a cattle tribunal? If you think justice among the cows is more important . . ."

He said he wasn't a particular friend of Osgood's, who as far as he was concerned was merely a member of the League, and that he would be at the Methodist tent no, fooling, within half an hour.

I got outside the ropes again, but instead of beating it I decided to hang around and wait for him. I watched the judging for a few minutes, but couldn't see very well on account of the mob, and so wandered along in front of the sheds. There was no one around at all, the judging being the current attraction, so naturally I observed the moving object that caught my eyes, especially since the first sight showed me that the object was familiar. It was Nancy Osgood, and the glance she cast behind her as she entered one of the sheds was either furtive or I was getting fanciful. Even if she was furtive it was none of my business, but a detective who minds his own business would be a contradiction in terms, so I slid over to the shed and inserted myself through the door.

She wasn't within view. There were plenty of cows, black and white this time, and a few visitors further down the aisle, but no Nancy. I strolled along between the rows of hind ends. Toward the middle of the shed there was a partitioned compartment on the left, containing no cow; but an instant's peep disclosed that it contained three other things: a large pile of straw with a pitchfork handle protruding from its center, Nancy Osgood, and Jimmy Pratt. I would have passed on, but I had been seen. Jimmy's voice was gruff and discourteous:

"Well?"

I shrugged. "Well enough. Hoping you are the same." I started to move on, but his voice came even gruffer:

"Wait and look and listen. The more you see and hear the more you can tell."

"Don't, Jimmy." Nancy sounded very distressed. She turned her eyes, more bloodshot than ever, in my direction: "Were you following me, Mr. Goodwin? What for?"

A couple of passers-by seemed disposed to linger, so I stepped inside the stall to keep it in the family. "Yes," I told her, "I was. For about 40 seconds. I happened to see you enter this shed looking behind you for bloodhounds, and followed you out of curiosity." I surveyed young Pratt. "It's a good thing you're training for architecture instead of the diplomatic service. You lack suavity. If this is a clandestine rendezvous and you suspected I might report it, it might be better to rub me with salve than sandpaper."

He reached for his pocket. "Oh, in that case—"

I let him go on. His hand emerged with a modest roll, from which, with unsteady fingers, he peeled a ten. He thrust it at me with an objectionable smile and asked, "Will that do?"

"Swell." I took it. "Munificent." My first impulse was to stick it in the pocket of Nancy's jacket and tell her to buy stocking with it, but at that moment our party was joined by a lanky guy in overalls carrying a pitchfork. With only a glance at us he rammed the fork into the pile of straw and started to lift the load. I stopped him by shoving the $10 bill under his nose.

"Here, brother. I represent the exposition management. We've decided you fellows are overworked. Take this as an expression of our esteem."

He stared. "What's that?"

"Don't try to understand it, just take it. Redistribution of wealth. A form of communism."

"From the exposition management?"

"Right."

"I'll be derned. They must be crazy." He took the bill and stuffed it in his pocket. "Much obliged to you."

"Don't mention it." I waved airily. He elevated the load of straw, a big one, about one-fourth of the entire pile, above his shoulder with an expert twist, and departed.

"You said salve, didn't you?" Jimmy Pratt sounded resentful. "How the hell could I know you're Robin Hood? After what you said about salve, wasn't it natural to take you for a chiseler?" He turned to Nancy. "He knows all about Bronson and the paper Clyde signed, anyway, since he was there when you told Wolfe. As far as your father hearing about our being together is concerned . . ."

I was extremely glad he had shifted to Nancy, because it gave me an opportunity I was badly in need of. I grant that I have aplomb, but I'm not constructed of wood, and it still surprises me that nothing on my face gave them alarm. What I had seen was something that had been uncovered by the removal of a portion of the straw. Making a movement, my toe had touched some object that wasn't straw, and a downward glance had shown me what it was. It was a brown custom made oxford perched on its heel, an inch of brown sock, and the cuff of one leg of a pair of Crawley trousers.

So, as I say, I was glad Jimmy had shifted to Nancy, for it gave me an opportunity to kick at the straw capriciously and thereby get the shoe and sock and trouser cuff out of sight again. Nothing was left visible but straw.

Nancy was talking to me: "Perhaps I shouldn't, after Mr. Wolfe said he would help me, but I met Jimmy this morning and we . . . we had a talk . . . and I told him about that paper and Bronson still having it . . . and he thought he could do something about it and I was sure he shouldn't try it without seeing Mr. Wolfe first . . . and we arranged to meet here at 2 o'clock and discuss it . . ."

I had unobtrusively got myself moved around to where I could reach the pitchfork handle which was protruding erect from the center of the pile of straw. With my eyes respectfully attending to Nancy, my hand idly played with the straw, which is nice to touch, and without much effort it found the spot where the handle of the fork joined the tines. Two of my fingers—feeling with the ends of their nails, which don't leave prints—explored downward along a tine, but not far, not more than a couple of inches, before they were stopped by something that was neither tine nor straw. I kept the fingers there half a minute, feeling, and then slowly withdrew my hand.

Jimmy demanded, "What's the use of deadpanning her? Either you and Wolfe are going to act as decent as he talked—"

"Deadpan?" I grinned. "Not on your life. I wouldn't know about decency, but Wolfe and I always do what he says. But you children are only going to make it harder by being indiscreet all over the fair grounds. Osgood is a difficult enough client already. For God's sake postpone this reunion for a day or two. Everybody in the county knows you, and here you stand in plain view. If you'll do what I say I'll guarantee that

Wolfe and I will be as decent as doves . . . and Osgood will never see that paper."

Jimmy was frowning. "Well?"

"Separate. Disunite. Immediately. You go out at the other end and I'll take her this way."

"He's right, Jimmy. It was awfully foolish, but you insisted—"

"Come on, beat it. Ten people have stopped to look in here at us in the last three minutes."

"But I've got to know—"

"Damn it, do what I say!"

"Please, Jimmy."

He took her hand and looked her in the eye and said her name twice as if he was leaving her bound to a railroad track, and tore himself away. I told her to come on and left the stall and turned right with her, toward the door by which I had entered. Outside I took her elbow and talked as we walked:

"I've got work to do and I'm leaving you. You've acted like a female nincompoop. It's true that emotions are emotions, but brains are also brains. To go running to Jimmy Pratt for help when you already had Nero Wolfe's! You get away from here. I suppose you have a date to meet your father somewhere. If so, go there and wait for him and practice thinking."

"But I haven't . . . you talk as if—"

"I don't talk as if anything. Don't worry about how I talk. Here's where I turn off. See you in kindergarten."

I left her in the middle of a crowd, thinking that was as good a place as any, and elbowed my way across the current to where I could make better time without displaying any indications of panic. It took less than five minutes to get from there to the Methodist tent. Wolfe was still there, at the table, looking massively forlorn on the folding chair. He had probably never before digested good food under such difficult circumstances.

He frowned up at me. "Well? Mr. Bennett?"

I sat down and nodded and restrained my voice. "I have to make a brief but tiresome report. Item 1, Mr. Bennett will be here in 10 minutes or so. He said. Item 2, I found Nancy Osgood and Jimmy Pratt in a cowshed, discussing means of getting the paper which I have in my pocket. Item 3, in the same shed I found Mr. Bronson lying under a pile of straw, dead, with a pitchfork stuck through his heart. No one knows of the last item but me . . . or didn't when I left."

Wolfe's eyes went shut, then came half-open again. He heaved a deep sigh. "The fool. I told that man he was a fool."

15

I NODDED. "Yeah. You also told him you were beginning to suspect that he was engaged in an enterprise which might prove to be a big blunder. Madam Shasta, in a booth down the line, calls it reading the future and charges a dime for it." I fished for a pair of nickels and shoved them across at him. "I'll bite. How did you know it?"

He ignored my offer. "Confound it," he muttered. "Too late again. I should have phoned Saul or Fred last evening to take a night train. Bronson should have been followed this morning. Once compelled to talk, he would have been all the evidence we needed. I am not myself, Archie. How the devil can I be, dashing around in all this furor . . . I have that scoundrel Shanks to thank for it. Well." He sighed again. "You say no one knows it?"

"Correct. Except the guy that did it. I was waiting around for Bennett and saw Nancy enter a cowshed and followed her in. She joined Jimmy Pratt in a stall which also contained a pile of straw. I made it three and we conversed. A cow nurse came and removed part of the straw, exposing a shoe and a trouser cuff. No one saw it but me and I kicked straw over it. A pitchfork was thrust into the pile, upright, with straw covering it part way up the handle, and I took a sounding with my hand and discovered what its pincushion was. Right through his chest. His pump was gone. I accused Romeo and Juliet of indiscretion and hustled them out in separate directions, and came here."

"Then the discovery awaits removal of more straw."

"Yes. Which may have already happened, or may not occur until tomorrow."

"But probably sooner. You came away to escape clamor?"

"To notify you. And to tell you about Bennett. And to save Nancy from being annoyed, by her father for the company she keeps, and by the cops for practically sitting on a corpse."

"You were all seen by the man who removed the straw."

"Sure, and by various others. Shall I go back now and discover him?"

Wolfe shook his head. "That wouldn't help. Nor, probably, will there be a trail for the official pack, so there's no hurry. I wouldn't have guessed Bronson would be idiot enough to give him such a chance, but of course he had to meet him somewhere. But it is now all the more imperative—ah, thank goodness! Good afternoon, sir."

Lew Bennett, still in his shirt sleeves, out of breath, stood beside him and curtly acknowledged the greeting. "You want to see me? Worst time you could have picked. The very worst."

"So Mr. Goodwin has told me. I'm sorry, but I can't help it. Be seated, sir. Have some coffee?"

"I'll just stand. If I once sat down . . . what do you want?"

"Have you had lunch?"

"No."

"Preposterous." Wolfe shook his head at him. "In the midst of the most difficult and chaotic problems, I never missed a meal. A stomach too long empty thins the blood and disconcerts the brain.—Archie, order a portion of the fricassee.—For God's sake, sir, sit down."

I doubt if Wolfe influenced him much, it was the smell of food. I saw his nostrils quivering. He hesitated, and when I flagged a Methodist and told her to bring it with an extra dime's worth of dumplings, which was an idea Wolfe had invented, he succumbed and dropped into a chair.

Wolfe said, "That's better. Now. I've been hired by Mr. Osgood to solve a murder, and I need to know some things. You may think of my questions irrelevant or even asinine; if so you'll be wrong. My only serious fault is lethargy, and I tolerate Mr. Goodwin, and even pay him, to help me circumvent it. 48 hours ago, Monday afternoon on Mr. Pratt's terrace, you told him that there were a dozen members of your league waiting for you to get back, and that when they heard what you had to say there would be some action taken. You shouted that at him with conviction. What sort of action did you have in mind?"

Bennett was staring at him. "Not murder," he said shortly. "What has that got—"

"Please." Wolfe wiggled a finger at him. "I've told you I'm not an ass. I asked you a simple straightforward question. Can't you simply answer it? I know you were shouting at Mr. Pratt in a rage. But what sort of action did you have in mind?"

"No sort."

"Nothing whatever?"

"Nothing specific. I was furious. We all were. What he intended to do was the most damnable outrage and insult—"

"I know. Granting your viewpoint, I agree. But hadn't ways and means of preventing it been discussed? For example, had anyone suggested the possibility of removing Hickory Caesar Grindon secretly and putting another bull in his place?"

Bennett started to speak, and stopped. His eyes looked wary. "No," he said curtly.

Wolfe sighed. "All right. I wish you would understand that I'm investigating a murder, not a conspiracy to defraud. You should eat those dumplings hot. It might be better to let this wait until you're through—"

"Go ahead. When I'm through I'm going."

"Very well. I didn't ask if some of you had substituted another bull or tried, I asked merely if it had been suggested in the heat of indignation. What I really want to know is, would such a plan have been feasible?"

"Feasible?" Bennett swallowed chicken. "It would have been a crime. Legally."

"Of course. But—please give this consideration as a serious question—might it have worked?"

He considered, chewing bread and butter. "No. Monte McMillan was there."

"If Mr. McMillan hadn't been there, or had been a party to the scheme, might it have worked?"

"It might have."

"It would have been possible to replace Caesar with another bull sufficiently resembling him so that the substitution would be undetected by anyone not thoroughly familiar with his appearance, without a close inspection?"

"It might have."

"Yet Caesar was a national grand champion." Wolfe shifted, grimacing, on the folding chair. "Didn't he approach the unique?"

"Hell no. There's plenty of good bulls, and quite a few great ones. The grand champion stuff is all right, and it's valid, but sometimes the margin is mighty slim. Last year at Indianapolis, Caesar scored 96 and Portchester Compton 95. Another thing of course is their get. The records of their daughters and sons. Caesar had 51 A R daughters—"

"And 9 A R sons. I know. And that of course would not be visible to the eye. But still I am not satisfied. If another bull was to be substituted for Caesar by . . . well, let us say

Clyde Osgood . . . it couldn't be a near-champion, for the bull was destined to be butchered, and near-champions are valuable too. Would it be possible for an average bull, of comparatively low value, to have a fairly strong resemblance to a champion?"

"Might. At a distance of say a hundred yards. It would depend on who was looking."

"How does a bull score points?"

Bennett swallowed dumplings. "The scale of points we judge on has 22 headings, with a total of 100 points for perfection, which of course no bull ever got. Style and symmetry is 10 points. Head 6, horns 1, neck 3, withers 3, shoulders 2, chest 4, back 8, loin 3, hips 2, rump 6, thurls 2, barrel 10, and so on. The biggest number of points for any heading is 20 points for Secretions Indicating Color of Product. That's judged by the pigment secretions of the skin, which should be a deep yellow inclining toward orange in color, especially discernible in the ear, at the end of the tailbone, around the eyes and nose, on the scrotum, and at the base of horns. Hoofs and horns should be yellow. There is a very close relationship between the color of the skin, the color of the internal fat, and the milk and butter. Now that heading alone is 20 points out of the 100, and you can only judge it by a close-up inspection. As far as value is concerned, a bull's A R record is much more important than his show record. In the 1935 auctions, for instance, the price brought by A R bulls averaged over $2000. Bulls not yet A R but with A R dams averaged $533. Bulls not A R and without A R dams averaged $157. That same year Langwater Reveller sold for $10,000."

Wolfe nodded. "I see. The subtleties rule, as usual. That seems to cover the questions of value and superficial appearance. The next point . . . I was astonished by what you told me on the telephone yesterday when I called you from Mr. Osgood's house. I would have supposed that every purebred calf would receive an indelible mark at birth. But you said that the only ones that are marked—with a tattoo on the ear—are those of solid color, with no white."

"That's right."

"So that if Caesar had been replaced by another bull it couldn't have been detected by the absence of any identifying mark."

"No. Only by comparing his color pattern with your knowledge of Caesar's color pattern or with the sketch on his Certificate of Registration."

"Just so. You spoke of sketches or photographs. How are they procured?"

"They are made by the breeder, at birth, or at least before the calf is six months old. On the reverse of the Application for Registration are printed outlines of a cow, both sides and face. On them the breeder sketches in ink the color pattern of the calf, showing white, light fawn, dark fawn, red fawn, brown and brindle. The sketches, filed in our office at Fernborough, are the permanent record for identification throughout life. Copies of them appear on the certificate of registration. If you buy a bull and want to be sure you are getting the right one, you compare his color and markings with the sketches."

"Then I did understand you on the telephone. It sounded a little haphazard."

"It's the universal method," declared Bennett stiffly. "There has never been any difficulty."

"No offense. If it works it works." Wolfe sighed. "One more thing while you have your pie and coffee. This may require some reflection. Putting it as a hypothesis that Clyde Osgood actually undertook to replace Caesar with a substitute, how many bulls are there within, say, 50 miles of here, which might have been likely candidates? With a fair resemblance to Caesar, the closer the better, in general appearance and color pattern? Remember it mustn't be another champion, worth thousands."

Bennett objected, "But I've told you, it couldn't have worked. No matter how close the resemblance was, Monte McMillan would have known. He would have known Hickory Caesar Grindon from any bull on earth."

"I said as a hypothesis. Humor me and we'll soon be through. How many such bulls within 50 miles?"

"That's quite an order." Bennett slowly munched a bite of pie, stirring his coffee, and considered. "Of course there's one right here, up at the shed. A Willowdale bull, 3-year-old. He'll never be in Caesar's class, but superficially he's a lot like him, color pattern and carriage and so on."

"Are you sure the one in the shed is the Willowdale bull?"

Bennett looked startled for an instant, then relieved. "Yes, it's Willowdale Zodiac all right. He was judged a while ago, and he's way down in pigment." He sipped some coffee. "There's a bull over at Hawley's, Orinoco, that might fill the bill, except his loin's narrow, but you might or might not notice that from any distance, depending on how he was standing. Mrs. Linville has one, over the other side of Crowfield, that would do even better than Orinoco, but I'm not sure if he's home. I understand she was sending him to Syracuse. Then of course another one would have been Hickory Buckingham Pell, Caesar's double brother, but he's dead."

"When did he die?"

"About a month ago. Anthrax. With most of the rest of McMillan's herd."

"Yes. That was a catastrophe. Was Buckingham also a champion?"

"Hell no. He and Caesar were both sired by old Hickory Gabriel, a grand and beautiful bull, but no matter how good a sire may be he can't be expected to hit the combination every time. Buckingham was good to look at, but his pigment secretion was bad and his daughters were inferior. He hadn't been shown since 1936, when he scored a 68 at Jamestown."

"In any case, he was dead. What about the Osgood herd? Any candidates there?"

Bennett slowly shook his head. "Hardly. There's a promising junior sire, Thistleleaf Lucifer, that might be figured in, but he's nearer brindle than red fawn. However, you might miss it if you had no reason to suspect it, and if you didn't have Caesar's pattern well in mind."

"What is Lucifer's value?"

"That's hard to say. At an auction, it all depends . . ."

"But a rough guess?"

"Oh, between $500 and $800."

"I see. A mere fraction of $45,000."

Bennett snorted. "No bull ever lived that was worth $45,000. McMillan didn't get that for Caesar as a proper and reasonable price for him. It was only a bribe Pratt offered to pull him in on a shameful and discreditable stunt. One or two of the fellows are inclined to excuse McMillan, saying that losing 80% of his herd with anthrax was a terrible blow and he was desperate and it was a lot of money, but I say nothing in God's world could excuse a thing like that and most of them agree with me. I'd rather commit suicide than let myself—hey, George, over here! I was just coming. What's up?"

One of the men I had noticed in the judging enclosure, a big broad-shouldered guy with a tooth gone in front, approached us, bumping the backs of chairs as he came.

"Can't they get along without me for 10 minutes?" Bennett demanded. "What's wrong now?"

"Nothin's wrong at the lot," the man said. "But we can't lead from the shed and back, on account of the crowd. There's a million people around there. Somebody found a dead man under a straw pile in the Holstein shed with a pitchfork through him. Murdered."

"Good God!" Bennett jumped up. "Who?"

"Don't know. You can't find out anything. You ought to see the mob . . ."

That was all I heard, because they were on their way out. A Methodist started after Bennett, but I intercepted her and told her I would pay for the meal. She said 90 cents, and I relinquished a dollar bill and sat down again across from Wolfe.

"The natural thing," I said, "would be for me to trot over there and poke around."

Wolfe shook his head. "It's after 3 o'clock, and we have business of our own. Let's attend to it."

He got himself erect and turned to give the folding chair a dirty look, and we departed. Outside it was simpler to navigate than formerly, because instead of moving criss-cross and every other way the crowd was mostly moving fast in a straight line, toward the end of the grounds where the cattle sheds were, in the opposite direction from the one we took. They looked excited and purposeful, as if they had just had news of some prey that might be pounced on for dinner. By keeping on one edge we avoided jostling.

Charles E. Shanks wasn't anywhere in sight around the orchid display, but Raymond Plehn, who was showing Laeliocattleyas and Odontoglossums, was there. It was the first we had seen of him, though of course we had looked over his entry, which wasn't in competition with ours. The building, with its enormous expanse of tables and benches exhibiting everything from angel food cake to stalks of corn 14 feet high, seemed to have about as many afternoon visitors as usual, who either hadn't heard the news from the Holstein shed or were contrary enough to be more interested in flowers and vegetables than in corpses.

Wolfe exchanged amenities with Plehn and then he and I got busy. One of our 18 plants had got temperamental and showed signs of wilt, so I stuck it under the bench and covered it with newspaper. We went over the others thoroughly, straightening leaves that needed it, re-staking a few, and removing half a dozen blossoms whose sepals had started to brown at the tips.

"On the whole, they look perky," I told Wolfe.

"Dry," he grunted, inspecting a leaf. "Thank heaven, no red spider yet.—Ah. Good afternoon, Mr. Shanks."

At 4 o'clock the judges came, with retinue and scale sheets.

One of them was a moonfaced bird from the Eastern States Horticultural Society and the other was Cuyler Ditson, who had been a judge several times at the Metropolitan. The pair started to squint and inspect and discuss, and a modest crowd collected.

It was such a pushover, and was over and done with so soon as far as the albinos were concerned, that it seemed pretty silly after all the trouble we had gone to, even though Wolfe got the medal and all three ribbons, and all Shanks got was a consoling pat on the back. But they both knew how it would look in the next issue of the American Orchid Gazette, and they knew who would read it. Shanks was dumb enough to get mad and try to start an argument with Cuyler Ditson, and Raymond Plehn gave him the horselaugh.

When the judges left the crowd dispersed. Wolfe and Plehn started to exercise their chins, and when that began I knew it would continue indefinitely, so I saw myself confronted by boredom. Wolfe had said that when the judging was over he would want to spray with nicotine and soap, and I dug the ingredients from the bottom of one of the crates, went for a can of water, and got the mixture ready in the sprayer. He did a thorough job of it, with Plehn assisting, put the sprayer down on the bench, and started talking shop again. I sat on a box and yawned and permitted my mind to flit around searching for honey in an idea that had occurred to me on account of one of the questions Wolfe had asked Bennett. But I hoped to heaven that wasn't the answer, for if it was we were certainly out on a limb, and as far as any hope of earning a fee from Osgood was concerned we might as well pack up and go home.

I glanced at my wrist and saw it was 10 minutes to 5, which reminded me that Lily Rowan was coming for orchids at 5 o'clock and gave me something to do, namely, devise a remark that would shatter her into bits. She had the appearance of never having been shattered to speak of, and it seemed to me that she was asking for it. To call a guy Escamillo in a spirit of fun is okay, but if you do so immediately after he has half-killed himself hurdling a fence on account of a bull chasing him, you have a right to expect whatever he may be capable of in return.

I never got the remark devised. The first interruption was the departure of Raymond Plehn, who was as urbane with his farewells as with other activities. The second interruption was more removed, when first noted, and much more irritating: I saw a person pointing at me. Down the aisle maybe ten paces he stood pointing, and he was unquestionably the lanky straw-handler in overalls whom I had last seen in the Holstein shed three hours previously. At his right hand stood Captain Barrow of the state police, and at his left District Attorney Waddell. As I gazed at them with my brow wrinkled in displeasure, they moved forward.

I told Wolfe out of the corner of my mouth. "Looky. Company's coming."

Apparently they had figured that the cow nurse would no longer be needed, for he lumbered off in the other direction, while the other two headed straight for their victim, meaning me. They looked moderately sour and nodded curtly when Wolfe and I greeted them.

Wolfe said, "I understand you have another dead man on your hands, and this time no demonstration from me is required."

Waddell mumbled something, but Barrow disregarded both of them and looked at me and said, "You're the one I want a demonstration from. Get your hat and come on."

I grinned. "Where to, please?"

"Sheriff's office. I'll be glad to show you the way. Wait a minute."

He extended a paw at me. I folded my arms and stepped back a pace. "Let's all wait a minute. I have a gun *and* a license. The gun is legally in my possession. We don't want a lot of silly complications. Do we?"

16

Wolfe said sweetly, "I give you my word, Captain, he won't shoot you in my presence. He knows I dislike violence. I own the gun, by the way. Give it to me, Archie."

I took it from the holster and handed it to him. He held it close to his face, peering at it, and in a moment said, "It's a Worthington .38, number 63092T. If you insist on having it, Captain—illegally, as Mr. Goodwin correctly says—write out a receipt and I'll let you take it from me."

Barrow grunted. "To hell with the comedy. Keep the damn gun. Come on, Goodwin."

I shook my head. "I'm here legally too. What are you after? If you want a favor, ask for it. If you want to give orders, show me something signed by somebody. You know the rules as well as I do. In the meantime, don't touch me unless you're absolutely sure you can pick up anything you drop."

Waddell said, "We know the law some, in a rustic sort of way. A murder has been committed, and Captain Barrow wants to ask you some questions."

"Then let him ask. Or if he wants a private conference let him request my company and not yap at me." I transferred to Barrow. "Hell, I know what you want. I saw that ape that came in with you pointing me out. I know he saw me this afternoon alongside a pile of straw in the Holstein shed, talking with two acquaintances. I also know, by public rumor, that a dead man has been found under a pile of straw in that shed with a pitchfork sticking in him. I suppose it was the same pile of straw, I'm lucky that way. And you want to know why I was there and what I and my acquaintances were talking about and what was my motive for sticking the pitchfork into the man, and the doctor said the man had been dead two hours and six minutes and will I therefore give a timetable of my movements from ten o'clock this morning up to 2:37 p.m. Right?"

"Right," Barrow said agreeably. "Only we're more interested in the dead man's movements than we are in yours. When did you see him last?"

I grinned. "Try again. I abandoned that trick years ago. First tell me who he is or was."

Barrow's eyes weren't wandering from my face. "His name was Howard Bronson."

"I'll be damned." I screwed up my lips and raised my brows in polite surprise. "Clyde Osgood's friend? Identified?"

"Yes. By Osgood and his daughter. When did you see him last?"

"At ten-thirty this morning, as he got out of Osgood's car in front of the hotel. Miss Osgood and Mr. Wolfe and I went on in the car."

"Did you know him well?"

"Never saw him before Monday afternoon."

"Any intimate relations with him?"

"Nope."

"Any close personal contacts with him?"

"Well—no."

"Well what?"

"Nothing. No."

"Any financial transactions? Did you pay him any money or did he pay you any?"

"No."

"Then will you explain how it happens that an empty brown leather wallet found in his pocket was covered with your fingerprints, inside and outside?"

Of course the boob had telegraphed the punch. If he hadn't, if he had fired that at me to begin with, he might have been gratified at a couple of stammers and a little hemming and hawing, but as it was he allowed me plenty of time for preparation.

I grinned at him. "Sure I'll explain. Last evening at Osgood's house I found a wallet on the veranda. I looked in it for papers to identify the owner, and found it was Bronson's, and returned it to him. It never occurred to me to wipe off my prints."

"Oh. You had it ready."

"Had what ready?" I demanded innocently. "The wallet?"

"The explanation."

"Yeah, I carry a big stock for the country trade." I compressed my lips at him. "For God's sake use your bean. If I had croaked the guy and frisked the wallet, or if I had found him dead and frisked it, would I have left my signature all over it? Do I strike you as being in that category? Maybe I can offer you a detail though. You say the wallet was empty. Last night when I found it, and when I returned it to him, it was bulging with a wad which I estimated roughly at 2000 bucks."

At that point Nero Wolfe's genius went into action. I say genius not because he concocted the stratagem, for that was only quick wit, but because he anticipated the need for it far enough ahead of time to get prepared. I didn't recognize it at the moment for what it was; all I saw, without paying it any attention, was that, apparently bored by a conversation he had no part in, he slipped the pistol into his coat pocket and picked up the sprayer and began fussing with the nozzle and the pressure handle.

"You advise me to use my bean," Barrow was saying. "I'll try. Did you remove anything from the wallet?"

"Today? I haven't seen it. I only found it once."

"Today or any other time. Did you?"

"No."

"Did you take anything from Bronson at all? His person or his effects?"

"No."

"Are you willing to submit to a search?"

My brain didn't exactly reel, but the wires buzzed. For half a second five or six alternatives chased each other around in a battle royal. Meanwhile I was treating Barrow to a grin to show how serene I was, and also, out of the corner of an eye, I was perceiving that Nero Wolfe's right index finger, resting half concealed by his coat on the pressure lever, was being wiggled at me. It was a busy moment. Hoping to God I had interpreted the wiggle correctly, I told Barrow affably, "Excuse the hesitation, but I'm trying to decide which would annoy you more, to deny you the courtesy and compel you to take steps, or let you go ahead and find nothing. Now that my gun is gone and you can't disarm me—"

The spray of nicotine and soap, full force under high pressure, hit him smack in the face.

He spluttered and squeaked and jumped aside, blinded. That was another busy moment. My hand shot into my breast pocket and out again and without stopping for reflection slipped my ostrich card case into the side coat pocket of District Attorney Waddell, who had stepped toward the captain with an ejaculation. Except for that I didn't move. Barrow grabbed for his handkerchief and dabbed at his eyes. There were murmurings from onlookers. Wolfe, offering his own handkerchief, said gravely:

"A thousand apologies, Captain. My stupid carelessness. It won't hurt you, of course, but nevertheless—"

"Shut it or I'll shut it for you." There were still pearly drops on Barrow's chin and ears, but he had his eyes wiped. He faced me and demanded savagely, "A goddam slick trick, huh? Where did you ditch it?"

"Ditch what? You're crazy."

"You're damn right I'm crazy." He whirled to Waddell: "What did he do when that fat slob sprayed my eyes shut?"

"Nothing," said Waddell. "He didn't do anything. He stood right here by me. He didn't move."

"I can add my assurance," Wolfe put in. "If he had moved I would have seen him."

Waddell glared at him savagely. "You're so slick you slide, huh?"

"I have apologized, sir."

"To hell with you. How'd you like to go along to the courthouse with us?"

Wolfe shook his head. "You're in a huff, Captain. I don't blame you, but I doubt if it's actionable. To arrest me for accidentally spraying you with soap would seem . . . well, impulsive—"

Barrow turned his back on him to confront Waddell. "You say he didn't move?"

"Goodwin? No."

"He didn't hand Wolfe anything?"

"Positively not. He wasn't within 10 feet of him."

"He didn't throw anything?"

"No."

A dozen or so onlookers had collected, down the aisle in either direction. Barrow raised his voice at them: "Did any of you see this man take anything from his pocket and hand it to the fat man or put it somewhere or throw it? Don't be afraid to speak up. I'm Captain Barrow and it's important."

There were head shakings and a few muttered negatives. A woman with a double chin said in a loud voice, "I was watching you, that spray in your face, it was like a scene in the movies, but if he'd done any throwing or anything like that I'm sure I'd have seen him because my eye takes in everything."

There were a couple of nervous giggles and Barrow abandoned his amateurs. He looked around, and I felt sorry for him. I still hadn't moved. There was no place within perhaps

6 feet where I could possibly have hidden anything. In the direction I faced were pots of orchid plants on the benches; behind me was the table of dahlia blooms in vases; both were way beyond my reach. I stood with my arms folded.

Barrow had pretty well regained his handsome and unflinching dignity. He composedly wiped with his handkerchief behind his ears and under his chin and told me: "I'm taking you to the courthouse for questioning in connection with the murder of Howard Bronson. If you're still trying to decide how to annoy me, it'll take me maybe twenty minutes to get a legal commitment as a material witness—"

"Permit me," Wolfe put in, purring. "We surely owe you some complaisance, Captain, after this regrettable accident. I don't believe I'd insist on a warrant, Archie. We really should cooperate."

"Whatever you say, boss."

"Go. After all, it is a little public here for a privy interview. I may join you later.—In the meantime, Mr. Waddell, if you can spare a few minutes, I'd like to tell you of a discovery I made last evening, touching both Clyde Osgood and Mr. Bronson. I questioned Bronson for nearly an hour, and I think you'll find it interesting."

"Well . . . I was going with Captain Barrow . . ."

Wolfe shrugged. "Now that Bronson has also been murdered, it is doubly interesting."

"What about it, Captain?"

"Suit yourself," Barrow told him. "You're the district attorney, you're in charge. I can handle Goodwin." He sounded as if all he required was a red-hot poker and a couple of thumbscrews. "Shall I go on?"

Waddell nodded. "I'll be along pretty soon."

I told Wolfe, "When the young lady comes for the orchids, tell her I've gone to pick huckleberries."

Walking the length of the main exhibits building to the exit, and through the crowds beyond the end of the grandstand, Barrow kept behind, with his left elbow about 10 inches back of my right one, proving that he had been to police school. A patrol car, with the top down and a trooper behind the wheel, was waiting there. I was instructed to get in with the driver and Barrow climbed in behind. His eyes weren't leaving me for a second, and I reflected that his hunch that I had something I would like to discard had probably been reinforced by Wolfe's performance with the sprayer

In 5 minutes, in spite of the exposition traffic, we were pulling up at the courthouse. Instead of entering at the front as with Osgood when calling on Waddell the day before, we went around to a side entrance that was on the ground level. The hall was dark and smelled of disinfectant and stale tobacco juice. The trooper preceding us turned the knob of a door marked SHERI F, with one F gone, and I followed him in with Barrow at my rear. It was a big dingy room with decrepit desks and chairs, at one desk in a corner being the only occupant, a bald-headed gentleman with a red face and gold-rimmed specs who nodded at us and said nothing.

"We're going through you," Barrow announced.

I nodded indifferently and struck a pose. I know that the whole included all its parts and that that was one of the parts, and it had been necessary for Wolfe to toss me to the dogs so that he could have a private interview with the district attorney's coat pocket. So I tolerated it, and got additional proof that they had been to police school. They did everything but rip my seams. When they had finished I returned the various items to their proper places, and sat down. Barrow stood and gazed down at me. I was surprised he didn't go and wash his face, because that nicotine and soap must have stung. Tough as they come, those weatherbeaten babies.

"The mistake you made," I told him, "was coming in there breathing fire. Nero Wolfe and I are respectable law-abiding detectives."

He grunted. "Forget it. I'd give a month's pay to know how you did it, and maybe I'll find out sometime, but not now. I'm not going to try any hammering. Not at present." He glanced to see that the trooper was ready at a desk with notebook and pencil. "I just want to know a few things. Do you maintain that you took nothing from Bronson at any time?"

"I do."

"Did you suspect him of being implicated in the murder of Clyde Osgood?"

"You've got the wrong party. Mr. Wolfe does all the suspecting for the firm, ask him. I'm the office boy."

"Do you refuse to answer?"

"No indeed. If you want to know whether I personally suspected Bronson of murder, the reply is no. No known motive."

"Wasn't there anything in his relations with Clyde that might have supplied a motive?"

"Search me. You're wasting time. Day before yesterday at 2 o'clock the Osgoods and Pratts and Bronson were all complete strangers to Mr. Wolfe and me. Our only interest in any of them is that Osgood hired us to investigate the murder of his son. You started investigating simultaneously. If you're discouraged with what you've collected and want our crop as a handout, you'll have to go to Mr. Wolfe. You said you wanted to question me in connection with the murder of Howard Bronson."

"That's what I'm doing."

"Go ahead."

He kicked a chair around and sat down. "Wolfe interviewed Bronson last night. What was said at that interview?"

"Ask Mr. Wolfe."

"Do you refuse to answer?"

"I do, you know. I'm a workingman and don't want to lose my job."

"Neither do I. I'm working on a murder, Goodwin."

"So am I."

"Were you working on it when you entered the shed this afternoon where Bronson was killed?"

"No, not at that moment. I was waiting for Lew Bennett to tear himself away from the judging lot. I happened to see Nancy Osgood going into the shed and followed her out of curiosity. I found her in there in the stall talking to Jimmy Pratt. I knew her old man would be sore if he heard of it, which would have been too bad under the circumstances, so I advised them to postpone it and scatter, and they did so, and I went back to the Methodist tent where my employer was."

"How did they and you happen to pick the spot where Bronson's body was?"

"I didn't pick it, I found them there. I don't know why they picked it, but it would seem likely that it wasn't cause and effect. I imagine they would have chosen some other spot if they had known what was under the pile of straw."

"Did you know what was under it?"

"I'll give you three guesses."

"Did you?"

"No."

"Why were you so eager to get them out of there in a hurry?"

"I wouldn't say I was eager. It struck me they were fairly dumb to feed gossip at this particular time."

"You wouldn't say that you were eager to keep it quiet that they had been there, and you had?"

"Eager? Nope. Put it that I was inclined to feel it was desirable."

"Then why did you bribe the shed attendant?"

Of course he had telegraphed it again. But even so it was an awkward and undesirable question.

"I was waiting for that," I told him. "Now you have got me where it hurts, because the only explanation I can offer, which is the true one, is loony. There are times when I feel kittenish, and that was one. I'll give it to you verbatim." I did so, words and music, repeating the conversation just as it had occurred, up to the departure of the beneficiary. "There," I said, "Robin Hood, his sign. And when a corpse was discovered there, the louse thought I had been bribing him with a measly tenspot, and so did you. I swear to God I'll lay for him tonight and take it away from him."

Barrow grunted. "You're good at explanations. The fingerprints on the wallet. I suppose a man like Bronson would leave a wallet containing two thousand dollars lying around on a veranda. Now this. Do you realize how good you are?"

"I told you it was loony. But lacking evidence to the contrary, you might assume that I'm sane. Do I look like a goof who would try to gag a stranger in a case of murder with a ten dollar note? Should I start serious bribing around here, the per capita income of this county would shoot up like a skyrocket. And by the way, does that clodhopper say that I made any suggestions about silence or even discretion?"

"We're all clodhoppers around here. You try telling a jury of clodhoppers that you're in the habit of tossing out ten dollar bills for the comic effect."

I snorted. "Unveil it, brother. What jury? My peers sitting on my life? Honest, are you as batty as that?"

"No." The Captain squinted at me and rubbed a spot on the side of his neck. "No, Goodwin, I'm not. I'm not looking forward to the pleasure of hearing a jury's opinion of you. Nor do I bear any grudge because you and your boss started the stink on the Osgood thing. I don't care how slick you are or where you come from or how much you soak Osgood for, but now that the bag has been opened it is going to be emptied. Right to the bottom. Do you understand that?"

"Go ahead and jiggle it."

"I'm going to. And nothing's going to roll out of my sight while I'm not looking. You say ask Wolfe, and I'm going to, but right now I'm asking you. Are you going to talk or not?"

"My God, my throat's sore now."

"Yeah. I've got the wallet with your prints all over it. I've got the bill you gave the shed attendant. Are you going to tell me what you got from Bronson and where it is?"

"You're just encouraging me to lie, Captain."

"All right, I'll encourage you some more. This morning a sheriff's deputy was in the hotel lobby when Bronson entered. When Bronson went to a phone booth and put in a New York call, the deputy got himself plugged in on another line. He heard Bronson tell somebody in New York that a man named Goodwin had poked him in the jaw and taken the receipt from him, but that he expected to pull it off anyway. Well?"

"Gee," I said, "that's swell. All you have to do is have the New York cops grab the somebody and run him through the coffee grinder—"

"Much obliged. What was the receipt for and where is it?"

I shook my head. "The deputy must have heard wrong. Maybe the name was Doodwin or Goldstein or DiMaggio—"

"I *would* like to clip you. Jesus, I would enjoy stretching you out." Barrow breathed. "Are you going to spill it?"

"Sorry, nothing to spill."

"On the hotel register you wrote your first name as Archie. Is that correct?"

"Yep."

He turned to his colleague. "Bill, you'll find Judge Hutchins waiting upstairs. Run up and swear out a material witness commitment. Archie Goodwin. Hurry down with it, we've got to shake a leg."

I raised the brows. The cossack made it snappy. I asked, "How's the accommodations?"

"Fair. A little crowded on account of the exposition. Any time you're ready to talk turkey—"

"No speak English. This will get you a row of ciphers and the finger of scorn and a bellyache."

He merely looked unflinching. We sat. In a few minutes his pal returned with a document, and I asked to see it and was obliged. Barrow took it and asked me to come on, and I went between them down the dark hall, around a corner and along another hall, and into another office smaller than the one we had left but not so dingy, with WARDEN on the door. A sleepy-looking plump guy sat at a desk which had a vase of flowers on it besides miscellany. He let out a low growl when he saw us, like a dog being disturbed in the middle of comfort. Barrow handed him the paper and told him:

"Material witness in the Bronson case. We've gone through

him; I suppose you'll want to take his jackknife. I'll stop in later for my copy or get it in the morning. Any time he asks for me, day or night, I want to see him."

The warden pushed a button on his desk, ran his eyes over the paper, looked at me, and cackled. "By golly, bud, you should have put on some old clothes. The valley service here is terrible."

.... was notion ...... to you. ....ingham, ... superfic...., but was ...... only a .... was alive and well. You announced that

17

It was certainly an antique. Apparently it was a whole wing of the ground floor of the court-house. The cells faced each other, two rows of them, one on either side of a long corridor. Mine was two doors from the far end. My cellmate was a chap in a dark blue suit with a pointed nose and sharp brown eyes and a thick mop of well-brushed hair. At the time I was locked in, which was around 6 o'clock, he was sitting on one of the cots brushing the hair. The dim light from the little barred window, too high to see out of, made things seem gloomy. We exchanged greetings and he went on brushing. Pretty soon he asked:

"Got any cards or dice with you?"

"Nope."

"They didn't strip you, did they?"

"They took my knife."

He put the brush down and nodded. "You can't kick on that. Were you working out at the grounds? I've never seen you around before."

"You wouldn't. My name is Archie Goodwin, and I'm from New York and am being squeezed." I waved a hand and sat down on the other cot, which was covered with a dirty gray blanket. "Forget it. Were you working out at the grounds?"

"I was until yesterday afternoon. Spoon-bean. Are you hungry?"

"I could eat. But I hesitate to send in an order—"

"Oh, not on the house. No. They feed at 5, and it's the usual. But if you're hungry and happen to have a little jack . . ."

"Go ahead."

He went over to the door and tapped three times with his fingernail on one of the iron bars, waited a second, and tapped twice. In a couple of minutes slow footsteps sounded in the corridor, and as they got to our apartment my mate said in a tone restrained but not particularly secretive, "Here, Slim."

I got up and ambled across. It wasn't the keeper who had

escorted me in, but a tall skinny object with an Adam's apple as big as a goose egg. I got out the Nero Wolfe expense wallet, extracted a dollar bill, and told him that I required two ham sandwiches and a chocolate egg malted. He took it but shook his head and said it wasn't enough. I told him I knew that but hadn't wanted to spoil him, and parted from another one, and asked him to include 5 evening papers in the order.

By the time he returned, in a quarter of an hour, my mate and I were old friends. His name was Basil Graham, and his firsthand knowledge of geography and county jails was extensive. I spread my lunch out on the cot with a sheet of the newspaper for a tablecloth, and it wasn't until the last crumb had disappeared that he made a proposal which might have withered the friendship in the bud if I hadn't been firm. His preparations were simple but interesting. From under the blanket of his cot he produced three teaspoons of the five and dime variety, and a small white bean. Then he came over and picked up one of my newspapers and asked, "May I?" I nodded. He put the newspaper on the floor and sat on it, and in front of him, on the concrete, ranged the three teaspoons in a row, bottoms up. He had nifty fingers. Under one of the spoons he put the bean and then looked up at me like the friend he was.

"You understand," he said, "I'm just showing you how it's done. It will pass the time. Sometimes the hand is quicker, sometimes the eye is quicker. It's not a game of chance, but a game of skill. Your eye against my hand. Your eye may be quicker than my hand, and we can only tell by trying. It never hurts to try. Which spoon is the bean under?"

I told him, and it was. He tried again, his fingers darting, and again it was. The next time it wasn't. The next three times it was, and he began to act flustered and surprised and displeased with himself.

I shook my head. "Don't do it, Basil," I said regretfully. "I'm not a wise guy exactly, but I'm a tightwad. If you go on working up indignation at yourself because my eye is so much quicker than your hand, you might get so upset you would actually offer to make a bet on it, and I would have to refuse. As a matter of fact, you are extremely good, both at manipulating the bean and at getting upset, but the currency you saw in the wallet is not my own, and even if it was I'm a tightwad."

"It don't hurt to try, does it? I just want to see—"

"No, I don't lather."

He cheerfully put the spoons and the bean away, and the friendship was saved.

It began to get dark in the cell, and after a while the lights were turned on. Somehow that only made it gloomier, since there was no light in the cell itself. The only way I could have read the paper, except for the headlines, which were screaming murder, would have been to hold it up against the bars of the door to catch the light from the corridor, so I gave it up and devoted myself to Basil. He was certainly a good-natured soul, for he had been nabbed after only one day's work at the exposition and expected to be fined 50 samoleons on the morrow, but I suppose if you embrace spoonbean as a career you have to be a philosopher to begin with. The inside of my nose was beginning to smart from the atmosphere. In a cell across the corridor someone started to sing in a thin tenor, *I'm wearing my heart away for you, it cries out may your love be true,* and from further down the line groans sounded, interrupted by a voice like a file growling, "Let him sing, let him sing, what the hell, it's beautiful."

Basil shrugged. "Just bums," he said tolerantly.

My wrist watch said 10 minutes to 8 when footsteps stopped at our address again, a key was turned in the lock, and the door swung open. A keeper I hadn't seen before stood in the gap and said, "Goodwin? You're wanted." He stepped aside to let me out, relocked the door, and let me precede him down the corridor. "Warden's office," he grunted.

Three men were standing in the office: Nero Wolfe, under self-imposed restraint, Frederick Osgood, scowling, and the warden, looking disturbed. I told them good evening. Osgood said, "Come on, Ollie, we'll step outside." The warden muttered something about the rules, Osgood got impatient and brusque, and out they went.

Wolfe stood and looked at me with his lips compressed. "Well?" he demanded. "Where were your wits?"

"Sure," I said bitterly, "brazen it out. Wits my eye. Fingerprints on the wallet. I bribed the shed attendant with ten bucks of Jimmy Pratt's money, which I'll explain to you some day if I don't rot in this dungeon. But chiefly, a deputy sheriff says that this morning at the hotel he heard Bronson tell somebody in New York on the telephone that a man named Goodwin poked him in the jaw and took a receipt away from him. Ha ha ha. Did you ever hear anything so droll? Even so, they don't think I'm a murderer. They only think I'm reticent. They're going to break my will. Of course if I *had* taken a receipt from Bronson and if they should find it—"

Wolfe shook his head. "Since you didn't, they can't. Which reminds me . . ."

His hand went into his pocket and came out again with my card case in it. I took it and inspected it, saw that it contained its proper items and nothing else, and put it where it belonged.

"Thanks. No trouble finding it?"

"None. It was quite simple. I had a talk with Mr. Waddell after you left and told him of my interview with Mr. Bronson last evening whatever I thought might be helpful. Then he went, and I telephoned the courthouse and could learn nothing. I found myself marooned. Finally I succeeded in locating Mr. Osgood, and his daughter came for me. She had been questioned, but not, I imagine, with great severity—except by her father. Mr. Osgood is difficult. He suspects you of arranging the meeting between his daughter and Mr. Pratt's nephew, God knows why. Watch him when he comes back in here; he might even leap at you. He agreed to control himself if I would question you about it."

"Good. You came to question me. I was wondering what you came for."

"For one thing . . ." He hesitated, which was rare. He went on, "For one thing, I came to bring that package for you. The Osgood housekeeper kindly prepared it."

I looked and saw a four-bushel bundle, wrapped in brown paper, on a table. "Saws and rope ladders?" I demanded.

He said nothing. I went and tore some of the paper off and found that it contained a pillow, a pair of blankets, and sheets. I returned to confront Wolfe.

"So," I said. "So that's the way it is. I believe you mentioned wits a minute ago?"

He muttered ferociously, "Shut up. It has never happened before. I have telephoned, I have roared and rushed headlong, and Mr. Waddell cannot be found. Since I learned you were detained—he's deliberately hiding from me, I'm convinced of it. The judge won't set bail without the concurrence of the District Attorney. We don't want bail anyway. Pfui! Bail for my confidential assistant! Wait! Wait till I find him!"

"Uh-huh. You wait at Osgood's, and I wait in a fetid cell with a dangerous felon for a mate. By heaven, I will play spoon-bean with your money. As for the package you kindly brought, take it back to the housekeeper. God knows how long I'll be here, and I don't want to start in by getting a reputation as a sissy. I can take it, and it looks like I'm going to."

"You spoke of money. That was my second reason for coming."

"I know, you never carry any. How much do you want?"

"Well . . . twenty dollars. I want to assure you, Archie—"

"Don't bother." I got out the expense wallet and handed him a bill. "I can assure you that I shall come out of here with bugs—"

"Once when I was working for the Austrian government I was thrown into jail in Bulgaria—"

I strode to the door and pulled it open and bellowed into the hall: "Oh, warden! I'm escaping!"

He appeared from somewhere in a lumbering trot, stumbling. Behind him came Osgood, looking startled. From the other direction came the sound of a gallop, and that proved to be the keeper, with a revolver in his hand. I grinned at them: "April fool. Show me to my room. I'm sleepy. It's the country air."

Osgood rumbled, "Clown." The warden looked relieved. I tossed a cheery good night to Wolfe over my shoulder, and started off down the hall with the keeper trailing me.

Basil was seated on his cot brushing his hair. He asked me what the yelling had been for and I told him I had had a fit. I asked him what time the lights went out and he told me 9 o'clock, so I proceeded to get my bed made. Having had the forethought to order 5 copies of the newspaper, there was more than enough to cover the cot entirely with a double thickness. Basil suspended the brushing momentarily to watch me arranging it with ample laps, and when I was nearly through he observed that it would rustle so much that I wouldn't be able to sleep and neither would he. I replied that when I once got set I was as dead as a log, and he remarked in a sinister tone that it might not turn out that way in my present quarters. I finished the job anyhow. Down the line somewhere two voices were raised in an argument as to whether February 22nd was a national holiday, and others joined in.

It was approaching 9 o'clock when the key was turned in our lock again and the keeper appeared in the door and told me I was wanted.

"Cripes," Basil said, "we'll have to install a telephone."

It couldn't be Wolfe, I thought. There was no one else it could be except Waddell or Barrow, and there wasn't a chance of getting put on the sidewalk by them, and if they wanted to harry me they could damn well wait until morning. I decided to be contrary.

"Whoever it is, tell him I've gone to bed."

Even in the dim light, I seemed to perceive that the keeper looked disappointed. He asked, "Don't you want to see her?"

"Her?"

"It's your sister."

"Oh. I'll be derned. My dear sister."

My tone must have been good, for there was no audible derision as for the second time I preceded the keeper along the corridor. I went for two reasons, the first being curiosity. It might conceivable be Nancy or Caroline, but my guess was Lily, and the only way of finding out was to go and see. Second, I felt I should cooperate. 9 o'clock at night was no visiting time at a jail, and if it was Lily she must have been liberal in her negotiations with the warden, and I hated to see money wasted. It was the first time I could remember that anyone had paid cash to have a look at me, and I thought it was touching. So I trotted along.

It was Lily. The warden was at his desk, and stayed there, and the keeper closed the door and stood in front of it. Lily was in a chair in a dark corner, and I crossed to her.

"Hello, sis." I sat down.

"You know," she said, "I was wondering last night what would be the best thing to do with you, but it never occurred to me to lock you up. When you get out of here I'll try it. When will that be, by the way?"

"No telling. In time to spend Christmas at home, I hope. How are dad and ma and Oscar and Violet and Arthur—"

"Fine. Is it cosy?"

"Marvelous."

"Have you had anything to eat?"

"Plenty. There's a caterer."

"Have you got money?"

"Sure, how much do you want?"

She shook her head. "No, really. I'm flush." She opened her bag.

I reached and shut it. "No, you don't. Jimmy Pratt gave me 10 dollars today and that's partly why I'm here. Money is the root of all evil. Is there anything I can do for you?"

"Why, Escamillo. I came to see you."

"I'm aware of that. Did you bring any bedding?"

"No, but I can get some. Do you want some?"

"No, thanks. I was just curious. I have plenty of newspaper. But would you like to do me a favor?"

"I won't sleep if I can't do you a favor."

"Will you be up at midnight?"

"I can stay up."

"Do so. At midnight get Osgood's on the phone and ask to speak to Mr. Nero Wolfe. Tell him you're Mrs. Titus Goodwin and that you are at the Crowfield Hotel, having just come in an airplane from Cleveland, Ohio. Tell him that you got a telegram from your son Archie saying that he is in jail, stranded and abandoned and in despair. Tell him you want to know what the hell he had me put in jail for and you'll have the law on him, and you'll expect to see him first thing in the morning and he must be prepared to rectify his ghastly mistake without delay. And atone for it. Tell him he'll have to atone for it." I considered. "I guess that will do."

She nodded. "I've got it. Is any of it straight?"

"No, it's firecrackers."

"Then why don't I rout him out tonight? Make him come to the hotel right away and look for me. I mean at midnight."

"My God, no. He'd kill me. That will be sufficient. You follow instructions."

"I will. Anything else?"

"Nope."

"Kiss me."

"I can't until I wash my face. Anyway, I told you that wasn't a precedent. I have to be careful. I kissed a girl once in the subway and when she came to she was on top of the Empire State Building. She had floated out through a grating and right on up."

"Goodness. Did you ever send one clear to heaven?"

"The place is full of them."

"When are you going to get out of here?"

"I don't know. You might ask Wolfe on the phone tonight."

"Well." She looked at me, and I was reminded how she had peeled me like a potato in the Methodist tent. "What I really came for. Any bail, any amount, I could have it arranged for by 11 o'clock in the morning. Shall I?"

"I might come high."

"I said any amount."

"I wouldn't bother. It would make Wolfe jealous. Thanks just the same."

The keeper's hoarse voice sounded:

"After 9 o'clock, chief. What about the lights?"

I got up and told him, "Okay, I'll help you. Good night, sis."

18

AT 9 O'CLOCK Thursday morning Basil sat on the edge of his cot brushing his hair. I sat on the edge of mine, with the newspapers still on it but a good deal the worse for wear, scratching my shoulder and my thigh and my right side and my left arm, with my forehead wrinkled in concentration, trying to remember the title of a book on prison reform which I had observed on Wolfe's library shelves at home but had never bothered to look at. It was a shame I hadn't read it because if I had I would have been much better prepared for a project which I had already got a pretty good start on. The idea of the project had occurred to me during breakfast for which meal I had limited myself to the common fare of my fellows for the sake of the experience, and I had got the start during the fifteen minutes from 8:30 to 8:45, when we had all been in the corridor together for what was called morning exercise, with a keeper and an ostentatious gun stationed at the open end.

Basil asked, "How many have we got?"

I told him four signed up and three more practically certain. I gave up trying to remember the name of the book and took my memo pad from my pocket and looked over the sheets I had written on:

> For the Warden, the District Attorney, the Attorney-General, the State Legislature, and the Governor.

MINIMUM BASIC DEMANDS OF THE CROWFIELD COUNTY PRISONERS UNION

1. Recognition of the C.C.P.U.
2. The closed shop.
3. Collective bargaining on all controversial matters ex-

cept date of release and possession by our members of objects which could be used for attack or escape.

4. No lockouts.

5. Food. (Food may be defined as nutritive material absorbed or taken into the body of an organism which serves for purposes of growth, work or repair, and for the maintenance of the vital processes.) We don't get any.

6. Running water in all cells.

7. Abolition of all animals smaller than rabbits.

8. Cell buckets of first grade enamel with good lids.

9. Daily inspection of bedding by a committee of public-spirited citizens, with one member a woman.

10. Adequate supply of checkers and dominoes.

11. Soap which is free of Essence of Nettles, or whatever it is that it now contains.

12. Appointment by our President of a Committee on Bathing, with power to enforce decisions.

Signed this 15th day of September, 1938.
ARCHIE GOODWIN, *President.*
BASIL GRAHAM, *Vice-President, Secretary and*
Treasurer.

Four other signatures followed.

I looked up with a dissatisfied frown. It was all right for a start, but there were 21 people inhabiting that corridor by actual count. I said in a resolute tone, "It has to be 100 per cent before nightfall. The fact is, Basil, you may be all right as Vice-President and/or Secretary and/or Treasurer, but you're no damn good as an agitator. You didn't get anybody."

He put the brush down. "Well," he said, "you made 3 mistakes. Demand number 9 will have to be amended by striking out the last five words. They simply don't like the idea of a woman poking around the cells. Demand number 12 is bad in toto. Even when he's out of jail a man resents having his personal liberties interfered with, and when he's in jail the feeling is greatly intensified. But worst of all was your offering them a dime apiece to join. That made them suspicious and we're going to have a hard time overcoming it."

"I don't see you making any strenuous effort."

"Is that so. I could make a suggestion right now. Are you game to step it up to two bits per capita?"

"But you said—"

"Never mind what I said. Are you?"

"Well . . ." I figured it. "Three seventy-five. Yes."

"But you wouldn't play spoon-bean, a game of skill. It's a funny world." He arose and approached. "Give me that ultimatum." I tore off the sheet and handed it to him and he went to the door and tapped on a bar with his fingernail, 3 and 2. In a minute the skinny one with the Adam's apple appeared and Basil began talking to him in a low tone. I got up and sauntered over to listen.

"Tell them," Basil said, "that the offer of a dime to join is withdrawn. Tell them that the privilege of being charter members expires at noon and after that we may let them in and we may not. Tell them that our platform is Brotherhood, Universal Suffrage, and Freedom. Tell—"

"Universal Suffering?"

"No. Suf—leave that one out. Brotherhood and Freedom. Tell them that if they don't like the idea of a public-spirited woman coming around and the provisions with regard to bathing, the only way these demands can be changed is by the membership of the C. C. P. U., which is organized and functioning, and if they don't become members they can't help change them. Incidentally, our President will pay you two bits for each and every one you get to sign."

"Two bits? That's on the level?"

"Absolutely. Wait a minute, come back here. Since you're a trusty and are therefore technically one of us, you're eligible to join yourself if you want to. But you don't get any two bits for signing yourself up. It wouldn't be ethical. Would it, President Goodwin? Wouldn't that be *e pluribus unum corpus delicti?*"

"Right."

"Okay. Go ahead, Slim. Noon is the deadline."

Basil went back and sat down and picked up the brush. "No damn good as an agitator?" he inquired sarcastically.

"As an agitator, above average," I admitted. "As a treasurer, only so-so. You're inclined to overdraw."

I don't know to this day what the C. C. P. U. membership amounted to at its peak. When Slim had got 4 new members signed up he came to our cell and requested a dollar before proceeding further, and I paid him, and by 10 o'clock he had 4 more and got another dollar, but at that point I was removed from the scene by a keeper coming to get me. I started out, but Basil interposed to say that I had better leave the other $1.75 with him, since I had assumed the obligation, just in case. I told him he shouldn't be so pessimistic about the President but agreed that his point was valid, and shelled out.

Captain Barrow, still with no sign of flinching, was waiting in the hall outside the warden's office. He told me curtly to come on, and from behind my elbow directed me out of that wing of the building, up two flights of stairs, and along an upper corridor to a door which I had entered on Tuesday afternoon in the company of Osgood and Wolfe. We passed through the anteroom to the inner chamber, and there sat District Attorney Waddell at his desk, with bleary eyes that made him look pudgier than ever.

I marched up to the desk and told him offensively, "Nero Wolfe wants to see you, mister."

Barrow snarled, "Sit down, you."

I sat, and scratched my thigh and shoulder and side and arm ostentatiously.

Waddell demanded, "What about it? Have you changed your mind?"

"Yes," I said, "I have. I used to think that the people who make speeches and write books about prison reform are all sentimental softies, but no more. They may or may not—"

"Turn it off," Barrow growled. "And quit scratching."

Waddell said sternly, "I advise you not to be flippant. We have evidence that you possess vital information in a murder case. We want it." He laid a fist on his desk and leaned forward. "We're going to get it."

I grinned at him. "I'm sorry, you'll have to excuse me. My head is fairly buzzing with this new idea I've got and I can't think of anything else, not even murder." I erased the grin and pointed a finger at him and made my tone ominous: "Your head will soon be buzzing too. Don't think it won't. The C. C. P. U. is going to clean up, and how would you like to be kicked out of office?"

"Bah. You damn fool. Do you think Osgood runs this county? What's the C. C. P. U.?"

I knew he'd ask, since elected persons are always morbid about organizations. I told him impressively, "The Crowfield County Prisoners Union. I'm President. We'll be 100 per cent by noon. Our demands include—"

I stopped and got my feet under my chair ready for leverage, because Barrow had got up and taken two steps and from his expression I thought for a second he was going to haul off and aim one. He halted and said slowly, "Don't get scared, I couldn't do it here. But there's a room down in the basement or I could take you out to the barracks. Get this. You cut the comedy."

I shrugged. "If you fellows really want to talk seriously, I'll tell you something. Do you?"

"You'll find out how serious we are before we finish with you."

"Okay. First, if you think you can scare me by threats about basements you're too dumb for a mother's tears. Common sense is against it, the probabilities are against it, and I'm against it. Second, the comedy. You asked for it by starting it, yesterday afternoon. You have no judgment. It's perfectly true that there are people who can be opened up by making faces at them and talking loud, but if I was one of them how long do you think I'd last as Nero Wolfe's favorite employee, eating with him at his table? Look at me, anyhow! Can't you tell one kind of mug from another kind? Third, the situation we're in. It's so simple I understand it myself. You think I have knowledge which is your legal property because you're cops working on a murder, and I say I haven't. Under those circumstances, what can I do? I can keep my mouth shut. What can you do? You can arrest me and put me under bond to appear on demand. Finally, when you've gathered up everything you can find and put it in order, you can either pin something on me, like obstruction of justice or accessory or perjury if I've been under oath, or any of that crap, or you can't. I return for a moment to your objection to my comedy. You deserved it because you've acted like a pair of comics yourselves."

I turned my palms up. "Were any of the words too long for you?"

Barrow sat down and looked at Waddell. The District Attorney said, "We don't think you have knowledge of facts, we know you have. And that's no comedy. Will you give them to us?"

"Nothing to give."

"Do you know your jeopardy? Have you had legal advice?"

"I don't need it. Didn't you hear my lecture? Find a lawyer that can beat it."

"You mentioned a bond. If you apply for release on bail, I'll oppose it. If your application is granted, it will be as high as I can make it."

"That's jake. Don't start worrying your little head about that on top of all your other troubles. I don't believe a rustic judge can look me in the eye and hold me without bail. The amount is a matter of indifference. My sister's father is a rich sewer tycoon."

"Your father? Where?"

"I said my sister's father. My family connections are none of your business, and besides, they're too complicated for you to understand. He is also occasionally my mother's father, on account of the fact that on the telephone last night my sister was my mother. But he isn't my father because I've never met him."

Barrow's head was twisted with his eyes fixed on me searchingly. "By God, I don't know," he said in a tone of doubtful surprise. "Maybe we ought to have Doc Sackett examine you."

Waddell disagreed. "It would cost 5 dollars and it's not worth it. Put him back in the cooler. If he's starting any trouble down there with this C. C. P. U. stuff, tell Ollie to put him in solitary. Tell Ollie he'd better investigate—"

The door popped open and Nero Wolfe walked in.

He looked neat and rested, with a clean yellow shirt on and the brown tie with tan stripes which Constanza Berin had sent him from Paris, but his shoes hadn't been shined. My glance took in those details as he crossed the room to us with his customary unhurried waddle. I scratched my leg furiously.

He stopped in front of me and demanded, "What are you doing? What's the matter?"

"Nothing. I itch."

"Look at your coat. Look at your trousers. Did you sleep in them?"

"What do you think I slept in, silken raiment? I'm glad you stopped in, it's nice to see you. We've been chatting. They're just sending me back to the you know. Did you hear from my mother? She's stricken."

He muttered, "Pfui," turned from me and looked at the other two and said good morning, and cast his eyes around. Then he took a step toward Barrow and said in his best manner, "Excuse me, Captain, but you have the only chair that is endurable for me. I'm sure you wouldn't mind changing." Barrow opened his mouth, but shut it again and got up and moved.

Wolfe nodded thanks, sat down, and directed a composed gaze at the district attorney. "You're a hard man to catch, sir," he observed. "I spent hours last evening trying to find you. I even suspect I was being evaded."

"I was busy."

"Indeed. To any effect?"

Barrow growled. Waddell leaned forward again with his

fist on his desk. "Look here, Wolfe," he said in a nasty tone. "I've concluded you're no better than a waste of time, and probably worse. Thinking over what you told me about your talk with Bronson, what does it add up to? Zero. You were stringing me. You talk about evading! For the present I've only got one thing for you: a piece of advice. Either instruct your man here to open up and spill it, or do so yourself."

Wolfe sighed. "You're in a huff. Yesterday Captain Barrow, now you. You gentlemen are extraordinarily touchy."

"I'm touchy enough to know when I'm being strung. I don't enjoy it. And you're making a mistake when you figure that with Fred Osgood behind you, you can get away with anything you want to. Osgood may have owned this county once, but not any more, and he may be headed for a disagreeable surprise himself."

"I know." Wolfe was mild, and look resigned. "It's incredible, but judging from rumors that have reached Mr. Osgood you are actually entertaining a theory that Bronson killed his son, and the killing of Bronson was an eye for an eye. Mr. Waddell, that is infantile. It is so obviously infantile that I refuse to expound it for you. And your suggestion that I rely on Mr. Osgood's position and influence to protect me from penalties I have incurred is equally infantile. If I palaver with you at all—"

"You don't need to," Waddell snapped. "Peddle it somewhere else." Abruptly he stood up. "For two cents I'd stick you in with Goodwin. Beat it. On out. The next time I listen to you it will be in a courtroom. Take Goodwin down, Captain."

"Oh, no." Wolfe was still mild. "No, indeed. I bothered to see you only on Mr. Goodwin's account. You'll listen to me now."

"And who'll tell me why?"

"I will. Because I know who murdered Clyde Osgood and Howard Bronson, and you don't."

Barrow straightened. Waddell stared. I grinned, and wished Basil was there to tell me which spoon the bean was under.

"Furthermore," Wolfe went on quietly, "there is a very slim chance that you could ever find out, and no chance at all that you would ever be able to prove it. I have already found out, and I shall soon have proof. Under the circumstances, I should say it is even your duty to listen to me."

Barrow snapped, "I'd suggest having a judge listen to you."

"Pfui. For shame, Captain! You mean threaten me with the same treatment you have given Mr. Goodwin? I merely tell the judge I blathered. If he proves to be also an imbecile and holds me, I procure bail and then what do you do? You are helpless. I assure you—"

Waddell exploded, "It's a goddam cheap bluff!"

Wolfe grimaced. "Please, sir. My reputation . . . but no, I have too much respect for my reputation—"

"You say you *know* who murdered Clyde Osgood? And Bronson?"

"I do."

"Then by God you're right. I'll say I'll listen to you." Waddell sat down and pulled his phone over, and after a moment barked into it, "Send Phillips in."

Wolfe raised his brows. "Phillips?"

"Stenographer."

Wolfe shook his head. "Oh, no. You misunderstand. I only came for Mr. Goodwin. I need him."

"You do? So do we. We're keeping him. I repeat to you what I've told him, if there's an application for bail I'll oppose it."

The door opened and a young man with pimples appeared. Waddell nodded at him and he took a chair, opened his notebook, poised his pen, and inquired, "Names?" Waddell muttered at him, "Later. Take it."

Wolfe, disregarding the performance, said in a satisfied tone, "Now we've arrived at the point. It's Mr. Goodwin I want. If you hadn't eluded me last night I'd have got him then. Here are the alternatives for you to choose from. It is simplified for me by the fact that the sheriff, Mr. Lake, happens to be a protégé of Mr. Osgood's, while you are not. I understand you and Mr. Lake are inclined to pull in opposite directions.

"First. Release Mr. Goodwin at once. With his help I shall shortly have my proof perfected, and I'll deliver it to you, with the murderer, alive or dead.

"Second. Refuse to release Mr. Goodwin. Keep him. Without his help and therefore with more difficulty, I'll get the proof anyway, and it and the murderer will go to Mr. Lake. I am told that the Crowfield Daily Journal will be glad to cooperate with him and see that a full and correct account of his achievement is published, which is fortunate, for the public deserves to know what it gets for the money it pays its servants. It's a stroke of luck for you that you have Mr. Goodwin. But for that, I wouldn't be bothering with you at all."

Wolfe regarded the district attorney inquiringly. "Your choice, sir?"

I grinned. "He means take your pick."

Barrow growled at me, "Close your trap."

Waddell declared, "I still think it's a bluff."

Wolfe lifted his shoulders a quarter of an inch and dropped them. "Then it's Mr. Lake."

"You said you know who murdered Clyde Osgood and Howard Bronson. Do you mean one man committed both crimes?"

"That won't do. You get information after my assistant is released, not before,—and when I'm ready to give it."

"In a year or two, huh?"

"Hardly that long. Say within 24 hours. Less than that, I hope."

"And you actually know who the murderer is and you've got evidence?"

"Yes, to the first. I'll have satisfactory evidence."

"What kind of evidence?"

Wolfe shook his head. "I tell you it won't do. I'm not playing a guessing game, and I won't be pumped."

"Convincing evidence?"

"Conclusive."

Waddell sat back, pulled at his ear, and said nothing. Finally he turned to the stenographer and told him, "Give me that notebook and beat it." That command having been obeyed, he sat again a minute and then looked at Barrow and demanded sourly, "What about it, Captain? What the hell are we going to do?"

"I don't know." Barrow compressed his lips. "I know what I'd like to do."

"That's a big help. You've had 6 or 8 men on this thing and they haven't dug up a single solitary fragment, and this smart elephant knows who did it and will have conclusive evidence within 24 hours. So he says." Waddell suddenly jerked up his chin and whirled to Wolfe: "Who knows it besides you? If Lake or any of his deputies have been holding out on me—"

"No," Wolfe assured him. "That's all right. They're in the boat with you and Captain Barrow, with no hooks and no bait."

"Then when did you pick it up? Where have you been? Goodwin certainly didn't help any, since we collared him soon after Bronson's body was found. By God, if this is a stall . . ."

Wolfe shook his head. "Please. I've known who killed Clyde Osgood since Monday night; I knew it as soon as I saw the bull's face; and I knew the motive. Your incredulous stare only makes you look foolish. Likewise with Mr. Bronson; the thing was obvious."

"You knew all about it when you were sitting there in that chair Tuesday afternoon? Talking to me, the district attorney?"

"Yes. But there was no evidence—or rather, there was, but before I could reach it it had been destroyed. Now I must find a substitute for it, and shall."

"What was the evidence that was destroyed?"

"Not now. It's nearly 11 o'clock, and Mr. Goodwin and I must be going. We have work to do. By the way, I don't want to be annoyed by surveillance. It will be futile, and if we're followed I shall consider myself released from the bargain."

"Will you give me your word of honor that you'll do just what you've agreed to do, with no reservations and no quibbling?"

"Not a word of honor. I don't like the phrase. The word 'honor' has been employed too much by objectionable people and has been badly soiled. I give you my word. But I can't sit here talking about it all day. I understand that my assistant has been legally committed, so the release must be legal too."

Waddell sat and pulled at his ear. He frowned at Barrow, but apparently read no helpful hint on the captain's stony countenance. He reached for his telephone and requested a number, and after a little wait spoke into it: "Frank? Ask Judge Hutchins if I can run up and see him for a minute. I want to ask him to vacate a warrant."

19

I ASKED, "Shall I go get him?"

Wolfe said, "No. We'll wait."

We were in a room at the exposition offices, not the one where we had met Osgood Tuesday afternoon. This was smaller and contained desks and files and chairs and was cluttered with papers. It was noon. On leaving the courthouse with Wolfe I had been surprised to find that our sedan was parked out front; he explained that an Osgood employee had brought it from where I had left it the day before. He had instructed me to head for the exposition grounds, and our first stop had been the main exhibits building, where we gave the orchids an inspection and a spraying, and Wolfe arranged with an official for their care until Saturday, and the crating and shipping when the exposition closed. Then we had walked to the offices and been shown to Room 9. I was allowed to know that we expected to meet Lew Bennett there, but he hadn't arrived, and at noon we were still waiting for him.

I said, "If you ask my opinion, I think the best thing we can do is disguise ourselves as well as possible and jump in the car and drive like hell for New York. Or maybe across the line to Vermont and hide out in an old marble quarry."

"Stop that scratching."

I stuck my hands in my pockets. "You realize that I have been studying your face for 10 years, its lights and its shadows, the way it is arranged, and the way you handle it. And I say in all disrespect that I do not believe that the evidence which you mentioned to those false alarms is in existence."

"It isn't."

"I refer to the evidence which you promised to deliver within 24 hours."

"So do I."

"But it doesn't exist."

"No."

"But you're going to deliver it?"

"Yes."

I stared. "Okay. I suppose it was bound to happen sooner or later, but it's so painful to see that I wish it had happened to me first. Once at my mother's knee, back in 1839 I think it was—"

"Shut up, I'm going to make it."

"What? The bughouse?"

"The evidence. There is none. The bull was cremated. Nothing else remained to demonstrate the motive for murdering Clyde, and even if there had been other incriminating details—and there were none—they would have been useless. As for Bronson, Mr. Lake reports a vacuum. No fingerprints, except yours on the wallet, no one who remembers seeing him enter the shed, no one who saw him in anybody's company, no one with any discoverable motive. From the New York end, tracing his phone call. so far nothing—and of course there can be nothing. A complete vacuum. Under the circumstances there is only—ah! Good morning, sir."

The Secretary of the National Guernsey League, having entered and shut the door behind him, approached. He looked like a man who has been interrupted, but nothing like as exasperated as he had been the preceding day. His greeting was affable but not frothy, and he sat down as if he didn't expect to stay long.

Wolfe said, "Thank you for coming. You're busy of course. Remarkable, how many ways there are of being busy. I believe Mr. Osgood told you on the phone that I would ask a favor in his name. I'll be brief. First the relevant facts: the records of your league are on file in your office at Fernborough, which is 110 miles from here, and the airplane belonging to Mr. Sturtevant, who takes passengers for hire at the airport at the other end of these grounds, could go there and return in 2 hours. Those are facts."

Bennett looked slightly bewildered. "I guess they are. I don't know about the airplane."

"I do, I've inquired. I've even engaged Mr. Sturtevant's services, tentatively. What I would like to have, sir, before 3 o'clock, are the color pattern sketches of Hickory Caesar Grindon, Willowdale Zodiac, Hawley's Orinoco, Mrs. Linville's bull whose name I don't know, and Hickory Buckingham Pell. Mr. Sturtevant is ready to leave at a moment's notice. You can accompany him, or Mr. Goodwin can, or you can merely give him a letter."

Bennett was frowning. "You mean the original sketches?"

"I understand no others are available. Those on certificates are scattered among the owners."

Bennett shook his head. "They can't leave the files, it's a strict rule. They're irreplaceable and we can't take risks."

"I understand. I said you can go yourself. When they come you can sit me here at this table with them and they can be constantly under your eye. I need only half an hour with them, possibly less."

"But they mustn't leave the files. Anyhow, I can't get away."

"This is the favor requested by Mr. Osgood."

"I can't help it. It . . . it isn't reasonable."

Wolfe leaned back and surveyed him. "One test of intelligence," he said patiently, "is the ability to welcome a singularity when the need arises, without excessive strain. Strict rules are universal. We all have a rule not to go on the street before clothing ourselves, but if the house is on fire we violate it. There is a conflagration here in Crowfield— metaphorically. People are being murdered. It should be extinguished, and the incendiary should be caught. The connection between that and the sketches in your files may be hidden to you, but not to me; for that you will have to accept my word. If it is vital, it is essential, that I see those sketches. If you won't produce them as a favor to Mr. Osgood, you will do so as obligation to the community. I must see them."

Bennett looked impressed. But he objected. "I didn't say you couldn't see them. You can, anybody can, at our office. Go there yourself."

"Preposterous. Look at me."

"I don't see anything wrong with you. The airplane will carry you all right."

"No." Wolfe shuddered. "It won't. That's another thing you must accept my word for, that to expect me to get into an airplane would be utterly fantastic. Confound it, you object to violating a minor routine rule and then have the effrontery to suggest—have you ever been up in an airplane?"

"No."

"Then for heaven's sake try it once. It will be an experience for you. You'll enjoy it. I'm told that Mr. Sturtevant is competent and trustworthy and has a good machine. Get those sketches for me."

That was really what decided the question, 5 minutes later— the chance of a free airplane ride. Bennett gave in. He made a notation of the sketches Wolfe wanted, made a couple of phone calls, and was ready. I went with him to the landing field; we walked because he wanted to stop at the Guernsey cattle shed on the way. At the field we found Sturtevant, a good-looking kid with a clean face and greasy clothes, warming up the engine of a neat little biplane painted yellow. He said he was set and Bennett climbed in. I backed out of harm's way and watched them taxi across the field, and turn, and come scooting across the grass and lift. I stood there until they were up some 400 feet and headed east, and then walked back to the exposition grounds proper, to meet Wolfe at the Methodist tent as arranged. One rift in a gray sky was that I was to get another crack at the fricassee, and after my C. C. P. U. breakfast I had a place for it.

But it wasn't a leisurely meal, for it appeared that we had a program—that is, Wolfe had it and I was to carry it out. After all his gab about violating rules, he kept his intact about the prohibition of business while eating, and since he was in a mood there wasn't much conversation. When the pie had been disposed of and the coffee arrived, he squirmed to a new position on the folding chair and began to lay it out. I was to take the car and proceed to Osgoods, and bathe and change my clothes. Since the house would be full of funeral guests, I was to make myself as unobtrusive as possible, and if Osgood himself failed to catch sight of me at all, so much the better, as I was still under suspicion of having steered his daughter to a rendezvous with the loathsome Pratt brat. I was to pack our luggage and load it in the car, have the car filled with gas and oil and whatever else it had an appetite for, and report at the room where we had met Bennett not later than 3 o'clock.

"Luggage?" I sipped coffee. "Poised for flight, huh?"

Wolfe sighed. "We'll be going home. Home."

"Any stops on the way?"

"We'll stop at Mr. Pratt's place." He sipped. "By the way, I'm overlooking something. Two things. Have you a memorandum book with you? Or a notebook?"

"I've got a pad. You know the kind I carry."

"May I have it? And your pencil. It would be well to use the kind of pencil that is carried, though I think it will never get to microscopes. Thank you." He frowned at the pad. "Larger sheets would be better, but this will serve, and it wouldn't do to buy one in Crowfield." He put the pad and pencil in his pocket. "The second thing, I must have a good and reliable liar."

"Yes, sir." I tapped my chest.

"No, not you. Rather, in addition to you."

"Another liar besides me. Plain or fancy?"

"Plain. But we're limited. It must be one of the three

persons who were there when I was standing on that rock in the pasture Monday afternoon."

"Well." I pursed my lips and considered. "Your friend Dave might do for a liar. He reads poetry."

"No. Out of the question. Not Dave." Wolfe opened his eyes at me. "What about Miss Rowan? She seems inclined to friendship. Emphatically, since she visited you in jail."

"How the devil did you know that?"

"Not knowledge. Surmise. Your mother's voice on the telephone was hers. We'll discuss that episode after we get home. You must have suggested that performance to her, therefore you must have been in communication with her. People in jail aren't called to the telephone, so she couldn't have phoned you. She must have gone to see you. Surely, if she is as friendly as that, she would be pliant."

"I don't like to use my spiritual appeal for business purposes."

"Proscriptions carried too far lead to nullity."

"After I analyze that I'll get in touch with you. My first impulse is to return it unopened."

"Will she be?"

"Good lord, yes. Why not?"

"It's important. Can we count on it?"

"Yes."

"Then another detail is for you to telephone, find her, and make sure she will be at Mr. Pratt's place from 3 o'clock on. Tell her you will want to speak to her as soon as we arrive there." He caught the eye of a Methodist, and when she came to his beckoning requested more coffee. Then he told me, "It's after 1 o'clock Mr. Bennett is over halfway to Fernborough. You haven't much time."

I emptied my cup and left him.

The program went without a hitch, but it kept me on the go. I phoned Pratt's first thing, for Lily Rowan, and she was there, so I checked that off. I warmed up the concrete out to Osgood's, and by going in the rear entrance and up the back stairs avoided contact with the enraged father. I probably wouldn't have been noticed anyway, for the place was nearly as crowded as the exposition. There must have been a hundred cars, which was why I had to park long before I got to the end of the drive, and of course I had to carry the luggage. Upstairs I caught a glimpse of Nancy, and exchanged words with the housekeeper in the back hall downstairs, but didn't see Osgood. The service began at 2 o'clock, and when I left the only sound in the big old house, coming from the part I stayed away from, was the rise and fall of the preacher's voice pronouncing the last farewell for Clyde Osgood, who had won a bet and lost one simultaneously.

At 5 minutes to 3, with clean clothes and a clean body, not to mention the mind, with the car, filled with luggage and the other requisites, parked conveniently near, and without any satisfactory notion of the kind of goods Wolfe's factory was turning out in the line of evidence, though I had a strong inkling of who the consignee was to be, I sought Room 9 in the exposition offices. Sturtevant had apparently made good on his schedule, for the factory was in operation. Wolfe was there alone, seated at a table, with half a dozen sketches of bulls, on small sheets of white paper about 6 by 9 inches, arranged neatly in a row. One of them, separate, was directly under his eye, and he kept glancing back and forth from it to the sheet of my memo pad on which he was working with my pencil. He looked as concentrated as an artist hell bent for a masterpiece. I stood and observed operations over his shoulder for a few minutes, noting that the separate sheet from which he seemed to be drawing his inspiration was marked "Hickory Buckinham Pell," and then gave it up and sat down.

"What about Bennett keeping his sketches under his eye?" I demanded. "Did you worm yourself into his confidence, or bribe him?"

"He went to eat. I'm not hurting his sketches. Keep quiet and don't disturb me and don't scratch."

"I don't itch any more."

"Thank heaven."

I sat and diverted myself by trying different combinations on the puzzle we were supposed to be solving. At that point, thanks to various hints Wolfe had dropped, I was able to provide fairly plausible answers to most of the questions on the list, but was still completely stumped by the significance of the drawing practice he was indulging in. It seemed fanciful and even batty to suppose that by copying one of Bennett's sketches he was manufacturing evidence that would solve a double murder and earn us a fee and fulfil his engagement with Waddell, but the expression on his face left no doubt about his expectations. He was, by his calculations, sewing it up. I tried to work it into my combinations somehow, but couldn't get it to fit. I quit, and let my brain relax.

Lew Bennett entered with a toothpick in his mouth. As he did so Wolfe put my memo pad, with the pages he had worked on still attached, into his breast pocket, and the pencil.

Then he sighed, pushed back his chair and got to his feet, and inclined his head to Bennett.

"Thank you, sir. There are your sketches intact. Guard them; preserve them carefully; you already thought them precious; they are now doubly so. It is a wise precaution for you to insist that they be made in ink, since that renders any alteration impossible without discovery. Doubtless Mr. Osgood will find occasion to thank you also. Come, Archie."

When we left, Bennett was leaning over the table squinting at the sketches.

Down at the parking space Wolfe climbed into the front seat beside me, which meant that he had things to say. As I threaded my way slowly along the edge of the darting crowds, he opened up: "Now, Archie. It all depends on the execution. I'll go over it briefly for you. . . ."

20

AT PRATT's place I parked in the graveled space in front of the garage, and we got out. Wolfe left me and headed for the house. Over at a corner of the lawn Caroline was absorbed in putting practice, which might have been thought a questionable occupation for a young woman, even a Metropolitan champion, on the afternoon of her former fiancé's funeral, but under the circumstances it was open to differing interpretations. She greeted me from a distance as I passed by on my way to meet Lily Rowan as arranged on the phone.

Lily stayed put in the hammock, extending a hand and going over me with a swift and comprehensive eye.

I said, "You're not so hot. Wolfe recognized your voice on the telephone last night."

"He didn't."

"He did."

"He agreed to meet me at the hotel at six in the morning."

"Bah. You laid an egg, that's all. However, you got him out of bed at midnight, which was something. Thank you for doing me the favor. Now I want to offer to do you one, and I'm in a hurry. How would you like to take a lesson in detective work?"

"Who would give it to me?"

"I would."

"I'd love it."

"Fine. This may be the beginning of a worthwhile career for you. The lesson is simple but requires control of the voice and the facial muscles. You may not be needed, but on the other hand you may. You are to stay here, or close by. Sometime in the next hour or two I may come for you, or send Bert—"

"Come yourself."

"Okay. And escort you to the presence of Mr. Wolfe and a man. Wolfe will ask you a question and you will tell a lie.

It won't be a complicated lie and there is no possibility of your getting tripped up. But it will help to pin a murder on a man, and therefore I want to assure you that it is not a frame-up. The man is guilty. If there were a chance in a million that he's innocent—"

"Don't bother." The corner of her mouth went up. "Do I have any company in the lie?"

"Yes. Me; also Wolfe. What we need is corroboration."

"Then as far as I'm concerned it isn't a lie at all. Truth is relative. I see you've washed your face. Kiss me."

"Pay in advance, huh?"

"Not in full. On account."

After about 30 or 32 seconds I straightened up again and cleared my throat and said, "Whatever is worth doing at all is worth doing well."

She was smiling and didn't say anything.

"This is it," I said. "Now quit smiling and listen."

It didn't take long to explain it. Four minutes later I was on my way to the house.

Wolfe was on the terrace with Pratt and Jimmy and Monte McMillan. Jimmy looked sullen and preoccupied, and I judged from his eyes that he was having too many high-balls. McMillan sat to one side, silent, with his eyes fixed on Wolfe. Pratt was raving. He appeared to be not only sore because the general ruction had spoiled his barbecue plans and ruined the tail end of his country sojourn, but specifically and pointedly sore at Wolfe for vague but active reasons which had probably come to him on the bounce from District Attorney Waddell. Even so his deeper instincts prevailed, for when I arrived he interrupted himself to toss me a nod and let out a yell for Bert.

But Wolfe, who, I noticed, had already disposed of a bottle of beer, shook his head at me and stood up. "No," he said. "Please, Mr. Pratt. I don't resent your belligerence, but I think before long you may acknowledge its misdirection. You may even thank me, but I don't ask for that either. I didn't want to disturb you. I needed to have a talk with Mr McMillan in private. When I told him so on the phone this morning and we tried to settle on a meeting place that would ensure privacy, I took the liberty of suggesting your house. There was a special reason for it, that the presence of Miss Rowan might be desirable."

"Lily Rowan? What the hell has she got to do with it?"

"That will appear. Or maybe it won't. Anyhow, Mr. Mc-Millan agreed to meet me here. If my presence is really offensive to you we'll go elsewhere. I thought perhaps that room upstairs—"

"I don't give a damn. But if there's anything on my mind I'm in the habit of getting it off—"

"Later. Indulge me. It will keep. If you'll permit us to use the room upstairs? . . ."

"Help yourself." Pratt waved a hand. "You'll need something to drink. Bert! Hey, *Bert!*"

Jimmy shut his eyes and groaned.

We got ourselves separated. McMillan, who still hadn't opened his mouth, followed Wolfe, and I brought up the rear. As we started up the stairs, with the stockman's broad back towering above me, I got my pistol from the holster, to which it had been previously restored, and slipped it into my side coat pocket, hoping it could stay there. There was one item on Wolfe's bill of fare that might prove to be ticklish.

The room was in apple-pie order, with the afternoon sun slanting in through the modern casement windows which Wolfe had admired. I moved the big upholstered chair around for him, and placed a couple more for McMillan and me. Bert appeared, as sloppy and efficient as ever, with beer and the makings of highballs. As soon as that had been arranged and Bert had disappeared, McMillan said:

"This is the second time I've gone out of my way to see you, as a favor to Fred Osgood. It's sort of getting monotonous. I've got 7 cows and a bull at Crowfield that I've just bought that I ought to be taking home."

He stopped. Wolfe said nothing. Wolfe sat leaning back in the big upholstered chair, motionless, his hands resting on the polished wooden arms, gazing at the stockman with half-shut eyes. There was no indication that he intended either to speak or to move.

McMillan finally demanded, "What the hell is this, a staring match?"

Wolfe shook his head. "I don't like it," he said. "Believe me, sir, I take no pleasure from it. I have no desire to drag it out, to prolong the taste of victory. There has already been too much delay, far too much." He put his hand in his breast pocket, withdrew the memo pad, and held it out. "Take that, please, and examine the first three sheets. Thoroughly.—I'll want it back intact, Archie."

With a shrug of his broad shoulders, McMillan took the pad and looked it over. His head was bent and I couldn't see his face. After inspecting the sheets twice over he looked up again.

"You've got me," he declared. "Is there a trick to it?"

"I wouldn't say a trick." Wolfe's tone took on an edge. "Do you identify those sketches?"

"I never saw them before."

"Of course not. It was a bad question. Do you identify the original they were drawn from?"

"No I don't. Should I? They're not very good."

"That's true. Still I would have expected you to identify them. He was your bull. Today I compared them with some sketches, the originals on the applications for registration, which Mr. Bennett let me look at, and it was obvious that the model for them was Hickory Buckingham Pell. Your bull that died of anthrax a month ago."

"Is that so?" McMillan looked the sheets over again, in no haste, and returned his eyes to Wolfe. "It's possible. That's interesting. Where did you get these drawings?"

"That's just the point." Wolfe laced his fingers across his belly. "I made them myself. You've heard of that homely episode Monday afternoon, before your arrival. Mr. Goodwin and I started to cross the pasture and were interrupted by the bull. Mr. Goodwin escaped by agility, but I mounted that boulder in the center of the pasture. I was there some 15 minutes before I was rescued by Miss Pratt. 1 am vain of my dignity, and I felt undignified. The bull was parading not far off, back and forth, and I took my memorandum pad from my pocket and made those sketches of him. The gesture may have been childish, but I got satisfaction from it. It was . . . well, a justification of my point of vantage on the boulder. May I have the pad back, please?"

McMillan didn't move. I arose and took the pad from him without his seeming to notice it, and put it in my pocket.

McMillan said, "You must have a screw loose. The bull in the pasture was Caesar. Hickory Caesar Grindon."

"No, sir. I must contradict you, for again that's just the point. The bull in the pasture was Hickory Buckingham Pell. The sketches I made Monday afternoon prove it, but I was aware of it long before I saw Mr. Bennett's official records. I suspected it Monday afternoon. I knew it Monday night. I didn't know it was Buckingham, for I had never heard of him, but I know it wasn't Caesar."

"You're a goddam liar. Whoever told you—"

"No one told me." Wolfe grimaced. He unlaced his fingers to wiggle one. "Let me make a suggestion, sir. We're engaged in a serious business, deadly serious, and we'll gain nothing by cluttering it up with frivolous rhetoric. You know very well what I'm doing, I'm undertaking to demonstrate that Clyde Osgood and Howard Bronson died by your hand. You can't refute my points until I've made them, and you can't keep me from making them by calling me names. Let's show mutual respect. I can't expose your guilt by shouting 'murderer' at you, and you can't disprove it by shouting 'liar' at me. Nor by pretending surprise. You must have known why I asked you to meet me here."

McMillan's gaze was steady. So was his voice: "You're going to undertake to prove something."

"I am. I have already shown proof that Caesar, the champion, was never in that pasture."

"Bah. Those drawings? Anybody would see through that trick. Do you suppose anyone is going to believe that when the bull chased you on that rock you stood there and made pictures of him?"

"I think so." Wolfe's eyes moved. "Archie, get Miss Rowan."

I wouldn't have left him like that if he had had the sketches on him, but they were in my pocket. I hotfooted it downstairs and across the lawn and under the trees to the hammock, which she got out of as she saw me coming. She linked her arm through mine, and I had to tolerate it for business reasons, but I made her trot. She offered no objections, but by the time we got upstairs to our destination she was a little out of breath. I had to admit she was a pretty good pupil when I saw her matter-of-fact nods, first to Wolfe and then to McMillan. Neither of them got up.

Wolfe said, "Miss Rowan. I believe Mr. Goodwin has informed you that we would ask you for an exercise of memory. I suppose you do remember that on Monday afternoon the activity of the bull marooned me on a rock in the pasture?"

She smiled at him. "I do."

"How long was I on the rock?"

"Oh . . . I would say 15 minutes. Between 10 and 20."

"During that time, what was Miss Pratt doing?"

"Running to get her car and driving to the pasture and arguing with Dave about opening the gate, and then driving to get you."

"What was Dave doing?"

"Waving the gun and arguing with Esca . . . Mr. Goodwin and arguing with Caroline and jumping around."

"What were you doing?"

"Taking it in. Mostly I was watching you, because you made quite a picture—you and the bull."

"What was I doing?"

"Well, you climbed to the top of the rock and stood there 2 or 3 minutes with your arms folded and your walking stick hanging from your wrist, and then you took a notebook or something from your pocket and it looked as if you were writing in it or drawing in it. You kept looking at the bull and back at the book or whatever it was. I decided you were making a sketch of the bull. That hardly seemed possible under the circumstances, but it certainly looked like it."

Wolfe nodded. "I doubt if there will ever be any reason for you to repeat all that to a judge and jury in a courtroom, but if such an occasion should arise would you do it?"

"Certainly. Why not?"

"Under oath?"

"Of course. Not that I would enjoy it much."

"But you would do it?"

"Yes."

Wolfe turned to the stockman. "Would you care to ask her about it?"

McMillan only looked at him, and gave no sign. I went to open the door and told Lily, "That will do, Miss Rowan, thank you." She crossed and stopped at my elbow and said, "Take me back to the hammock." I muttered at her, "Go sit on your thumb. School's out." She made a face at me and glided over the threshold, and I shut the door and returned to my chair.

McMillan said, "I still say it's a trick. And a damn dirty trick. What else?"

"That's all." Wolfe sighed. "That's all, sir. I ask you to consider whether it isn't enough. Let us suppose that you are on trial for the murder of Clyde Osgood. Mr. Goodwin testifies that while I was on the rock he saw me looking at the bull and sketching on my pad. Miss Rowan testified as you have just heard. I testify that at that time, of that bull, I made those sketches, and the jury is permitted to compare them with the official sketches of Caesar and Buckingham. Wouldn't that satisfactorily demonstrate that Buckingham was in the pasture, and Caesar wasn't and never had been?"

McMillan merely gazed at him.

Wolfe went on, "I'll answer your charge that it's a trick. What if it is? Are you in a position to condemn tricks? As a matter of fact, I do know, from the evidence of my own eyes, that the bull was Buckingham. I had the opportunity to observe him minutely. Remember that I have studied the official sketches. Buckingham had a white patch high on his left shoulder; Caesar had not. The bull in the pasture had it. The white shield on Buckingham's face extended well below the level of the eyes; on Caesar it was smaller and came to a point higher up. Not only did I see the face of the bull in the pasture on Monday afternoon, but that night I examined it at close range with a flashlight. He was Buckingham. You know it; I know it; and if I can help a jury to know it by performing a trick with sketches I shall certainly do so. With Mr. Goodwin and Miss Rowan to swear that they saw me making them, I think we may regard that point as established."

"What else?"

"That's all. That's enough."

McMillan abruptly stood up. I was on my feet as soon as he was, with my gun in sight. He saw it and grinned at me without any humor, with his gums showing. "Go ahead and stop me, son," he said, and started, not fast but not slow, for the door. "Make it good though."

I dived past him and got to the door and stood with my back against it. He halted three paces off.

Wolfe's voice came, sharp, "Gentlemen! Please! If you start a commotion, Mr. McMillan, the thing is out of my hands. You must realize that. A wrestling match would bring people here. If you get shot you'll only be disabled; Mr. Goodwin doesn't like to kill people. Come back here and face it. I want to talk to you."

McMillan wheeled and demanded, "What the hell do you think I've been doing for the past month except face it?"

"I know. But you were still struggling. Now the struggle's over. You can't go out of that door; Mr. Goodwin won't let you. Come and sit down."

McMillan stood for a minute and looked at him. Then slowly he moved, back across the room to his chair, sat, put his elbows on his knees, and covered his face with his hands.

Wolfe said, "I don't know how you feel about it. You asked me what else. If you mean what other proof confronts you I repeat that no more is needed. If you mean can I offer salve to your vanity, I think I can. You did extremely well. If I had not been here you would almost certainly have escaped even the stigma of suspicion."

Wolfe got his fingers laced again. I returned the gun to my pocket and sat down. Wolfe resumed: "As I said, I suspected

Monday afternoon that the bull in the pasture was not the champion Caesar. When Clyde offered to bet Pratt that he would not barbecue Hickory Caesar Grindon, he opened up an amusing field for conjecture. I diverted myself with it while listening to Pratt's jabber. How did Clyde propose to win his bet? By removing the bull and hiding him? Fantastic; the bull was guarded, and where could he be hid against a search? Replace the bull with one less valuable? Little less fantastic; again, the bull was guarded, and while a substitute might be found who would deceive others, surely none would deceive you, and you were there. I considered other alternatives. There was one which was simple and plausible and presented no obstacles at all: that the bull in the pasture was not Hickory Caesar Grindon and Clyde had detected it. He had just come from the pasture, and he had binoculars, and he knew cattle. I regarded the little puzzle as solved and dismissed it from my mind, since it was none of my business.

"When the shots fired by Mr. Goodwin took us all to the pasture Monday night, and we found that Clyde had been killed, it was still none of my business, but the puzzle gained in interest and deserved a little effort as an intellectual challenge. I examined the bull, looked for the weapon and found it, and came to this room and sat in this chair and satisfied myself as to the probabilities. Of course I was merely satisfying myself as a mental exercise, not the legal requirements for evidence. First, if the bull wasn't Caesar you certainly knew it, and therefore you had swindled Pratt. How and why? Why, to get $45,000. How, by selling him Caesar and then delivering another bull, much less valuable, who resembled him. Then where was Caesar? Wouldn't it be highly dangerous for you to have him in your possession, since he had been legally sold, and cooked and eaten? You couldn't call him Caesar, you wouldn't dare to let anyone see him. Then you didn't have him in your possession. No one did. Caesar was dead."

Wolfe paused, and demanded, "Wasn't Caesar dead when you took the $45,000 from Pratt?"

McMillan, his face still covered with his hands, was motionless and made no sound.

"Of course he was," Wolfe said. "He had died of anthrax. Pratt mentioned at dinner Monday evening that he had first tried to buy Caesar from you, for his whimsical barbecue, more than six weeks ago, and you had indignantly refused. Then the anthrax came. Your herd was almost entirely destroyed. One morning you found that Caesar was dead. In your desperation an ingenious notion occurred to you. Buckingham, who resembled Caesar superficially but was worth only a fraction of his value, was alive and well. You announced that Buckingham had died, and the carcass was destroyed; and you told Pratt that he could have Caesar. You couldn't have swindled a stockman like that, for the deception would soon have been found out; but the swindle was in fact no injury to Pratt, since Buckingham would make just as good roast beef as Caesar would have made. Of course, amusing myself with the puzzle Monday evening, I knew nothing of Buckingham, but one of the probabilities which I accepted was that you had delivered another bull instead of Caesar, and that Caesar was dead.

"Clyde, then, had discovered the deception, and when you heard him propose the bet to Pratt, and the way he stated its terms, you suspected the fact. You followed him out to his car and had a brief talk with him and got your suspicions confirmed, and he agreed to return later that evening and discuss it with you. He did so. You were supposed to be asleep upstairs. You left the house secretly and met Clyde. I am giving you the probabilities as I accepted them Monday evening. Clyde informed you that he knew of the deception and was determined to expose it in order to win his bet with Pratt. You, of course, faced ruin. He may have offered a compromise: for instance, if you would give him $20,000 of the money Pratt had paid you he would use half of it to settle his bet, keep the other half for himself, and preserve your secret. I don't know, and it doesn't matter. What happened was that you knocked him unconscious, evolved a plan to make it appear that he had been killed by the bull, and proceeded to execute it. I was inclined to believe, looking at the bull's horns Monday night, that you had smeared blood on them with your hands. You should have been much more thorough, but I suppose you were in a hurry, for you had to wash off the pick and get back to the house and into the upstairs room unobserved. You didn't know, of course, whether the thing would be discovered in 5 minutes or 5 hours, since Mr. Goodwin was on the other side of the pasture talking to Miss Rowan."

Wolfe opened his eyes. "Do I bore you or annoy you? Shall I stop?"

No movement and no response.

"Well. That was the way I arranged the puzzle Monday evening, but, as I say, it was none of my business. It didn't become my business until the middle of Tuesday afternoon when I accepted a commission from Mr. Osgood to solve the murder, having first demonstrated that there had been one. At that moment I expected to have the job completed within a few hours. Only two things needed to be done to verify the solution I had already arrived at: first, to question everyone who had been at Pratt's place Monday evening, for if it turned out that you could not have left the house secretly—for instance, if someone had been with you constantly—I would have to consider new complexities; and second, to establish the identity of the bull. The first was routine and I left it to Mr. Waddell, as his proper province, while I investigated Clyde's background by conversing with his father and sister. The second, the proof that the bull was not Caesar, I intended to procure, with Mr. Bennett's assistance, as soon as I heard from the district attorney, and that delay was idiotic. I should not have postponed it one instant. For less than 3 hours after I had accepted the case I learned from your own lips that the bull was dead and his carcass was to be immediately destroyed. I tried; I phoned Mr. Bennett and learned that there was no single distinguishing mark or brand on Guernsey bulls, and Mr. Goodwin rushed over to take photographs; but the bull was already half consumed by fire. You acted quickly there, and in time. Of course you gave him the anthrax yourself. It would be . . . perhaps you would tell me how and when you did it."

McMillan said nothing.

Wolfe shrugged. "Anyhow, you were prompt and energetic. As long as the bull was destined to be cooked and eaten—this was to be the day for that, by the way—you ran little risk of exposure. But when all thought of the barbecue was abandoned, and it was suspected that Clyde had been murdered, the bull's presence, alive or dead, was a deadly peril to you. You acted at once. You not only killed him, you did it by a method which insured that his carcass would be immediately destroyed. You must have been prepared for contingencies.

"As for me, I was stumped. You had licked me. With all trace of the bull gone but his bones, there seemed no possible way of establishing your motive for murdering Clyde. I had no evidence even for my own satisfaction that my surmise had been correct—that the bull was not Caesar. Tuesday evening I floundered in futilities. I had an interview with you and tried to draw you out by suggesting absurdities, but you were too wary for me. You upbraided me for trying to smear some of the mess on you, and left. Then I tried Bronson, hoping for something—anything. That kind of man is always impervious unless he can be confronted with facts, and I had no facts. It's true that he led me to assumptions: that Clyde had told him how and why he expected to win the bet, and that Bronson therefore knew you were guilty—might even have been there himself, in the dark—and that he was blackmailing you. I assumed those things, but he admitted none of them, and of course I couldn't prove them.

"Yesterday morning I went for Bennett. I wanted to find out all I could about identifying bulls. He was busy. Mr. Goodwin couldn't get him. After lunch I was still waiting for him. Finally he came, and I got a great deal of information, but nothing that would constitute evidence. Then came the news that Bronson had been murdered. Naturally that was obvious. Suspecting that he was blackmailing you, I had told the man he was a fool and he had proved me correct. There too you acted promptly and energetically. Men like you, sir, when once calamity sufficiently disturbs their balance, become excessively dangerous. They will perform any desperate and violent deed, but they don't lose their heads. I wouldn't mind if Mr. Goodwin left me with you in this room alone, because it is known that we are here; but I wouldn't care to offer you the smallest opportunity if there were the slightest room for your ingenuity."

McMillan lifted his head and broke his long silence. "I'm through," he said dully.

Wolfe nodded. "Yes, I guess you are. A jury might be reluctant to convict you of first degree murder on the testimony of my sketches, but if Pratt sued you for $45,000 on the ground that you hadn't delivered the bull you sold, I think the sketches would clinch that sort of case. Convicted of that swindle, you would be through anyway. About the sketches. I had to do that. 3 hours ago there wasn't a shred of evidence in existence to connect you with the murders you committed. But as soon as I examined the official sketches of Buckingham and Caesar I no longer surmised or deduced the identity of the bull in the pasture; I knew it. I had seen the white patch on the shoulder with my own eyes, and I had seen the extension of the white shield on his face. I made the sketches to support that knowledge. They will be used in the manner I described, with the testimony of Miss Rowan and Mr. Goodwin to augment my own. As I say, they will certainly convict you of fraud, if not of murder."

Wolfe sighed. "You killed Clyde Osgood to prevent the exposure of your fraud. Even less, to avoid the compulsion

of having to share its proceeds. Now it threatens you again.
That's the minimum of the threat."

McMillan tossed his head, as if he were trying to shake
something off. The gesture looked familiar, but I didn't remember having seen him do it before. Then he did it again,
and I saw what it was: it was the way the bull had tossed
his head in the pasture Monday afternoon.

He looked at Wolfe and said, "Do me a favor. I want
to go out to my car a minute. Alone."

Wolfe muttered, "You wouldn't come back."

"Yes, I would. My word was good for over 50 years. Now
it's good again. I'll be back within 5 minutes, on my feet."

"Do I owe you a favor?"

"No. I'll do you one in return. I'll write something and
sign it. Anything you say. You've got it pretty straight. I'll
do it when I come back, not before. And you asked me how
I killed Buckingham. I'll show you what I did it with."

Wolfe spoke to me without moving his head or his eyes.
"Open the door for him, Archie."

I didn't stir. I knew he was indulging himself in one of
his romantic impulses, and I thought a moment's reflection
might show him its drawbacks; but after only half a moment
he snapped at me, "Well?"

I got up and opened the door and McMillan, with a heavy
tread but no sign of the blind staggers, passed out. I stood
and watched his back until the top of his head disappeared
on his way downstairs. Then I turned to Wolfe and said
sarcastically, "Fortune-telling *and* character-reading. It would
be nice to have to explain—"

"Shut up."

I kicked the door further open and stood there, listening for the sound of a gunshot or a racing engine or whatever I might hear. But the first pertinent sound, within the
5 minutes he had mentioned, was his returning footsteps on
the stairs. He came down the hall, as he had promised, on
his feet, entered without glancing at me, walked to Wolfe
and handed him something, and went to his chair and sat
down.

"That's what I said I'd show you." He seemed more out
of breath than the exertion of his trip warranted, but otherwise under control. "That's what I killed Buckingham with."
He turned his eye to me. "I haven't got any pencil or paper.
If you'll let me have that pad . . ."

Wolfe held the thing daintily with thumb and forefinger,

regarding it—a large hypodermic syringe. He lifted his gaze. "You had anthrax in this?"

"Yes. Five cubic centimeters. A culture I made myself from the tissues of Caesar's heart the morning I found him dead. They gave me hell for cutting him open, but—" He shrugged. "I did that before I got the idea of saying the carcass was Buckingham instead of Caesar. I only about half knew what I was doing that morning, but it was in my mind to use it on myself—the poison from Caesar's heart. Watch out how you handle that. It's empty now, but there might be a drop left on the needle, though I just wiped it off."

"Will anthrax kill a man?"

"Yes. How sudden depends on how he gets it. In my case collapse will come in maybe twenty minutes, because I shot more than two cubic centimeters of that concentrate in this vein." He tapped his left forearm with a finger. "Right in the vein. I only used half of it on Buckingham."

"Before you left for Crowfield Tuesday afternoon."

"Yes." McMillan looked at me again. "You'd better give me that pad and let me get started."

I got out the pad and tore off the three top sheets which contained the sketches, and handed it to him, with my fountain pen. He took it and scratched with the pen to try it and asked Wolfe, "Do you want to dictate it?"

"No. Better in your own words. Just—it can be brief. Are you perfectly certain about the anthrax?"

"Yes. A good stockman is a jack of all trades."

Wolfe sighed, and shut his eyes.

I sat and watched the pen in McMillan's hand moving along the top sheet of the pad. Apparently he was a slow writer. The faint scratch of its movement was the only sound for several minutes. Then he asked without looking up:

"How do you spell 'unconscious'? I've always been a bad speller."

Wolfe spelled it for him, slowly and distinctly.

I watched the pen starting to move again. My gun, in my pocket, was weighting my coat down, and I transferred it back to the holster, still looking at the pen. Wolfe, his eyes closed, was looking at nothing.

21

THAT WAS two months ago.

Yesterday, while I was sitting here in the office typing from my notebook Wolfe's dictated report on the Crampton-Gore case, the phone rang. Wolfe, at his desk in his oversize chair, happening not to be pouring beer at the moment, answered at his instrument. After a second he grunted and muttered:

"She wants Escamillo."

I lifted my receiver. "Hello, trifle. I'm busy."

"You're always busy." She sounded energetic. "You listen to me a minute. You probably don't know or don't care that I seldom pay any attention to my mail except to run through it to see if there's a letter from you. I've just discovered that I did after all get an invitation to Nancy's and Jimmy's wedding, which will be tomorrow. I know you did. You and I will go together. You can come—"

"Stop! Stop and take a breath. Weddings are out. They're barbaric vestiges of . . . of barbarism. I doubt if I'd go to my own."

"You might. You may. For a string of cellophane pearls I'd marry you myself. But this wedding will be amusing. Old Pratt and old Osgood will be there and you can see them shake hands. Then you can have cocktails and dinner with me."

"My pulse remains steady."

"Kiss me."

"Still steady."

"I'll buy you some marbles and an airgun and roller skates . . ."

"No. Are you going to ring off now?"

"No. I haven't seen you for a century."

"Okay. I'll tell you what I'll do. I'm going to the Strand tomorrow evening at 9 o'clock to watch Greenleaf and Baldwin play pool. You can come along if you'll promise to sit quietly and not chew gum."

"I wouldn't know a pool from a pikestaff. But all right. You can come here for dinner—"

"Nope. I'll eat at home with my employer. I'll meet you in the lobby of the Churchill at 8:45."

"My God, these public assignations—"

"I am perfectly willing to be seen with you in public."

"8:45 tomorrow."

"Right."

I replaced the instrument and turned to my typewriter. Wolfe's voice came:

"Archie."

"Yes, sir."

"Get the dictionary and look up the meaning of the word 'spiritual.'"

I merely ignored it and started on paragraph 16 of the report.

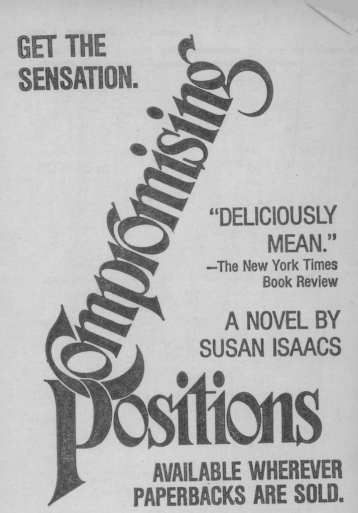